THEI
A WILD
COLONIAL
BOY

JOHN BOYD ROE

ISBN-13: 978-1533362056
ISBN-10: 153336205X

CONTENTS

PROLOGUE

Rachel's Story

Awakening to sunshine gave me the same boost that it always did. It was the best part of the day, and I lost no time in grabbing a shower long before anyone else was around. The tropical kit was an heirloom from when my mum, Leah, had done her stint at a kibbutz. She persuaded me to take it when my turn came. By then the young Americans who outnumbered the rest of us set the trends in dress code. They wore designer jeans and T-shirts, and I followed suit. No way was I going to wear the grey drill and be mistaken for a Girl Scout.

Given that we shared a keener interest in fashion than our forebears, I suppose some of us might have been equally prepared to lay down our lives for the Promised Land. How different, to life in the Kimberleys. I've never felt so Jewish, or so English than I did in Australia. The grey drill finally seemed to be an appropriate uniform. How did the nearest small town, Kununurra, compare for intellectual stimulation? Well, I seldom heard any conversation concerning anything beyond booze, sport, and TV soaps.

To be fair, Australians lack the stimulus of shared danger to unite them. Believe me, I saw a lot of bigots in Israel, not to mention trigger-happy border guards and police, but believe me, they are very welcome when you are surrounded by fifty million hostile Arabs, hell-bent on exterminating Jews.

I have more in common with them than the sort of airy-fairy peace protesters that are always on the march in England. It was almost disappointing that I had reacted to Israel exactly as my dad, Neville, and Leah had done. There was evidently a lot more going for England than I had realised, and Israel was where our roots were, and it has a great climate too!

There had to be some angle to parlay getting my hands dirty in the kibbutz into a great gap year. I soon persuaded Neville that an internship at the Kimberley Research Station would be very relevant to taking a degree in botany. I have a six-month work permit that expires just before The Wet commences.

This is no Ivory Tower. We run controlled tests on cash crops suitable for local conditions. Some proved to be dead ends. Cotton and sorghum succumbed to pests, and sugar cane thrives, but won't be worth growing until a processing plant is built.

Mangoes, bananas, and sandalwood grow well through the wet season, but we are on black clay, which is totally unworkable until it dries out again. However, all cucurbits flourish, from the familiar cucumber to every kind of melon and squash.

Stringless beans are very successful, too.

I do my best to avoid to avoid lads of my own age that I work with, but no probs there. I have never had a problem with getting my own way, so when a new project came up to run a model mixed small-holding, I volunteered to care for the poultry, which necessitates 'living over the shop' in a trailer caravan, to feed them and see them safely in their shed every night, and collect eggs each morning. No-one else competed for this, because they need to live in town, where the pubs are.

Bruce is my project leader, and one morning, as I fed my charges, he came round showing a newcomer the ropes. She was a thirty-ish blonde, in slacks, shades, and a straw sun hat, sweating pinkly. He introduced me with his usual juvenile banter. "Rachel is our juvenile recluse, to work experience from your neck of the woods. She has ensnared our young bronzed surfies with her sultry beauty, but clearly prefers poultry." "Right on! A khaki Campbell is worth ten bronzed surfies, in my book." "You'll soon change your tune, girlie. Hazel Swindlehurst, meet Rachel Breslau." "Hi Hazel! If you didn't previously share my opinion of Australian men, that intro should convince you."

Ms Swindlehurst blushed at my outspoken attitude, and took control. "It's lovely to meet you, Rachel. I feel as though this is my first day at school. I hope to learn all about your project. I'm here on a short break from teaching. I believe that we both owe our acceptance here to Tim Clancy."

Bruce cut her short. "Why don't you get together in your lunch break? We've still got a lot to see before you start in the lab this arvo."

The canteen is pretty good. It serves the choicest local produce. Both Tiger Prawns and Barramundi usually feature on the menu. Hazel arrived at my table damp and glowing. "My, you do look cool. I'm smothered in sun cream, but I'd still get sun-burn if I didn't keep covered up, so I really feel overdressed for this heat. Tim Clancy is marrying my sister in a few weeks, and Ralph and I are her only relatives over here." "As you probably know, Ralph and I go way back. Is he here with you?" "He went straight from Darwin to Mount Isa, while we made our way to Kununurra. He is taking his Private Pilot's License."

"That's enterprising. Is he here to stay?" "He is on his school holiday, hopefully before taking up his place at Lancaster University." "Where are you staying?" "Helen and I share a tiny rented bungalow. She and Tim are spending their honeymoon finding somewhere to start their light aircraft sale agency. Once Helen moves out, I'll have space to put Ralph up. I'm sure Tim's mum would put him up, but we don't want to impose on her hospitality before we are better acquainted. Back home, Ralph's flying always took priority over Helen's arrangements." That figured. "What about Jane? She must have started at Aberystwyth."

"That's right. She got sponsorship for a three-year law degree. I do hope Ralph takes up his place. If he should stay on here, I doubt if they can keep up their relationship while she finishes her course, and then works through her commitment to the firm that sponsored her."

Hazel whipped out her diary. "I must remind Helen to invite you. Ralph will be delighted to see you, and Helen will be grateful for a twenty-five per cent increase on the bride's side of the church!"

"If it comes to a stoush, as they say here, I won't be able to hold back the barbarians for long. I'll be glad to face fearful odds on behalf of the Slingers and Swindlehursts, because Ralph is a mate. Besides, we went out with Jane once, and we all had a ball!"

I had to make that clear. At one time, he had run after me like a lovesick calf. Helen must have been relieved when he transferred his affections to Jane, the most clever (and most sporty) girl in his class. After all, that's what his gene-pool lacked, and while I could provide that, and more besides, Helen must have realised that she would find me much harder to manage! Anyway, he should be so lucky! He could keep up with Jane, both socially and financially.

We appreciate each other as mates. He lost his father a couple of years back, and I reckon I freed him from Helen's apron strings. I soon realised that he was out of his depth with me. Hazel's voice roused me from my wool-gathering. "Which local places have you visited?"

"I've been to Darwin and Broome. We scientists need a few dates and other numbers to make a proper dissertation of my ramblings. Darwin was developed in WW2 as a forward base against any attempted Japanese incursion. All the concrete defences date from then, and the older parts of the town were mostly swept away by Hurricane Tracy in '74. This led to a big investment in the town to attract tourists, hence the swish restaurants, hotels and shops.

"While it only supports a population of seventy

thousand, it has a vast catchment area because there is nowhere else to go! You would have to cross the state boundary to find another town as big, and you would be two thousand miles from the next city. Sydney, the biggest city in Oz, is two thousand five hundred miles away from Darwin. This is what most visitors to Australia fail to realise. You should not waste too much time travelling once you get here, but see everything of interest in your immediate locality."

Hazel stifled a yawn at this avalanche of unwanted information, muttering something about not bothering to hire a bicycle, in that case. "You mentioned Broome as well. What has that place got to offer?"

"It is about three hundred miles west of here. It originated as harbour for the pearl-fishing fleet, and supported a lot of Japanese pearl divers. In the thirties, this was the core of the oriental quarter. I imagine it might have been rather like Tahiti back then.

"I've visited the zoo, the Cable Beach Club, and Moonlight Bay. It shares Darwin's main problem as a tourist resort in that it is infested with small jellyfish called sea-wasps, and sharks as well."

"I'm not too keen on resort towns, anyway. I expect I will start by seeing as much as I can of the Orde Valley."

"Well the Institute kicked off in 1945, and the Orde Valley Scheme was their first project. The Diversion Dam was completed eleven years ago. Lake Argyle is the main storage reservoir, and is really quite dramatic, surrounded as it is by parched red hills like the Dead Sea. They make a great backdrop for the tourist village. There are boat trips and bush walks.

Hidden Valley National Park is worth a visit, too."

"That's exactly what I'm looking for. Tim and his mum remember the place before it boasted tourist attractions, so they tend to disparage them. Helen and I want to see them, because not having a car leaves us ill-equipped for serious exploration. We realise that their opinion of tourist attractions is irrelevant, because they aren't tourists!

"If that involves us in being shepherded around with the other 'common trippers' as Mother would have described us, it's preferable to hiring a car when we don't really need one. Helen and I would be delighted to have you round for tea, to tell us more."

"Thank you! I would be equally glad to escape my trailer for the afternoon." We compared diaries, and found a suitable day. "That's settled then," Hazel said. "We won't intrude on you too much, but you are welcome any time that you want to speak to someone other than your colleagues. Helen asked me to tell you that she really appreciates your moral support on her side of the church."

"I think they'll make a great couple. Who, other than Helen, could keep Tim on a tight rein?" Hazel laughed out loud. "Ralph and I often tease Helen about her bossiness, but whether she can subdue Tim remains to be seen. When he and Ralph get together, they have us in stitches!"

A couple of weeks later, I was knocking on the door of their bungalow, in my white two-piece. Tim answered the door, our first meeting. He was renewing his tan, in a Hawaiian shirt and shorts. He was tall and rangy, with a long horse face and hooded grey eyes. "Hello, Rachel darlin', you are as lovely as your press photos said you would be." I had indeed been featured in the press a couple of times. "Come through, we are on the back garden veranda. Helen will be with us as soon as she has brewed up. Sit here, in the shade."

"I'd like to thank you for your intro to the Research Station." "It won me nothing but notoriety at Australia House. When I did the same for Hazel, I think they suspected me of operating a 'white slave' racket."

"That is not very flattering to us! I imagine they would be more likely to worry that an augmented Clancy clan would threaten the balance of power in Kununurra."

"Ouch! So small-town life is touching a nerve, is it? We had wondered why you had sought a hermit's life in your trailer at the Research Station." "I hadn't intended to belittle your home town." "Forget it! Why did you think I left it to work abroad? It was worse before the population grew to three thousand. I used to think that everyone here was too concerned about me and my business. I was always aware (from their point of view) that if I trod on someone's toe, nearly half the town would be limping. That was just the relationships that everyone knew about. They all had more relations, those that were born 'on the wrong side of the blanket' as you Brits might say."

Helen made her entrance, carrying the tea-tray. "I'm afraid that Hazel will be a little late joining us. I heard Tim's inappropriate remarks about 'white slaving' and I apologise on his behalf. I'm sure your parents would consider it overfamiliar, especially on first meeting you."

"Thanks, but they've met other Ockers, and know what to expect. Whenever I decide to 'swap my beauty for your diamonds' Tim shall have first refusal, but only of the business arrangements, of course."

This went down like a lead balloon. Even Tim looked embarrassed for once in his life. Helen must have thought it an ill-mannered response to her apology on Tim's behalf. She registered my jibe with this mild response. "I had forgotten that your sophistication was more appropriate to my age, and vice versa. Here is your wedding invitation. We are so happy that you have accepted." I hope I had enough grace to blush. I got up to embrace her. "Thanks so much, Helen, I really appreciate it."

Helen was a couple of years older than her sister, not as pretty, but full of determination. Ralph had told me that Alec, a real tough nut, deferred to her in most business matters. He seldom deferred to anyone else. He had gone against her judgement in taking out an agricultural mortgage to fund a new dairy enterprise and a herd of cows, and then died in a stupid motorbike accident. She promptly sold off the cows and some of the sheep to repay the mortgage, to resume her management job at the dairy, leaving Ralph to cope with the reduced sheep in the hill flock.

"I ought to have contacted you earlier. It never dawned on me that shutting myself in with my poultry at the research station had attracted so much unwanted notice. I'm writing a journal to make sure that no part of my time here is wasted." Finally, a barbed response. "I shall ask Ralph to do the same, and at the wedding, and any other event where you are both present, it will be revealing to see how the two accounts differ."

I licked my finger, and made the gesture of 'chalking one up to her'.

CHAPTER 1

Pride Comes Before a Fall

As I parked the Cessna 150, and followed the chief flying instructor to the office, a Cessna twin taxied over to the Flying Doctor hangar. It was great to have achieved my private pilot's license at long last. This was the home of both the Flying Doctor service, and also the School of the Air. Thanks to gliding experience in the UK, plus twelve hours of dual in Tim's Super Cub, I had come here with background experience to help me on my way.

I had reached the required standard with thirty hours of solo flying, the minimum total that was permitted. Having been interested in flying for years, and being well read on the theoretical, technical, and legal requirements, I had no problem with the written and oral tests.

After flying cross-country in the UK, the triangular cross-country flight was a doddle. No more groping my way through English clag, I was blessed with gin-clear visibility at all times. I had spoken once to a young man who had been training pilots on a fighter jet delta-wing. He wanted to hire a light aircraft to fly to the Republic. He was familiar with cooling towers as an aid to navigation, but when he took off from Barton, at one thousand feet, fifteen were visible. Railway lines were also too thick on the ground to offer a lot of help.

No, the tough bit had been the hour-long flying test that I had just completed. "Good on yer, you've managed to scrape through. I always give PPL students a good rollicking in the course of the flying test, to see how you cope under pressure. You may be a shade less timid and tearful than the average young Pom, but that ain't saying much! Given a hundred hours in your log and you might fully grasp the essentials.

"It's all about managing to keep your machine in the air to eventually blunder (by pure chance) on your destination. If you can then get it down in one piece, you will once again have beaten the odds. I realise that you have to get the money first to do this training, and that means that you would probably be better suited to piloting a pedal rickshaw, and no doubt thousands of people now piloting rickshaws could well be natural pilots, who could be earning almost as much as footballers. That's life for you."

He took my logbook into the office to complete the entry in my flying log that would transform me from Clark Kent into Superman! It authorised me to act as 'pilot in charge' flying any Cessna 150 'days only'.

"You never told us that you've got a mate here."

"I have?"

"There's a furtive Fenian in the bar, gasping to bludge a stubby from you. He calls himself Costello, but nevertheless claims to hail from the Emerald Isle."

"Well then there are **some** things you don't know. I've got a relative named Robert Donbavand, descended from one of many shipwreck survivors to wash up on Irish soil from the Armada."

My mind was in turmoil as I made for the bar. We had met only two years ago, a poor start to what was to become a firm and lasting friendship. I was sweeping the floor in the clubhouse of the gliding club, when I heard Tim approach, in conversation with some Hispanic guy. I'm sure it was Tim's fault, but this guy insulted my mum, and then burst in through the door so I had to jump out of the way behind the door.

I gave him a kick on the backside that sent him sprawling across a table and head-first onto the floor. That was then, and this is now. I had avoided my fellow pupils, and had decided to give them a drink and then depart. There was nothing to keep me here now I had got my license, and I decided to ring Mum, give her my news, and head for Kununurra without further delay. I opened the bar door, my elation fast evaporating. It occurred to me that it would be best to keep my conversation with Sean free from interruption.

He probably shared this aim, because he was sat at a window table at the far end from the door. I clapped him on the back, and asked him what he was drinking. "Sure, a pint of porter would be welcome."

I laughed heartily. "The first time we spoke, you took my advice to be more like your Irish neighbours in good part. You said, 'I'll come on like I'm auditioning for Finian's Rainbow,' and now I finally believe you. You look prosperous, Sean, has the work permit come through?"

"Isn't that what I'm here to tell you? I've made down payments on a Pawnee crop-sprayer and a pickup truck. I finally drummed up several crop-spraying contracts. I need a cheap, strong, and simple errand boy to refill the Pawnee's hopper for me, and help maintain the spray system. The gas tanks have to be filled from drums by hand pump. The spray system has twenty nozzles and many filters to clean."

I must have cringed. "It's beginning to grab you already, right? Picture the scene; the Pawnee staggers towards the far boundary fence, like a goony bird hefting a sack of coal. It barely clears the fence, leaving you in a dust storm the length of the runway.

"That leaves you twenty minutes to collapse with heat-stroke and asphyxia before my bird hauls its butt over the fence to be gassed up and reloaded with insecticide. My casting director swears that in the absence of Errol Flynn, this has to be a starring vehicle for Ralph Swindlehurst!"

"Walking to the bar to meet you, I wondered what you might need from me. I decided that if it included some flying, I should accept the paltry wage and mediaeval working conditions that might be part of it. In short, I need to work while I'm here, and can think of nothing I'd rather do."

"Welcome on board! The job is a lot worse than

you think." He paused to weigh me up, wondering if his next suggestion might give offence. "Mind if I make a suggestion?" "Fire away, Sean." "Don't tell Helen about your PPL yet. Try the crop-spraying first, and when you are happy with it, that will be soon enough to tell her. In other words, let this be your decision, not hers. If things don't work out, I'll regret it but I guarantee to drop you off nearer to Kununurra than you were at the Isa. and you'll have picked up some flying hours and money in the bank. The first three jobs are at Barkly Table Lands. Get those under your belt, and then tell Helen.

"You'll get a small hourly wage, plus five per cent of the gross value of the contract. When I choose to drive the pickup, you will fly to the next venue, but you will get several flying hours a day on top of that. As you know, I can't pay you for the flying you do, but you will be accumulating flying hours without having to pay for them. I will pay for you to add the Pawnee to the list of aircraft in your log book.

"I guessed you would be up for it, so you will be checked out this afternoon when you've memorised the Pawnee handling notes regarding stalling speeds in various configurations of load and flap settings, best climbing speed, cruising speed and approach speed."

"Bloody hell! I thought I'd finished for the day."

"Tim told me that you were a quick study. Here's the handling notes, get with it."

My conversion to the Pawnee was soon completed. Clearly, dual instruction is not possible in a single-seater, so once I had mastered the handling notes I was given an oral test on them, and then demonstrated two touch-and-go landings (a power-on landing on the tarmac followed by one with half-flap on the grass. That finished my conversion, and the Pawnee was listed in my log book as a new type.

"We've time to grab a burger somewhere. You drive. You will find a surplus steel ammunition box bolted against the back of the cab. It has a Coleman petrol burning ring in it, and a cool box. There's a can of unleaded petrol for the burner and canned food and toilet paper. Each seat in the cab has a sleeping bag behind it, and under the tarp in the back there are two spare wheels, two jerricans of diesel, and enough lubricant for an oil change."

We ate our burgers while he showed me the route.

"There's a campsite and motel at Camooweal, where you must spend the night. Ring me at this number at twenty-two hundred hours, so I know my truck is still in one piece. That is 185 kilometres down the Barkly Highway. The client has provided the insecticide, and taken delivery of our avgas. The water in those bags on the bull-bars are a legal requirement, so if you use any, be sure to replace it at the first opportunity.

"Now drop me off at the airfield and hit the road. Watch out for the dust cloud raised by road trains. You might leave just enough space for an oncoming motorbike, and hit a wagon hidden in the dust."

"As in hitting a 'stuffed cloud' when flying over mountains in bad viz." "Exactly so!" "While you do the leg from Camooweal to our client at Gallipoli Station, I shall take it easy through the heat of the day, and I'm partly acclimatised. You'll find that we get up early to avoid the heat. Don't try to impress me by going at it 'like a bull at a gate', as you would say. If you sweat off all your electrolytes you will collapse with heat stroke, which can be serious."

I dropped him off, and made for Camooweal in the heat of the afternoon. Arriving after a three-hour drive, I was completely whacked. That hour-long flying test had felt like a day's work, and I had a headache from sun glare with the driving. I had only made one brief stop in the shade of a rock to drink a can of cola from the cool box, before pressing on again.

I booked in at the campsite, and made for the shower block with a change of clothes. I felt much refreshed when I emerged, to wipe the dust off the bonnet of the pickup, and spread the washed shirt and shorts to dry. The bonnet was almost too hot to touch. I bought a paperback to while away a few hours before I settled for the night.

Next morning I treated myself to a hearty cooked breakfast in the café. I then covered the final hundred kilometres to our client, arriving at the gantry marking the entrance. It bore two Australian Light Horse badges, with the word 'Gallipoli' between them. Just as I got to the barn and shearing shed, I heard the Pawnee fire up. I passed the homestead and its water tower, and made for a flatbed trailer beyond.

I saw a tall skinny guy in singlet and slacks with a bush hat stood on it, awaiting me. His eyes were hidden by goggles, and I realised why! The trailer bore forty-gallon avgas drums, with red plastic containers of insecticide lined up in the shade beneath. Everything was covered with red dust, and the next helping of it arrived as the Pawnee climbed into the sky. Our client indicated where I should park. "G'day, son, I'm Jim Daly."

I climbed onto the trailer to shake his hand, already stiff and sweating before I had started my first day's work. "Ralph Swindlehurst." "Pin your ears back, Ralph. On the subject of safety, I'm your link with the Flyin' Doctor. I'll have to leave my vital chores to give you first-aid, right? So make life a little easier for me by trying to avoid cocking up. This spot offers the best head of water; each red can is sufficient when you tip it in the hopper and fill to the top with water.

"I've rigged a shower so that you can decontaminate yourself if you get splashed with neat insecticide. Whip your duds off and wash yourself down. This evil stuff was developed from nerve gas. The board supporting the shower head also bears a squeeze bottle for irrigating your eyes, if necessary."

"I've got it. You've done us proud."

He hadn't finished. "The foam extinguisher is here, under the trailer. Your mate can relieve himself only while you are filling the hopper. While either of you pump fuel, the other must attend **holding the extinguisher.** If he puts the extinguisher down, **you** stop pumping avgas, do I make myself clear? Otherwise, I'll be on the phone to replace you before Noreen has even made room in the chest freezes for another charred carcass." "Relax, Mr Daly. I've been refuelling light aircraft by hand pump most weekends over the last two years, and I'm almost as keen to postpone my incineration as you seem to be!" "God Awmighty! I've taken a flamin' Pom to me bosom!" "For my part, I've seen better bosoms. Sean should have warned you about my shameful origins." "Forget it, son. Like the 'Ghans say about nutters, 'We must help those on whom Allah has laid so heavy a burden.'"

"Thanks for those few kind words. Now I shall depend on you to show how hospitable Australians can be, even to those who didn't originate in Ireland."

"We know how to make all our visitors well-fed and comfortable, no worries." He smiled at me, and winked.

Hearing Sean throttle back as he approached on finals galvanised me. I sloshed the avgas drum to judge how much it held. I saw the spare goggles hanging from the shower head, and wiped them clean before shoving them in a pocket and grabbed my own goggles and gauntlets from the truck, and put them on. The gauntlets immediately stuck to my sweaty hands. The Pawnee taxied close to the trailer, and Sean chopped the throttle, and then pushed it fully open to gulp air into the hot cylinders. The engine cowling shimmered with heat.

"Leave the fuel, Ralph. I don't need any extra weight. I opened the quick release catch on the hopper tank, and carefully emptied the insecticide in, taking great care to avoid any splashes. "Enjoy your drive here?" He poured himself lemonade from a large thermos flask. "Yeah, it was great. Here's your clean goggles." "What's bothering you, then? Has Jim been riding you?" "Too right. Is it just us, or do you reckon all newcomers are treated to his Mary Poppins act?"

I reached for the water hose, which had a nozzle with its own valve, to conserve precious water. I filled up with water, while holding the insecticide empty between my knees while I screwed the cap on.

"I guess that they all get it. Can't you see it through his eyes? To live here, you accept that you are on your own. When accidents happen, however trivial, you **must deal with them yourself** unless Jim or I are on hand.

"You might twist your ankle, and die as a result. Or a chip-pan fire might destroy the homestead. You'll know you've passed muster when he has nothing to say to you. By the way, it takes about fifteen minutes to fill up with water, and as we deplete the water tank, there will be less 'head' of water, reducing the flow."

"In motor racing, they used to refuel using a milk churn and a funnel." "That sounds both messy and dangerous to me. Every water splash on the wing would gather dust, increasing drag. Suppose you dropped a fuel can through the wing fabric, leaving an unsightly hole. It might occupy my darning needle for the rest of the day! Let's just carry on doing this the wrong way, until I come up with a better plan."

"I'm sorry. That was 'teaching my granny to suck eggs', Sean. I'll cope better when I'm used to the climate." He hadn't quite shut me up yet. "One final 'spiffing wheeze'. You know the safety 'gas nozzle' that gas stations use in the States? They shut off as soon as the fuel reaches the nozzle. That would allow me to refuel while the hopper filled up with water."

"Now you're 'cookin' with gas'! I'll get one, mail order, soonest. You could complete all the 'turn round' tasks in the time it takes to fill the hopper. A tip for you, in return. Always sit in the truck from when I start the engine tests until I level out, because you'll be in a dust storm."

He put on his goggles and climbed into the cockpit, slow and easy in the heat. I just made it to the cab and slammed the door shut, before he fired up the engine, with a roar from the exhaust stubs. He ran through the pre-takeoff checks in seconds, before lining up with the longest run into wind possible, with the tail only feet away from the boundary. It was hot enough in the cab to dry my lungs, forcing me out again before the dust had settled.

I had found a catering-sized peach can where they sorted the household waste, and I soaked my cleanest rag in it, and swabbed my face and head. I felt cleaner and cooler for nearly five minutes. Sean had only cleared the wire fence by ten feet at the most. No wonder he hadn't filled up with fuel. As the dust cloud drifted slowly downwind, it dawned on me that the siting of the airstrip could make or mar an outback homestead.

I found the line of empty insecticide containers, and added one to it. I thought they should be checkable, rather than throw them on a heap. Sean had sprayed his first run, and was flying in a gradually widening circle. This way, he didn't waste time turning at the end of each run, and he was always flying up-sun as he sprayed, so his last pass glistened in the sunlight, making it possible to avoid both gaps and over-sprays on the crop he was treating.

Mrs Daly emerged from the house, seeking Jim's attention. As he was watching the Pawnee, which drowned her shouts, this got her nowhere. Would she walk half a mile to speak to him? No way! There was a large brass shell-case hanging on the veranda, with a spanner hanging from a lanyard. She beat it urgently, causing Jim to sprint back to the homestead. This was evidently their fire alarm, and he was not the man to hope it was just a false alarm.

He was still absent when Sean landed. "Just half a tank of fuel, so you can have a bash." "Surely, I'm not allowed to." "Of course you are!" Why else did you get clearance on the Pawnee authorised at the Isa? That plus your PPL is all the law requires. All that is forbidden is being paid for it, as I explained.

"As soon as you reach operating altitude, dump flaps, and start the circulating pump for the spray, otherwise nothing will happen when you try to start spraying. Then initiate a half-rate turn up-sun. Hold the spray until you cross the fence, and then centralise the controls in that lazy turn, laying your swathe against the one I've just done.

"Be aware that you start with a full load, raising stalling speed to ten knots faster than when you last flew it." "What about half-filling the hopper? If Jim spots a half-full can of insecticide, he'll think we are cheating him." "That is a good point. The wind sock is showing an increased headwind, so I'm sure you'll be OK taking off with a full load. I'll do all the chores, just climb aboard and familiarise yourself with everything, including where the horizon is when she sits on her tail skid, 'cause that's where it will be at touchdown. Just do it!"

I got in, and adjusted the spare goggles to fit. I then checked the controls for 'for full and free movement' by moving the control column in the widest possible circle, then pushing each rudder bar back to the stops. It only remained to pull full flaps on, and check the heel brakes. "She's all yours, Ralph." I started the engine, then checked idling speed (too fast would result in taking more airfield to stop) then 'mag drop.

Piston-engined light aircraft have dual ignition, as a safety feature. To make sure they are both working, you switch one off, while checking that the rpm doesn't drop, then switch it back on and check the other. I checked the wind sock, and then turned as close as possible to the fence, to give me the maximum take-off run, dead into wind. I checked 'harness and hatches' (the canopy and door closed and my harness fastened) then selected half flap for take-off, and was ready to go.

I held her on the heel brakes before pushing the throttle full open, and checked the rev counter to confirm that the rpm showed that I was getting full power. Then I released the brakes, and once we were underway, I pushed the control column slightly to pick the tail up, to let her pick up speed in the 'ground effect', those few feet where the air sticks to the ground. This also causes 'paddle wheeling,' as the propeller digs into this static air, pushing the nose to the right. I therefore needed a boot full of left rudder just to proceed in a straight line. I soon picked up sufficient air speed to rotate into the climb as I approached the boundary fence.

I reset the throttles to 'best climbing speed' and trimmed to maintain that attitude. At three hundred feet above the airstrip, I pushed the nose forward slightly to compensate for the reduction in lift as I eased the flaps back in. I turned the circulating pump on, and re-trimmed for level flight as I initiated my half-rate turn up-sun. Sean's last swathe glistened in the sunlight. I trimmed nose down, to avoid 'low and slow' dangers, and turned the spray on to lay my swathe just touching Sean's.

I needed to fly as close to the ground as I dared, so that the prop wash would shake the crop sufficiently to wet both sides of each leaf. I needed to do the best job I could, without appearing reckless to Sean. It took absolute concentration to think what I would do if the engine died on me, while flying accurately and thinking fast.

I soon found that spot on the wing to align with the shining arc on the ground. I turned off the spray as I approached the boundary, and put on a little more power as I held it in that gentle turn. As I gained confidence, the thought occurred to me that if Jim had completed the task that Noreen required him for, he might not realise that Sean was no longer at the controls. Even he might have spotted a novice on my first run.

Several passes later, I noticed the stick and rudder becoming more responsive, as the hopper emptied. The Pawnee presented a lessening angle of attack, and the resulting reduction of drag had slightly increased the air speed, so I throttled back slightly. All too soon the hopper emptied, and I turned off the spray, followed by the pump.

I zoomed off excess speed to gain a little height to help me complete pre-landing checks during my downwind leg. I checked my drift after turning crosswind, then turned into wind on finals, at the right height, and speed. I applied half flap, and closed the throttle. She floated over the ground like a feather, before settling down for a decent three-point landing.

I taxied towards the trailer as slowly as possible to reduce the amount of dust I stirred up. I sidled up to the trailer, held her securely with the heel brakes, and turned off both ignition switches, immediately pushing the throttle open to spread oil on the cylinder walls, and gulp cool air into the hot engine. I undid my harness, opened the canopy, and stepped out.

"That wasn't bad, Ralph. Do you feel more confident now?" "I reckon I was all over the shop on my first pass, but feel I'm getting there now. She certainly needs fuel now, so I'll grab the extinguisher while you do the needful."

So the day passed; Sean and I pressed on until the light faded. It was only when we drove in the ground screws to picket the Pawnee that I realised how tired I was. My eyes were bloodshot, and I was caked with red dust. We grabbed clean clothes, and headed for the shower. I smelt a barbecue. Jim was right. They had indeed 'done us proud!'

Noreen apologised for serving mutton. We each had what Helen described as a 'Barnsley chop', the thick steak cut off the end of hind leg. It was served with their home-grown vegetables, and there was a bottle of good red wine to wash it down. Sean and I were on our best behaviour.

I was so ashamed of getting impatient with Jim that I insisted on washing up afterwards. There was deep satisfaction the previous day in which I had passed my PPL, been cleared to fly the Pawnee, and driven 185km to Camooweal. Today was my first full day in my new job, and with a few hours of flying, almost as rewarding.

That day set the pattern for finishing our first contract, and the others that followed were little different. At first, each farmer seemed eccentric to me, although I thought I knew something about farming. Sean empathised with all of them. He pointed out that when they distrusted us, it was usually as a result of their previous experiences with other contractors, rather than with us. Once they found that we were always ready to start at first light and get on with the job in hand until it was completed, they were easy to get on with.

"All these 'cocky farmers', as they call them, are tied to the land," Sean said. "Each has inherited a spread that only turns a profit in good years, so they barely get a living from it. They would be ashamed to sell up, because their fathers and grandfathers had survived hard times, too. If they chose to sell, where would they find a buyer? Unless they had a prosperous neighbouring farmer, their holding would be almost unsaleable. There are easier ways to earn a crust."

Finally, we finished the third contract, and I was able to tell Helen my good news. She sounded anxious. "Tim was sure you must have qualified a couple of weeks ago."

"He's right. Sean was waiting for me the morning I qualified. He wanted me to help with three crop-spraying contracts that he had signed up to. I got type qualification at the Isa for his Pawnee, and he suggested that I do these three contracts with him before telling you." "What is he paying you?" "A

26

small wage, in line with Australian wages, plus five per cent of the gross contract (which he shows me)." "In other words, you kept it from me until it was a 'fait accompli'." "I dare say you are right, but now I've done it, and I'm proud of it. You must agree that when I get home and say that I've got my PPL, friends will probably say, 'What good will that do you? It is a very expensive hobby for anyone not yet earning.' Well it has already paid for itself. I have a few hundred quid in the bank, and nearly a hundred hours solo that hasn't cost me a penny." "When will we see you?"

"I won't know until Sean finishes prospecting for new contracts nearby. He won't take on any work for the week running up to the wedding, and any time I want to leave, he promised to drop me off nearer to you than the Isa, where he took me on. Apart from keeping that week free, we are both visiting Darwin to get our wedding finery, and the usual presents."

"He certainly seems to be punctilious in his dealings with you. As long as you are happy, I am satisfied. Please promise me that you will never drive or fly when you are tired." "It is true that you learn more from your parents' faults than their virtues. I love Dad, but I will always strive to avoid unnecessary risks, and think about your anxiety." "Then for a start, ring me at least weekly, to give me your news." "I promise, Mum."

Sean and I settled in to a good working relationship. It was now clear to me that my anger with him at our first our first meeting had Tim's fingerprints all over it. He had a selfish streak, as when he upset Helen and Hazel on the Christmas when he and Dean were our guests. Tim had showed bad manners, and Sean had tried to tell him that his behaviour was inappropriate. Unfortunately, he now had to draw my attention to antisocial aspects that he saw in **my** approach to those of my own age.

"You don't seem to recognise trouble coming your way. The Queensland climate seems to have melted your English reserve. For goodness' sake, avoid bars used by itinerant workers. You have cast aside the way you behaved at home, because no-one knows who you are. I should also avoid fishermen. Many of them bring marijuana ashore. Smoking grass never made anyone aggressive, but dealing it does. Those that do so have valuable drugs and plenty of cash about them, and carry a knife or a gun to protect what they carry.

"Both groups tend to whoop it up, wherever there is booze and girls to be had. You are sure as Hell heading for a brawl, and likely to get involved with girls that you wouldn't like Helen or Hazel to meet. I would prefer you to bring a six-pack back here, and share it with me, rather than tolerate bad company, or drink on your own. I'll bring it here, if that suits you better. Have you got condoms in your wallet? You should carry them, rather than risk unprotected sex!"

"So that's how you see me, is it? Always on the lookout for a punch-up or an easy lay, whenever I go out for a quiet beer?"

"I am just telling you how most guys of your age behave as soon as they are away from their own turf. All your life you have lived in a tight little community where everyone knows you. Every minor transgression becomes common knowledge.

"It is the best guarantee of good behaviour known to man. Once away from that restraint, you tend to hit foreign soil like Genghis Khan, with every appetite demanding instant satisfaction, and you don't give a hoot in Hell for anyone whose feathers you ruffle. Little wonder that you can't settle for a pint of shandy and a packet of crisps." "Sometimes they have salted peanuts, too, and occasionally pork scratchings."

"Now you've got it! You've found achievable goals for a night out already. So much for pleasure, now for business I have achieved no less than six new contracts, and whenever we finish those, we head for Kununurra, by way of Darwin. Otherwise, we finish in time to reach Kununurra a week before the wedding, and put any remaining contracts on the back burner."

I rang Helen, who expected to be absent doing final shopping for at least the start of that pre-wedding week, but promised to set some time aside to catch up properly with my news, and tell me her timetable. I called Hazel next, and we set some time aside for the same mutual updating. I then sent a long newsy letter to Jane, and asked how everything was panning out for her at Aberystwyth. On completion of her shopping trip, Helen sent me an invitation for Sean.

I set about our remaining contracts with a will, ready to work all hours to bring them to completion. As a result, I soon felt physically drained, and felt forebodings that I was approaching the next watershed in my life, that would affect the rest of my working life.

I often awoke in the small hours, disturbed and troubled, or, more rarely, experiencing blazing exhilaration, but had no idea why. I had worked through my school days taking things one day at a time, according to a timetable dictated by the school syllabus. All I had to do was take each hurdle as it arrived. All that seemed to matter was to prepare for the next exam.

Because Dad had livestock to manage, the only difference between being at school or on holiday, were ten or so family outings each year, but never a family holiday. My current absence from the farm and other local roots led to the very trouble that Sean had warned me against.

Having carefully taken on board what was required of me at the wedding, I started the next contract knowing that it would be completed two or three weeks hence. I was saving money, and my solo hours were accumulating fast enough to offer the possibility of achieving a commercial rating no longer beyond my grasp. Each evening I totted up my hours flown with a sense of real satisfaction.

Then one evening, we stopped flying earlier to maintain the spray system. After a couple of hours, Sean said that I looked tired, and offered to complete the job on his own, should I wish to borrow the pickup.

I thanked him, and accepted his offer, hoping to have a drink in the nearest bar while I mulled over something that had arisen when I was socialising in Kununurra. As I pulled out onto the main road on which the bar was situated, I was gratified to find the car park almost empty. There were just a few truckers there, enjoying a drink before turning in for the night. I took my drink to the far end of the veranda, which was otherwise empty.

A speeding pickup truck sounded its horn to give us the opening bars of 'Dixie', before squealing brakes, followed by screeching tyres, signalled its arrival in the bar's car park, still travelling fast enough to broadside, leaving a cloud of red dust. Six guys jumped out, each clad in dirty shorts and singlet. The rear fender bore a confederate flag decal, to go with the musical horn. The first one into the bar immediately ran out again, shouting, "There's no action here tonight, let's try the next place."

The runt of the litter replied, "Suit yerselves, I'm stayin'." The speaker was short, dark, and skinny. He sported a bush hat, and a large Bowie knife on his belt. This would be a useful tool to anyone who regularly skinned buffalo or crocodiles, but in his case I expected that it was more of a fashion statement. "Pick me up on your way back!" he shouted.

They looked at me and sniggered, then one of them shouted, "OK, but be good 'til Mummy comes back." They piled into the truck, and the driver made the mistake of pulling out with his foot on the accelerator again, with more red dust, squealing tyres, and tyre marks on the road. An oncoming police car turned on its blue lights and siren.

I decided to finish my drink and leave. "What are you smirkin' at, sonny?" Shorty had got his drink and was approaching. He ignored his mates, who had pulled up on the verge, awaiting the two approaching constables, who had parked so as to block their access to the road.

"I intend to finish my beer and leave." "You've chosen the wrong place to squat. You are in my seat, just for starters. D'you know what I did last week?"

"No, but make it snappy, because I'm off as soon as I've finished my drink." "Just listen politely. I'll tell you when you can go. I reckoned that busy as it was, it was too quiet for me so I pulled me knife. You should have seen them. They piled out of the door like scared rabbits. That's why nobody sits at my table, unless they are man enough to square-up to me."

"You are welcome to the table. I'm off." I stood up, and turned my head to drain my pint without taking my eyes off him. He put his glass down, then put his hat next to it. I saw that he was older than I had thought. He could be anything from forty to late fifties, and looked wiry and fast-moving. I was suddenly 'switched on'. I seemed to hear Dad whisper in my ear, "He took his hat off to nut you!" I heard boots thunder along the veranda, but I didn't intend to take my eyes off my assailant.

"Stand right where you are, both of you!" Shorty grabbed the haft of his knife, to distract me from his real intention. I reached out to pin his skinny wrist to his belt. Might he pull the sheath away with his free hand? I blocked that move by clasping him to my chest, as though intending to tango down the veranda with him. Aware that I no longer had a free hand, he smiled sweetly at me, and whispered, "As soon as you let go, I'll have you."

Thinking what Dad would do in this situation, I butted him hard, just above the bridge of his nose. Both his eyes rolled up beneath his eyelids, as if he was a fruit machine. As he sank slowly to the boards, I twitched his knife out, and drove it deep into one of the boards.

"We are taking you in for affray. He will have to be examined by a doctor, in case he has suffered concussion, or worse. Place your little friend in the pickup, and get in our car."

"What did you expect me to do? He threatened to 'get me' as soon as I let go!" The speaker was a tall slim guy. "We only have your word for that. From what I saw, his knife remained in its sheath until after you nutted him. You can both have your say at the station. Now put your hands behind your back, so I can handcuff you."

The only small satisfaction I got was to see him unable to pull the Bowie knife out of the floorboard. He gave up trying to exert his biceps to emulate King Arthur pulling Excalibur out of the stone, and only after several hefty kicks with his boot was it loosened enough to pull out.

Noting my smirk, his short mate said, "You itinerants have run wild for long enough." The tall one handcuffed the other rebels to the 'roll over' bar behind the cab, cuffing one of them ankle to ankle with my would-be assailant, as he reclined in state on a folded tarpaulin, next to the tailgate. He then preceded the police car back to the station.

The desk sergeant wasn't too keen on me, either. "You might have killed the little bastard, nutting him like that. We shall hold you while the doc checks him for concussion, or other injuries. You could face more serious charges. Put him down, Constable." "Can I ring my mate? He lent me his pickup to visit that bar." "Where are you both working?" I told him. "I'll ring Mr Cameron, and ask him to pass the message on." He asked for my papers, and I offered my driving license and passport. "What are you doing over here?" "I came over to attend my mum's remarriage, and took the opportunity to qualify for my PPL." I instantly realised that I should have obtained a work visa first, and decided only to answer direct questions, rather than volunteering information. I then sat in my cell, and the tall road patrol officer took pity on me, and asked if I wanted his newspaper to read.

"Take it easy. Most of the public disorder is caused by itinerant labour, and the most cost-effective way of dealing with it is a night in the cells."

"Thanks for offering your newspaper, but I went to that bar hoping to get my head around what I do next, having sat my final exams at school. What I really need is the loan of a pen, and some scrap paper to write on. What better use could I make of your kind hospitality?"

"You sure you wouldn't prefer the sergeant to take notes, while you recline on your bed doing your 'stream of consciousness' bit?"

"To do so might impose further on his kindness than I deserve."

"You are dead right there, mate." He returned with a wad of obsolete sheep-scab forms, and a Bic ball pen. I thanked him, and he said, "That's the ticket. Keep your mind busy for a couple of hours, and it will be much easier to kip-down afterwards." I pitched in right away by writing a heading at the top of the first sheet.

CHAPTER 2

Time for Reconstruction

Losing Dad when I was just fifteen left a huge gap in my life. I stood in St Bartholomew's church yard, liking Mum close as his coffin was lowered into the grave, my ears still hearing 'Crossing the Bar'. The February rain beat down on all those who joined us for the interment to pay their respects to him. The acrid perfume of witch hazel was noticeable from a few twigs in a black Wedgwood urn on an adjacent grave bearing, a bundle of black twigs with their insignificant yellow flowers, each one a few short bristles. The hills hid their heads in the low clouds. I swear, that for the rest of my life, that scent will take me back to his graveside.

The need for a funeral service dawned on me. When someone we love passes beyond our senses, we really need this ritual to remind us of their life, and take the first step towards closure after the first blow of losing them. I lacked friends, which kept us close.

Big for my years, I felt clumsy and tongue-tied in company, moving carefully for fear of tripping over my feet.

We returned home, to offer hospitality to our guests. I hovered over them, passing plates and filling teacups. I hoped that keeping busy would get the day over with more quickly. Looking back, I recall that it was a proper farmhouse in those days. The garden wall only served to keep the livestock away from the house, because there was no evidence that it had ever contained a garden.

Our home was built in the early 19th century. I expect that it owed its existence to the Enclosures Act, although no doubt it had been preceded by several wooden dwellings, and probably even turf shelters before them. The oldest stone houses in the area boasted mid-17th century dates on their front-door lintel, which indicated that those who erected those earlier dwellings had given no thought to building for future generations.

Anyway, it looks as symmetrical as a doll's house, but once inside you find the parlour occupies about a third of the frontage, while the hall and kitchen occupy the remaining two thirds. The front door opens onto the hall, with the staircase (with a broom cupboard beneath) facing you on the right, leading to a half landing lit by a tall window set in the side wall with a nice arched top to it. The parlour is to your left, with the kitchen door facing. We live in the kitchen, with one tattered rug set in front of the cast iron kitchen range. Behind the parlour, the pantry and wash house lead off from the kitchen, the washhouse giving access to the back yard.

I'm sorry, I've launched into estate agent mode before even introducing myself. My name is Ralph Swindlehurst, for what that's worth. My forebears have lived hereabouts at least since the 13th century, when there was a forest grange here, and an ancestor, a lay-brother at one of the monasteries, was sent with one other to prepare a site as winter grazing for the deer.

It could only be accessed by the deer by jumping down from higher ground, the idea being that once inside with full bellies, they would find themselves unable to jump uphill to regain their freedom. This was to keep them 'in-bye' for the winter, to avoid them dying of starvation.

When spring came, they were released back into the forest. We are well known on our own stamping ground. There are so many of us in St Bart's graveyard (and Slingers too) that other locals must feel like an ethnic minority, and off comers must feel like intruders. Most of us have become 'heafed to the fell', like our flocks of ewes. This has its advantages and disadvantages. I would have to think long and hard before leaving my own patch, but it can lead to narrow-mindedness.

It was back to school the following day, and I braced myself for trying to get back into the routine while everyone else would feel they had to walk on eggshells in my presence. My classmates were subdued in my presence, as if bereavement was contagious. In assembly, the headmaster asked everyone to try to share my loss. It was with relief that I remembered it would be one of my favourites, history, with Mr Bradshaw.

"Your homework should launch you confidently

into the next topic that we will discuss today. Sonia has raised an interesting point."

This was so unusual that everyone looked at her, causing a bellow of nervous laughter from this red-haired girl, sat on the back row.

"I had asked each of you to choose a historical period, bracketing it with dates, to be filled in with your own research. In her usual pugnacious manner, Sonia spent more time challenging the question, than she did answering it. I think she has a valid point. Share it with the whole class."

"I asked me mam what she would suggest. The Battle of Hastings, probably the only thing she could remember from her time at school."

"That must be the first time you've followed your mam's advice, our Sonj!"

"Shut it, Stubbins, you big ape! I wondered how many people would give a toss about it, once the news reached them. Few round here would care who won. Whoever had been favoured by King Harold would lose by it, but they would be thin on the ground round hereabouts. Most people would be far more concerned about how good the harvest would be, and whether they would get their full share of it." She blushed, and sat down, to show she had finished. "This is the valid point. It underlines the direction in which the teaching of history is leading us. We call it 'learning by empathy'. In fairness to the victor, King William, I should point out that his reign, despite his notorious 'ravaging of the north', brought several advantages to his humblest subjects.

"He ended slavery, and developed defences that

finally ended the succession of invasions from the continent. He also endowed monasteries which developed vast sheep runs, a new way of land management that is still visible in the landscape over most of the hill-sheep farming countryside. So much for England as a whole. Now let us focus on our locality. Domesday describes the locals as 'few, intractable, and wild'."

This brought general laughter, so he knew he had our attention. "Much later, the War of the Roses brought us roving plunderers, a common enemy to unite us. The Talbots, of Bashall Eaves, were little more than robber barons. When Richard the Third ruled, their name was commemorated in the couplet; 'The Cat (Caton), the Rat (Stanley) and Talbot the Dog, ruled all England under the Hog'. The hog, of course, was the wild boar which Richard chose as his emblem.

"Forest Law was administered by the King's Officers. These included the Abbots of Cockersands, Whalley, and Sawley Abbeys. Each ran granges in Bowland forest, on which they established sheep runs. The Parkers of Browsholme Hall took their name from their forest stewardship, which bore down heavily on the few forest residents.

"Many gentlemen living locally were quick to seize their opportunity when the forest system finally collapsed around 1500. Those that aspired to their own manor found that land and timber were theirs for the taking.

"Other King's Officers had already plundered what had been placed in their care. By the way, an interesting survival was the Forest Court, which occupied the first floor of 'the Hark to Bounty' inn', in Slaidburn, which was still sitting in the 1920s.

"By the time of the Civil War, little timber remained. It was only ever a forest in the sense that it was a hunting preserve for royalty, rather than woodland. What timber there was would have been open oak woodland, because it provides the best environment for deer. At this time, the human population doubled.

"'Bowland' meant 'Land of Cattle' which I take to refer to its pre-Norman use for raising beef cattle. An interesting facet of social history was the fact that John King was parish priest at St Bart's from the reign of James the First, through the Civil War and the Commonwealth, to the time of Charles the Second, proof that here at least, religious tolerance was the order of the day. Charles Fox, who taught Quaker beliefs, said, 'Seek that of God in every man,' which we tried to do."

I lost track of what he was saying at this point, as I remembered what Dad had to say on the subject. "To put down roots often requires that we make do with less, and bend to the wind, rather than reject all change. In times of religious persecution, both Catholics and Freethinkers were sheltered. Wesley preached in our church. We tried to respect other faiths, and judge a man on his merits. I believe not only that these values were commonly held in our local community, but that they were long-established family values that must be honoured."

"You have given me your attention so far, but I see that I'm starting lose some of you. You must know me well enough by now to realise that this discourse would introduce your next subject for an essay. Some of you are looking forward to university life, where you will be expected to be more self-motivated, and work on your own. You will be expected to manage your own time, to avoid being left behind.

"You are **all** capable of achieving better results than you have yet achieved, so this time you can't crib other people's work, or lift whole passages from an encyclopaedia. You are capable of researching less accessible sources in the school library, or a public library. This essay must cover the same period that you chose to bracket previously, but must concern local matter **only.**

"This means that you can quote national or local government legislation, but only to mention how it affected **this** locality. I will be happy to help you, but **only** after you have shown me what you have found for yourself. Ralph, please remain after class. The rest of you, dismissed!"

This was his message for me. "I'll make this deal with you. I can definitely get you through English language and history exams, if you follow my rules. You can easily manage English lit. on your own. I am sure that your actual exam paper this year will include at least three questions that you are given in your forthcoming 'mock' exams.

"Each year, we list the questions, and assume that there are only a fixed number of them in each subject, and that they more or less get repeated in a three-year cycle, so we can usually predict at least half of each year's questions. As you know, you are able to **choose** from a list of questions, a further opportunity to **avoid** what you can't answer!

"Firstly, **you** lack confidence, so must be methodical in your approach. You wouldn't believe the number of pupils that don't answer the question that has been set. They sit down, hoping for certain questions, and through not reading and re-reading what lies before them, they answer what they **hoped** was the question, but was not.

"You must take time to retrieve what you know from your memory. Secondly, take advantage of your good visual memory. Seek an image you link to a period, or a place, before trawling for dates and numbers. Thirdly, consciously seek to pigeon-hole what you hope to memorise. New data must be consciously placed in order.

"For instance, many journalists keep lists of 'news hooks', scraps of local information that can add colour to breaking news. Once you have accumulated your own database, you will be surprised how often you will know something about random places that are featured in the news. Eventually, what you already know may make some of these news items seem either unlikely, highly improbable, or simply from someone who hasn't understood what they are reporting.

"If you pass, I'll know then that you are ready to hear what little I know of your father's experiences, and some things I think he would have told you, if he had the time to do so. I did speak to him about why he bought himself out of the army.

"After all, he wanted to make it his career, and had been successful so far, and the Paras wanted to keep him. If you don't pass, I can only conclude that you weren't trying, and may not yet be mature enough to hear what I have to say. So much for generalities, what will your essay be about?"

"My last ramble was as far northwards on Salter Fell to the county boundary. I know it was a packhorse route, but neither where the salt came from, nor where it was going to."

"Then I'll give you a head start. This was used originally in the Dark Ages, when written records were almost non-existent. The best evidence was in the place names. As an example, by far the majority of English river names are Celtic in origin, but during the tenth century the North West saw an influx of Vikings from Ireland, where they had previously settled. A lot of the salt pans were built by them.

"As this was settlement, rather than invasion, they tended to trade, or farm sheep. Those Angles already settled there were among the first to use iron plough shares, so they occupied the heavy clay soils that gave them good yields of wheat, but were unusable to those still using wooden ploughshares.

"The salt had to be distributed, and the other very useful source is the Ordnance Survey publication 'Britain Before the Norman Conquest.' In the absence of written records, place names and viable routed are pretty much all we have to go on.

"A further unusual feature of that era is what is known as the 'Dublin-Jorvik axis'. Dublin was originated by Vikings, not Irish Celts. Although York flourished under the Romans who called it 'Eboracum', in Viking times it was known as Jorvik, and it was an important trading post for Vikings who traded from Kiev to Sicily, and on to Constantinople.

"Dublin did a lot of slave trading, and there was

thriving trade both ways along this axis. So presumably eastbound salt would head through Bainbridge (Viking 'Bein' meant 'the direct way') to York. Northbound salt might have gone by sea, and southbound along the existing Roman road towards Clitheroe, which was on another Roman thoroughfare from Ribchester (a major hub on the Roman road system). Oh dear. I am rambling on a bit.

"I'll lend you the dictionary, and can find you a textbook containing an excerpt of the map which covers North West England. Another textbook covering the settlement of North West England by Vikings from Ireland. Give me ten minutes to find the books, and then get home and look after your mother."

As soon as I got home, Mum asked how I had got on. She was relieved to hear about my chat with Mr Bradshaw. "You sound quite excited about your next essay. It so happens that I am taking social history in my WEA classes, and I can ask the tutor if he knows the possible source of the salt pan, north west of Hornby. I should be able to take you for a nosy round on Sunday."

Sunday arrived, and we set off. Mum drove us north to Caton, where we picked up the Kirkby Lonsdale road, forking right for Hornby. Mum's tutor had tipped 'The Salting' at Arnside as being almost certainly the source. We drove there via Gressingham and Borthwick, finding 'The Saltings' opposite the train station.

Mum decided it was time for lunch, and she fancied 'The Ship' at Sandside. Once we were comfortably settled, and had placed our order, we pored over the maps. Our oldest relevant one inch to the mile was for Preston, published in 1947. Thanks to the War intervening, it was based on the 1920 survey, with some amendments.

What amazed us was that the Salter Fell track **was not shown at all**, despite appearing on later OS maps! In its absence, the Roman Road was included, but with a gap in it, which extended from the pass dividing White Hill (near the county boundary with Yorkshire West Riding) and south to the 'remains of Croasdale House'. This track is not only clearly marked on the ground, but prior to Ted Heath's county boundary changes, was in regular use by Lancashire Constabulary, as a training ground for police motor cyclists.

I suggested, "Perhaps, two years after the end of WW2, someone in Ordnance Survey still anticipated a German invasion, and didn't want German Panzer divisions to use it as a handy shortcut?" Mum replied, "Such a person would soon find himself posted out to the 'Min. of Ag. and Fish.' to join like-minded colleagues." "Where do you reckon the salt went to from Arnside?" "I think northbound, it would either go by boat for longer journeys, or else by packhorse using the over-sand route. Westwards, it would cross the river at Gressingham or Hornby, and then pick up the Roman Road to York from Ribchester.

"It would have been much shorter to cross the Lune, and make for the Trough road towards Clitheroe, so I assume that the nearest ford to Lancaster (at the site of the Roman camp) must have been where the Duke of Lancaster, or someone else, exacted a toll for passing freight.

"I think, 'Dark Ages' or not, it is reasonable to

assume that they were as capable as we are at choosing the best option. In other words, whatever their technology was capable of, someone would have tried it."

"So, where shall we go to now?"

"We no longer have time to include Clitheroe, so might I suggest that (not to make a toil out of a pleasure) we linger over our lunch, then cover the whole of the Salter Fell track, and when we reach Newton, make for Dunsop Bridge, returning home by the Trough road.

"After all, you've already walked from Newton to the county boundary, so you will have already explored that stretch on foot."

What had Mr Bradshaw said about 'the best option'? I asked if I could have pudding and a coffee, in that case. I was quite happy to be driven, rather than walk, particularly having walked half the route already!

We set off, leaving Hornby by the Salter Fell track; driving slowly, we tried to take in as much as possible. She told me that once we crossed the boundary, she would tell me all she knew about our surroundings. "The quarry on our right was opened by the Fylde Water Board in the early 1920s to provide stone for building Stocks Reservoir, plus the handsome office building, in the style of a country house, standing just above water level, in addition to the treatment plant and pumping station at the foot of the dam.

"A light railway had been constructed to carry the stone to its destination. From the quarry, it took the shortest route to cross the Croasdale Beck, and then follow the side of Lamb Hill. The tarmac road to Newton starts at the gated cattle grid next to Higher Woodhouse Farm. Most of the track is just limestone chippings, but from the quarry to the cattle grid, it had been concreted at the time, but is now quite broken up by rain and frost."

I had noticed a weird track, not far from the cattle grid, that consisted of two deep ruts that would leave a Land Rover sat on its axles with the wheels barely touching the mud, I pointed this out to Mum. "Residents of Slaidburn have turbiary rights to cut turf here, for fuel.

Originally, they would remove it by sledge, using cart horses, but it is still used, towing the sledge by tractor. Indeed, the Lamb Hill shepherd (a friend of Grandpa) still cuts a year's supply, which he stacks under a corrugated shelter against the gable end of his cottage. Although the cottage is less than two miles distant, he has to transfer the load from sledge to wheeled trailer, and drive nine miles via Slaidburn, because the road he used to use is at the bottom of the reservoir!

Mum pointed out that until the 20s, even the road over Waddington Fell was unsealed, consisting of loose limestone chippings. Everything that passed in dry weather raised limestone dust, so that the surrounding sour wet heather, still has a bright green stripe of sweet grass. Prior to it being sealed, coal would have been brought from Clitheroe mainly by horse and cart. In fact Slaidburn was still using bucket sanitation in the 60s!

As Mum turned right at Newton for Dunsop Bridge, she gave me two other nuggets of local history. "The big house we are about to pass on our right is called 'The Heanings'. The Quaker gentleman who built it used the Roman road as his drive, so the Hodder is only a few yards beyond, and the Romans must have forded it here.

"Had we continued through the village and on to Waddington, where Henry the 6th was hiding after the battle of Hexham, having sheltered at various other houses on his way south. The Talbots got wind of this, and although he had fled on foot, they caught up with him at 'the hipping stones' where the Ribble was forded before a bridge was built." After these interesting facts, Mum remained silent, evidently going over something in her mind. From past experience, this was going to be bad news for me.

Eventually, she spoke. "I'm going to grab a bath first. You must write up the events of the day while it is all fresh in your mind. While you have your bath, I'll brew up. I must say, when I agreed to this outing, I never guessed how engrossing it would be. You are growing up fast, Ralph. This has been such a special day. Let it 'sugar the pill' of some unwelcome news for you.

"I am well aware how important the livestock was for Alec, and still is for you. I consider that the dairy herd to be a hobby that we can no longer afford. Alec bought the herd, and built the required dairy, by taking out an agricultural mortgage, at a time of historically high lending rates.

"As marginal dairy farms go, Alec did well to achieve a five per cent return on capital. Unfortunately, the loan bears an interest rate of fifteen per cent at the present. Hence my claim that this is 'hobby farming' which threatens us with bankruptcy, when that enterprise is under-staffed, and will remain so.

"At current values, selling the herd, plus some of the sheep, would clear the loan, and leave as a little working capital." She held up her hand to stop my reply. "Hear me out. You cannot cope with school work and manage the livestock as well. This whole business following Alec's untimely death, demonstrates the drastic state of hill-sheep farming. This proves that your education is much more necessary than the future of the farm, and your progress at school so far shows that you have a lot to catch up with before School Cert. That is my case, what is your response?"

Having expected bad news, it didn't take me long to decide on a course of action. She thought much faster than I did, and it was probable that I had missed a flaw in her argument. I clearly needed to keep her onside, as disagreement would be a festering sore in a relationship that demanded we act as one. If I worked out what that flaw was, it would have to be dealt with later. "Whatever you decide, I must accept as a fait accompli, whatever my dad might have thought about it. Let's hear the rest of your plan. As the milk cheque paid most of the bills, how do you plan to replace it?"

Her face lit up. "I have been offered first refusal of my management job at the creamery. I would far prefer having my salary, than watch you wear yourself out, as Alec did, tending livestock to the point that your education goes down the pan when hill-sheep farming can no longer provide a living. Here is how I see the pros and cons.

"You want to keep livestock, whether or not you

can afford to do so profitably. I firmly intend to sell the herd, now, and rent out the grazing. This provides a reversible decision which leaves us my salary, plus the grazing rental, plus a little cash in the bank, rather than an under-manned hill sheep and dairy enterprise burdened by debt."

She was well rehearsed, and had presented her case to appeal to the male mind. Unlike her, I believed that my empathy for livestock (and Dad's) is a strong point, not mere sentiment. As she well knew, it would take me time to spot the flaw in her argument, and the job offer demanded a swift response from her. My only course was to make the best of a bad job by accepting the inevitable with a good grace, while resolving that if she had pulled a fast one, I would not get mad, but get even! Alec would expect me to eventually inherit **his** farm, even if it had dropped in value.

"Is the manager's job what you want, Mum?" "I shall fly up Windy Street like a rat up a drain!" "Then go for it, and the best of luck!" That seemed to settle it. I'd expected Cock Hill to provide my livelihood. I saw myself as a mould, in which the passing years would add concrete, until out would pop a concrete gnome.

No-one would expect 'Belerephon astride winged Pegasus' to emerge from a naff rubber mould, would they? I was sitting for my School Cert. that year, and remember little of the farm sale, just another chunk of my life gone forever. As soon as it was over, Mum was on the phone to the local NFU office, to advertise the grazing to rent. They had welcome news for her.

The North Lancs. Gliding Club had contacted them seeking a site within reach of what they described as 'the bowl', consisting of that slope between Parlick and Fairsnape which offers hill slope soaring whenever the wind funnelled into it. The problem was, they had been offered a grant from the Sports Council, and an interest-free loan from another source, each conditional on security of tenure, meaning that they must **own** the site, rather than rent it. However, they could not afford the buildings as well.

Mum got her solicitor to contact the club, and after a couple of months during which they got no other offer, he was able to conclude a favourable deal with them. I had the option of renting the grazing, subject to keeping a stock-proof fence around it, and my agreement to enclose the sheep in a pound on flyable weekends.

This enabled them to secure an Agricultural Drainage Grant from the Ministry of Agriculture and Fisheries, as the land was to be kept in agricultural use. The grant was sufficient to pay for all the material and (second-hand) machinery that was necessary, so long as the club members provided the labour.

Mum was the best landowner they could have hoped to buy from, because she intended to live there, and I would clear the sheep when necessary. I told them I wanted to join the club, which increased the probability that their airstrip would be cleared when flying was due to commence. From the club's point of view, everything fitted together like a jigsaw, with one massive flaw that only affected me.

You have probably already spotted what it was. Mum's so-called 'reversible decision' had remained so for only weeks, rather than months! Her exchange of contracts limited my future use of Tewitts' Field as a hill-sheep farm.

These thoughts filled my mind one morning, as I prepared a garden (at Mum's insistence) before the club brought their equipment. I had explained that there was something decadent about a farmhouse 'tarted up' with a garden. It advertised the fact that what used to be farm, is now merely a dwelling.

"Just get digging, and that means **now!** Get all those bulbs planted, and don't forget the two window boxes, which need to be secured to the wall." There was a vast accumulation of rubbish to be disposed of before I could even start any gardening. Having made my feelings clear, without changing her intentions, I rolled my sleeves up, and got stuck in with my gardening on that bright October morning.

Not a moment too soon, because that was the day that some of the club members arrived to install a cattle grid ten yards in from the gate. This was so that they could improve access for their thirty-foot long glider trailers. There were only two members with any knowledge of dry-stone wall building, and they started by demolishing about ten yards each side of the gate posts, which had to be dug out, and re-sited either side of the cattle grid.

Life was looking up. As farmers, we had always been considered part of the entertainment laid on for weekend country-goers. It was great to find all these strangers taking on unfamiliar tasks for us to gawp at! The only stone-walling skill they were confident with was tearing the wall down either side of the grid. I ambled over, to clarify two issues.

"As there are sheep in the field, you will have to

replace what you have demolished with a temporary fence of sheep wire. Have you allowed for the fact that the two arcs that you are about to build will require more stone than you have demolished?" No, they hadn't. I showed them where there was a short run of redundant wall that they could cannibalise, but pointed out that the field would have to be stock-proof before they left.

"Eventually, you will have to re-site the gate posts. I think each one will extend two feet below ground level, and will weigh well over a ton, so you need a lot of help, and a tractor to drag them to their new position. We had to sell ours off, at the farm sale." They explained that they had one, and chains to drag the posts. They also had a JCB to help prepare the new sockets.

"OK, I'll find you some fence posts and sheep wire, and pen the sheep up, but it will still need to be stock-proof when you leave, because none of you will be here again until the weekend." It was panic stations as I returned to my gardening. The upshot was, that the gate remained on its posts, all the demolished wall was replaced with sheep wire, and the gate posts would have to be re-sited once their groundwork kit moved in.

It was quite a disappointment, weeks later, to see a slow convoy advancing towards the farm. At first, I could only identify the winch truck which was leading. A motley procession of cars and Land Rovers which were towing thirty-foot long trailers, each housing a de-rigged glider. Only after they had crossed the cattle grid, could I make out more detail.

The winch truck, bearing the winch engine, was an ex-service five-tonner, stripped of all bodywork other than the cab and mudguards. The winch I found, was a bus engine and gearbox sat on engine bearers of roughly burnt-off H-section steel. The winch driver had a seat, and was protected by a steel cage, made necessary by frequent cable brakes. The cage was covered with strong mesh, to allow the driver to see both cable and glider.

There was an elderly JCB, weeping expensive hydraulic oil at every connection, and with several full containers of this fluid in its bucket. The last vehicle was a single-cylinder diesel dump-truck, spewing out dense smoke, and carrying shovels, pry-bars, pick axes, and anything else that a navvy might lean on.

I have long realised that I am too quick to judge people at first acquaintance. Should they prove even slightly less vile than I anticipated, I am equally hasty in believing the best of them. In fact, I am as putty in their hands. Once again, I came to scoff, and stayed to pray. I was almost prepared to admit having joined their number. I fully anticipated being a sixth-former next autumn. Sixth form men require a certain cachet. Lacking the means to run a string of polo ponies, being a gliding club member seemed a cheap way to cut a dash at school.

Hence, I failed to spot that they seemed suspiciously keen to recruit a simple, trusting country boy. There was an awful lot of hard graft to complete before I would be competing with them for a launch. I might well be a burnt-out shell of my former self, when I finally pushed aside my Zimmer frame to climb into a glider cockpit. Like any other dispossessed peasant, I grappled with the intractable boulder clay of Tewitts' Field through a seemingly endless succession of cold, wet, weekends, despite not seeming to profit for my efforts. My new friends and I grubbed-out hedges, dug ditches for land drains, and then back-filled them and laid road-stone.

What a welcome change it was for everyone, when Guy Fawkes Night arrived. Festivities flowered abundantly, despite makeshift surroundings. Norman Gill, who owned a pub in Baxenden, ran the bar. Burgers and sausages sizzled on the barbecue. Everyone who attended seemed to bring fireworks, parkin, or treacle toffee. It was a fundraising event for the club, but Jack Aked, founder and ex-CFI, invited Mum as she would be disturbed by the noise; she might as well be there enjoying it. He was an ex-RAF instructor, and a real gentleman.

Most of those present who had actively involved themselves had only seen the site in autumn weather. It brought out their party spirit to be able to enjoy food and drink, and good company, while crackling flames put cold and darkness to flight. As entertainment, it certainly beat digging drains.

I've always been childishly excited around bonfires. I must have been dashing around like a mad arsonist, because Jack flagged me down from my third brisk lap around the fire. "Ralph, why don't you present yourself at the bar, and try to pass yourself off as an adult? I'm pretty sure that Jack will serve you a pint." This seemed a good time to collect Mum, and stand her a glass of wine.

I took this as a typically tactful ploy to dissuade me from scattering more screaming maidens into the outer darkness. Mum declined, introducing me to a work colleague, and saying that they were both about to go back home for a coffee. I got my pint, and tuned in to Tug Wilson, who was with his wife, Sue, in conversation with a fellow Scouser.

He had visited Paris with Kirby Karate Club. "We were hell-bent on demonstrating Scouse culture to Parisians, who clearly thought there wasn't any culture beyond their city limits. Each bout ended in a knock-out, with another Parisian smeared across the canvas like a work by Jackson Pollack.

"However, on each occasion, before our cheers had died away, the referee had disqualified our contender for using excessive force. Karate? They seemed to expect a Diddy men's tickling-stick contest!" I was impressed. I must be careful not to boast around these guys until I had something to boast about.

The evening wore on, and people started to drift away. Memories returned of other bonfire nights when I had helped Grandpa, and then Dad. I sought Mum out, and as the party dispersed, silence and solitude returned. We sauntered back to our kitchen in quiet harmony, with the scent of wood smoke clinging to our clothes.

The dull remaining weeks to Christmas crept by, and at weekends it was with ever-increasing reluctance that I climbed into cold, damp wellies to resume navvying. I must have been in a dull stupor, because I was startled to hear a strange voice address me, when I thought I was alone. "Now then, young man!" I turned to see a man in his early thirties, tall and broad, with long fair hair.

He had a long nose and blue eyes, and his big hands were black from working with the club's machinery.

He peered from under the neb of a US Army fatigues cap. "You can hold the funnel for me while I top the oil. Are you a new member here? I'm Ben."

"Yes, my name is Ralph, and I live here."

"Good man! I'm sure we'll find some way of cashing in on that. For a start, do you have any heavy grease?"

"We certainly do. It's where we keep our Land Rover, because it used to be the tractor shed."

I helped him complete servicing the JCB, and then he showed me on his own car how to trace 'failure to start' problems on a petrol engine. He tended machinery for a motorway-building contractor as his 'day job'. I was always willing to help him out with an extension lead, or torch, or even a hot drink on the many occasions when he arrived mid-week to finish some self-imposed task. It seemed little enough to do for someone who had driven here after a hard day's work, and with a fifty-mile drive home ahead of him!

The following Saturday, a load of road-stone arrived on site. It was two-inch limestone chippings intended for a roadway which had already been prepared with hardcore. Ben mounted his beloved JCB, and dispersed along the length to be finished. We labourers seized our rakes, and spread it as evenly as possible. I must say, the others looked to be ill-prepared for the job.

Only the sensible few were dressed in old worn clothes and stout boots. To use any long-handled tool outdoors, you need a snag-proof jacket, that won't rip on hedges of 'T' handles. To dig effectively, or even shovel, you need boots. Some were wearing ski-wear, which soon ripped on spade handles, thorns, or barbed wire. Others had buttons or pockets that soon snagged on 'T' handles. I never commented on this, but enjoyed feeling superior to these strange beings, to whom outdoor work was evidently a novelty.

Eventually, fading light brought work to an end. I watched my work-mates trudge towards the welcoming tea urn in the clubhouse. They no longer had a spring in their step. Their wet and muddy jeans stuck to their legs. Their hands were blistered beneath the mud that they had rashly failed to wipe off their hands. Ben, still fresh as a daisy, jumped back into the JCB, having decided to use it as a toad-roller. He charged up and down the freshly laid road drunk with power.

The JCB might have been clapped out, but when its front wheels struck a bump going uphill, I'll swear that he could coax a brief wheelie from it! One by one, the weary workforce turned to witness the total destruction of all that they had wrought, along with tons of expensive road stone, which was swallowed by the hungry clay sub-soil. Not an oath passed their lips. In my imagination, I saluted them. I had misjudged them. I had not yet achieved manhood, but all of them had done so.

Ben bedded down his favourite toy, and hailed everyone as he cleaned up for the drive home. "That was a belter! I dare say we'll need some hardcore and another load of road stone, if we are to finish the job next weekend. See you then, lads!"

Silence returned, by ruddy evening light. The farm house snuggled into the slope, beneath sheltering elms, etched black against a pink-to-turquoise sky. Parlick, our Pennine outlier, brooded like an old hen over its clutch of boulder-clay drumlins. A welcoming carpet of yellow light spilled towards me from the kitchen window, across the flagstones, as Mum prepared dinner.

Once inside, I filled the bath and laid out clean clothes before wallowing in the relaxing warmth of it. Everything I had worn except my boots was in the wash basket. As I followed the smell of chicken casserole into the kitchen, it dawned on me that she had made further changes. The windows had been dressed with cheerful gingham curtains, and a new pine welsh dresser stood against the hall wall. On it was displayed her best crockery, which had rarely seen the light of day.

Mum clocked me weighing up her efforts. "I had considered kitchen units, but knew you would disapprove. How do you like my changes?"

"I think I'm going to enjoy being a colour-supplement countryman. It's a real pleasure rising later on these cold, dark winter mornings."

"As this is where we spend most time indoors, it's worth splashing out to make it cosier." Mum bridled with pleasure, patting her hair. She looked years younger.

"Gosh, Mum! I really like the highlights. When did you have your hair done? Should I have noticed it a month ago?" "Fortunately for you, it was only done today. You men are all the same. If the three witches from Macbeth prepared your breakfast, you'd go to school without noticing my absence." "Sounds interesting. You must introduce me to the rest of your coven some time."

CHAPTER 3

Alec's Final Thoughts

Too many things in my life have gone pear-shaped, and they have been mostly my own fault. Musketeer was not. Anthony Eden committed us to Operation Musketeer when he was stricken with dementia. How did this happen? Within the cabinet, the PM is said to be 'first amongst equals', so why did they all defer to him? They were all equally responsible, but they let him behave like an American president. The very name of the op gives the game away, by indicating the involvement of three parties. Our brigade was ready in Cyprus between June and October, so there was no element of surprise, either.

A lot of Egyptian civilians died in the preliminary bombing, with no thought of British army families still resident in the Canal Zone. Fortunately for them, their own servants held off the mob that turned out to take revenge on them. I always knew that any action UK forces are involved in is at the behest of our political masters. I am the **only one** to blame for finding myself dying in a ditch.

I know that I only chose to ride the bike today because I felt nervous about doing so. How stupid was that? Helen was against the dairy enterprise, and I just proved her right, thus making Ralph's future more difficult!

I suppose my next experience will be a white light that I'm supposed to walk towards, in search of growing my soul to prepare for my afterlife. Only that isn't my priority. I won't be ready to move on until I've stretched every sinew to help my nearest and dearest out of the financial difficulties that they have inherited from me.

CHAPTER 4

Dreams for the Future

I sleep better at the weekends, probably because I spend more time in the open air. So when I was suddenly wakened by frantic barking, it took some time for me to gather my wits enough to turn on the light and check the time. It was 3am, and Blue, our wall-eyed Border Collie, was raising hell in the yard. It was only when she paused for breath that I was able to hear the commotion from the chicken shed which housed my ornamental bantams. They were terrified.

I groaned as I realised that I had to get up and sort this situation as quickly as possible, if only to let Mum go back to sleep. I went downstairs, collected the big rubber torch, pulled on my overcoat and wellies, and stepped outside.

I went straight to Blue, who wagged her tail and jumped up. I quietened her down, and then slipped her lead on, and unfastened her chain. She dragged me to the chicken shed, where it was evident that a fox had started digging at the bottom of the chicken-wire enclosure.

As her kennel was too heavy to move, I fastened her to one of the corner posts while I found an empty steel drum, and put plenty of straw in it to serve as a temporary kennel. I placed it next to the run, and left her chained up to the post. That would serve as a stop-gap defence until I shot the fox, which would only stop when either it killed all the banties, or else I shot it. There was no way it could get in the shed, even if it got in the run. But that wouldn't stop it from trying, so we would both suffer many sleepless hours until I dealt with it.

If only I had a brother like Phil Mitchell In East Enders, I would only have to tell him about it, and he would get out his baseball bat and pop outside for half an hour, and he would return, saying, "Sorted!" before putting the bat back under his bed. No such luck in my case. It was up to me. It was four o'clock when I washed my hands at the yard tap so as not to disturb Mum by going in the bathroom.

Dad's words came back to me, when he found me sleepless. "Don't turn the light on, don't get cold, those things will only stimulate your brain, so try to avoid lying there thinking. You need to empty your mind and just consciously relax."

It seemed best to warm myself with hot milk with some honey in it as it only took a minute, and it was useless going back to bed while my muscles were stiff with cold. Sure enough, I was not long in getting back to sleep. As is often the case, when I awoke in the morning, it was with a full-fledged plan of action in my mind.

In other words, I knew what Dad would have proposed. "Don't give it the chance to pit its brain against yours, to find a way through your defences. Your best chance is to kill it with one shot, in your first ambush." I loathe being kept from my bed, so I liked the logic of putting in all the work before using the shotgun. Hence the phrase, 'do it right, and do it once.'

The shed was raised about two feet above the ground, because rats would smell the chicken feed, and tunnel their way in unseen. I must make my hide beneath it, with the twin aims of sheltering myself from rain, and making certain that my birds could never be in my field of fire. I made a slight hollow for a groundsheet and an old sleeping bag,

I arranged two car spotlights on the two corners of the run either side of where I would lie, converging on a spot about ten feet away. I made sure the shed floor would shade me, as I had no wish to be dazzled by them. I then wired them through a domestic pendant switch to a battery that normally powered an electric fence.

I had a late supper, and tied Blue up in an outhouse, safely out of the way. I put on thick corduroys, a thick sweater. I added a balaclava, mittens, and gym shoes before taking to the sleeping bag. I needed to leave the last ten inches unzipped, because the loaded shotgun would share the bag with me. Of course, it would have been more sporting to have taken that risk if the odds were even between shooting the fox, and shooting myself.

However, Dad's maxim, "Always play to win,"

ruled this strategy out. I had the pendant switch under my pillow, and the shotgun next to the zip, where I could ease it into the firing position and thumb-off the safety catch. I must have soon dozed off, because I next recall being startled into consciousness by the rooster's alarm call, quickly followed by Blue's distant bark.

After briefly wondering why I wasn't in bed, it all came back to me. I slowly rolled on to my belly as I slid the gun into the firing position, thumbing off the safety. I laid the pendant switch next to the front end of the stock, so that I could switch it on before resuming my grip on the gun. My left forefinger switched on the lights as my right took the first pressure on the trigger.

Nothing stirred in the spotlights' glare, and all the bantams took up the rooster's call. For a second or more the fox remained belly down before me, yellow eyes completely dazzled, before it took a load of buck shot in the chest, from the choke barrel of my gun. I deflated like a burst balloon. Killing it had been so easy, that it now seemed unnecessary.

I had thought of making something for Mum out of the skin, but I knew now that she wouldn't want it. As I looked at the shredded blood-soaked carcass, it was hard to guess if it would yield enough to make a pair of gloves. The action was over, and I felt strangely weary. I buried the remains in the dung heap. I left the sleeping bag in the outhouse, because it smelt strongly of chicken crap, and washed my hands. Going upstairs to bed, I saw Mum's light on, so I knocked on the door to report the night's events. I opened the gun cupboard first, and as I spoke I screwed a brush on the cleaning rod, and dipped it in gun oil. I passed it through the clean barrel and then the choke barrel. I changed the brush for a flannel patch, and wiped both barrels with it, before using it to wipe every bit of the blued steel.

I then took a clean duster from the cupboard and wiped the whole of the walnut gun furniture to remove finger marks and stray gun oil. Only then did I look at her properly for the first time. My tiredness must have made me look older and more thoughtful at this ungodly hour, because I sensed that for a brief moment, her Alec stood before her once again. She looked at me with sad eyes, and then gave me a big hug before sending me off to bed.

Next morning I overslept. I generally rise first, so was not surprised that Mum also overslept. I woke her up, and asked her to make me sandwiches instead of breakfast, as I could eat them while she drove me to school. I strove to remember what my first lesson was, and was pleasantly surprised to recall that it was English lit., no longer taught by Mr Bradshaw, but by Miss Rossi, our American student teacher on work experience.

I must admit that I found her very attractive in the Latin manner. Rather than conceal her thick black eyebrows, she chose to emphasise them by wearing large and stylish horn-rimmed glasses. As I drew near, gulping down my last butty, I gathered my school bag for a sprint down the corridor. Once I reached the classroom door, I heard shouts of protest from my classmates. "Oh, **no** Miss!"

I burst in as she restored order. She raised her hand to silence any excuse for my lateness. "Right, Ralph, you are **it!** First off, why are you so late?" "I stayed up to shoot a fox that was after my bantams, and didn't get to bed until two." "Did you get it?" "Yes, Miss," I simpered modestly. "Right on! You will now relate the facts, not in your own words, but in the style of, this is a tough one, Edgar Alan Poe!"

I was feeling pretty euphoric, and here was a chance to show off. I had the attention of the whole class, each one relieved that someone else would make a fool of themselves for them to sneer at. I marshalled my thoughts, assembling the first paragraph, and then launched myself into it, haltingly at first, and then, establishing myself in my Victorian voice, more fluently.

"It was a dark and foggy evening as my tired eyes forced me to tear myself away from reading Gibbon's 'Decline and Fall' by lamplight. I lit a candle before snuffing the oil lamp, and preceding my guttering shadows up the creaking staircase to my celibate couch."

"Aaah!" my classmates chorused, and one wit hummed 'Hearts and Flowers'. From the back of the class Tony Stubbins shouted, **'Get on with it!'** "I donned my night shirt and knelt to make my peace with God. No sooner had my head touched the pillow, than sleep overtook me." **"Everything** overtakes you, Swindlehurst!" shouted Tony, which was really witty, for him.

"Imagine my surprise when a stranger of threatening appearance was revealed by my candle, which he must have lit. He wore a shallow-crowned top hat, as favoured by John Bull, or in his case, river-boat gamblers.

"His hat-band was decorated with a sunburst of ornamental bantam feathers, which boded ill for my own flock. He had chosen to decorate his features with a minimal moustache of ginger colour, and long 'sideboards' emphasised his wide and prominent cheekbones. His wary yellow eyes constantly scanned the room in a shifty way, sliding from side to side, alert and predatory. 'Just toss me your keys, sodbuster,' he said, fingering my gun nervously.

"I clearly needed to calm him down. I spoke slowly, in a soothing way. 'I am but a humble son of the soil. My few possessions scarcely merit the cost of a good lock on the door. In fact, it is mostly left open, even when business takes me elsewhere. You must be the first to have ever coveted anything of mine.'

"He seemed irritated by my meek exposition. 'Forget the damned keys! You can show me round, and if I find so much as one drawer or cupboard locked, I'll blow the lock off. You'd better find something I want, or I'll kill your bantams and take them with me. Back in the US of A, it ain't prudent to walk the streets without cash in your wallet. Muggers would be despised by other muggers, if they failed to kick the crap out of any victim found to be without cash.'

""The time for violence passed when you decided against killing me as I slept. Either humanity or common sense stayed your hand.'

"His hoots of laughter failed to allay my fears. 'Get you! I love being described as humane or intelligent, except by some **dumb mother** looking down the barrel of his own gun! Suppose you were Albert Einstein (which you sure ain't), and Tony Stubbins said 'I wish I was as good at sums as you are.' Would that surpass winning the Nobel Prize? I don't think so.'"

Tony responded with loud applause, evidently in the belief that any publicity was better than none at all. I continued. "'Look where you will. I can't conjure up valuables where none exist.' "'There go the bantams then. It won't matter to them which of us ends their lives.'

"'That is not so! They are pedigree breeding stock, and when they are stop breeding, they live out their natural lifespan with their offspring. You need to know what I keep the gun for. To keep any livestock requires a store for feed-stuff. Rats smell this, and like all creatures, their numbers are only limited by the amount of food available to them. The gun is only used for ratting. It is only licensed to me because the police believe I will store it in a secure place.

"'I have betrayed this responsibility, which means persuading you to give it back to me. If you do so, I'll find gifts for you. I'll give you all the food you can eat, plus sandwiches to take with you, and will not lay a complaint against you with the police. If you leave as an armed robber, taking my gun will result in relentless pursuit by the police, as an armed robber. They are equipped with all the technology that you lack, in the form of instant intelligence by telegraph, silent approach by police mounted on velocipedes, and night-time searches using bulls-eye lanterns!'

"'So, lead the way! I need to see what you are offering before I consider accepting your terms.'

"It looked as if he would accept. 'First things first!'

I walked to the gun cupboard, and opened it. 'Unload that gun and return it whence it came.' He leered at me as he broke the gun to reveal two empty chambers. What had I got that was flash enough for him and readily portable? My father had brought me two gifts from Hong Kong might fill the bill.

"'My papa, a military man, told me once that anyone who has his weapon used against him, only has himself to lame. Better to be a jester, belaboured by his bladder on a stick, than a tyrant knelt beneath his own guillotine. Would you concur?'

"'I saw your scatter-gun, and immediately pictured my brains spread against your bedroom wall. I couldn't feel safe until it was in my hands. I still need to see your gifts.' 'They are a silk dressing gown featuring a hand-embroidered gold dragon, covering it collar to hem, and a Rolex watch that may not be genuine.' 'They seem appropriate to me. Go get 'em.'" His eyes lit up when he saw them. "'I'll repair to the kitchen to prepare your breakfast.'

"'The watch looks great, and the dressing gown too. I feel like I could eat a horse, but then, I always do when house-breaking.' I didn't stint him. I cooked a whole Cumberland sausage, a gammon steak, fried eggs, and toast and marmalade to fill up with. While he ate, I made sandwiches to take with him. I took them to him in a box. He seemed determined not to leave any toast. 'You really meant it when you said you wouldn't report me to the police?'

"'Of course I meant it! I never break my word. Take your sandwiches, and I will return to the arms of Morpheus, for what little remains of the night.' 'Whatever turns you on, man!' I was still puzzling over what he meant by this, the following day."

"That was great, Ralph. I knew you could do it off the cuff! You would only have felt inhibited if you had been there for the briefing I gave to your classmates."

There followed a burst of raucous laughter from the others. Or maybe it was nervous laughter? They still had their turn to come. "I've never heard him string together more than six words, Miss. He must fancy you rotten!"

"Eat your heart out, Sonia! Ralph, I told the others that creative writing almost always involves speaking of our feelings and motives. We are loath to do this, because it reveals things that we feel shy about. That is why it is easier when one is speaking 'in voice' as a character, which cloaks our inner life. You explored your own feelings, as well as those of the fox, in a little story put together with humour and imagination. Now class, what message did you get from Ralph's story?"

As usual, Nigel was the first to raise his hand. "He stepped into the Victorian Gothic voice, as to the manor born. One wonders, and not for the first time, what else might lurk in the dark recesses of this loser's mind?" "I expected a put-down from you, Nigel. What do you have to say, Sonia?"

"I've only got as far as guessing that a 'celibate couch' must be a slang name for a bed. Celibacy may be OK for beds, and even extend their life, but a lusty farm lad should consider his other options." This caused more noisy laughter.

"Keep your suggestion until after school, Sonia. It

is too obvious to require the attention of the class. Now I would like to hear the different judgement we get when Ralph's effort has been filtered through a brain. You're on, Jane."

"Well the previous speakers, no doubt relieved not to be in the hot seat themselves, resorted to negative criticism. It should be judged as a first draft, and we have all read poorer efforts in 'rag day' magazines. I liked the way the narrator kept up the 'Gothic' voice, while choosing a James Hadley Chase, or Mike Hammer voice as the fox."

"Right, Jane. That's a great **style** analysis, but I want your judgement on the content." "Oh, Miss! This is embarrassing!" she resumed, in tones of exaggerated drama. "I can reveal that he has removed the veil from two levels of consciousness. The pompous opening was to impress us, but difficult to maintain while seeking an ending. It led us to expect he would cast himself in a heroic light, but he chose instead to steal the plot of 'The Bishop's Candlesticks'. The second veil was that 'one of the lads' got on his feet to swank, only to sit down 'a new man' This illustrates what Catholics must been by the phrase 'Redemption can come between the stirrup and the saddle.'"

Miss Rossi clapped her hands above her head until the class settled down. "That was very good, Jane. Ralph laid his head on the block by opening up to us. Your assessment was the first to rise to his level of communication. I don't want to hear any more negative criticism, as each of you have to take your turn, and I don't want your efforts to sacrifice openness and originality to fear of ridicule. Who else wants to have their say before I choose the next victim?"

Tony Stubbins, another farm boy, raised his hand. No-one could remember a previous occasion when this happened, so he got our attention. "Folk seldom get close enough to t'fox to kill it. If you was looking for rabbits, say, and you put up a fox, you would waste a shot, unless you were closer than fifty yards. Even then, you wouldn't do much damage with bird shot. Ralph had put in so much effort, worthy of a tiger hunt or summat, that it left him no option bar killin' it. The fairy-tale endin' shows his regret at havin' done so."

"Attaboy, Tony, you are diggin', ahem! Digging deep now." She should never have encouraged him. I think he had her tagged as an anti-Vietnam War activist, and posing as a kindred soul. "Suppose our Ralph hadn't made a military ambush out of his shoot. I guess he had his dad in mind, and felt he must do what Dad would have done. It took that to rouse his killer instinct. That might explain why thousands of American lads might have donned their country's uniform, and taken the first step towards genocide!

"You are cynical beyond your years, Tony. I think I catch your drift. I doubt that you know **Ralph's** motivation, and you'll never guess what pushes **my** button!" All the girls jeered Tony to signify their approval of Miss Rossi.

"Hey, guys! Why so noisy today? I've overlooked your barracking today, because you finally demonstrated some involvement! I'll make a deal with you, but only if a majority support me. With this degree of involvement, we could stage a play for the end-of-term entertainment. What I require in return, is that you read all the set books in your **own time**, to make room in the syllabus. We could all gain a lot through involvement in a stage play. The deal is, that I'll bring in a script for your approval. I intend to cast the play next week. Everyone not cast will either understudy one of the cast, or else be involved in the stage management. Give me a show of hands if you are in favour."

A clear majority did so. This day marked the point at which I started to come out of my shell by joining in more with school activities. I felt flattered by Jane's efforts to understand me, but mistook this as evidence that she fancied me. It was discouraging to think that Tony had been thinking about my circumstances, and hit the nail on the head about how often Dad was in my thoughts, but I would never value his opinion. Similarly, Sonia's pretence of lusting after me was really taking the mickey, and making a laughing stock of me.

This glimpse of reality should have given me the message that I was merely one schoolboy out of about two hundred pupils, not anyone special. Among the new contacts I made, the boys formed cliques or gangs, whereas the girls were both more sociable, and more friendly. All the girls managed to get on with each other, whereas those boys not in a clique or gang, were loners, as I had been. In all my contacts, mimicking staff members always seemed an easy way to get a laugh, Miss Rossi's rehearsals role-playing and workshops taught me to empathise with those I had previously disliked.

Christmas that year was better than Mum and I

had anticipated. Mum continued to make our home more comfortable. She was involved with festivities at work that she had avoided in the past, and also carol singing with the church choir. She roped me in for the carols, and I felt proud to stand beside her when we were out. As I approached manhood, we seemed closer in years. Now she could afford regular hairdressing and spend more on clothes and shoes, she looked years younger than when Dad died.

At the gliding club, the social side was in full swing, as gliding could not return before March, at the earliest. Of course we had ground-training sessions each weekend. Lectures were arranged to cover winch launching, theory of flight, and navigation. Each member rummaged their local library for textbooks that we illegally photocopied and pirated.

The nightly screaming of speed-dating vixens reminded me that nearly a year had passed since we lost Dad. There had been a great many changes since then. The first fruits of my gardening appeared, as aconites, snowdrops and croci showed their leaves. The club's refurbishment was making progress, too.

By the end of February, we had the toilets ready. We were already able to prepare food in the clubhouse, having removed the concrete stalls to open up the space in the shippon. Fluorescent lighting had been installed, which drew attention to the structural steel overhead, with hay bound by pigeon droppings and dust.

Dad had built the dairy, by adding a building-block lean-to to the outer side-all. This had to have tiled walls and a concrete floor topped with a special Granolithic cement topping to withstand any milk, as this turns to lactic acid, which quickly erodes normal cement. The whole area was designed to facilitate cleaning and sterilisation. The water supply necessary for cleaning, and also the milk cooler was more than sufficient for our clubhouse and toilets.

Dad had also added a feed-store. This had been converted into a kitchen, and a serving counter had been placed against the entrance to the clubhouse, complete with tea urn and cash till. When I considered what progress had been made already, it re-fired my keenness to join by club-mates in seeing things through to completion. The muck on the roof structure was merely part of a shabby chrysalis that would yield something really attractive!

CHAPTER 5

First Steps in Gliding

I always look forward to the end of February, which is my least favourite month, in the belief that the worst of the frost should be behind us. Of course, the pessimists rubbish this, quoting the saying, 'As the days lengthen the cold strengthens.' This time round, February came to an end, and March crept slowly on with no forecast of when gliding might resume. Weekend after weekend passed without offering flyable conditions. On one of these occasions, I was helping Ben check the winch over, when a van arrived, and the driver sought help to offload some heavy reels.

"That will be the new braided cable, which should greatly reduce the cable breaks that cause such delay in our launch rate," said the duty instructor. "Don't get too excited, we have loads of piano wire to use up before it will be used." It seems that it is dearer, but still more cost-effective because it increases the hour's flow, on which the club's income depends.

By now, prioritising the flying rota had gathered political overtones. The committee had to encourage volunteers for all the ground work. Having already made sure that all work was logged to enable assessment of these 'Stakhanovite workers', they then made two later revisions to the point-scoring system which infuriated those people who had topped the first list. Some (angrier still) had already topped both lists, and still had to compete with craftier members who had ignored two previous efforts to get some work out of them.

One wonders what damage this caused to future efforts to draw volunteers, as so many who had previously offered their services must have felt that they had been lied to. No member of the committee was religious enough to remind us of Jesus' parable of the casual labour hired by a farmer to harvest his crop. Some only offered their labour when most of the crop had been harvested, but the farmer decided that they should all receive the same amount. This has always baffled me, because the only reason the farmer could justify this must have been to resist his labour pool becoming unionised!

Firstly, we were given work cards, which recorded on which days they had turned up, and the total hours worked. Each day worked would earn one launch. Then, ab initio pupils were annoyed to find that despite their work, solo pilots would take priority because they provided more hours flown per launch, boosting club earnings per launch. All these solo pilots had to be cleared for flying from Tewitts' Field, more difficult due to it being a slope-soaring site, rather than Samlesbury, with its mile-long runway, and vast acreage of mown grass.

That was why the solo pilots must hone rusty skills (most had not flown for well over a year) and satisfy the CFI that they could cope with slope soaring, and a small, rough, and wet grass field, without endangering themselves or others.

Then an even newer ranking of worthiness was decided upon. Those of us who had not soloed felt cheated that the Blanik, a tandem two-seater sailplane, would be reserved for the use of these site checks, for as long as it took. The rest of us would rank after those awaiting a site check, on a first-come, first-served basis.

Obviously many of us who had regularly volunteered, felt cheated. Some who had stayed away until the work was finished could now show up, and get priority. To be fair this new dispensation favoured me in particular, because I only had to walk a hundred yards to find the duty officer and enter my name on the flying list.

Others might turn up later and fly before me, but I was in with a chance of getting a launch before the next solo pilot turned up! I never rubbed salt into my fellow members' wounds by climbing into a glider in my pyjamas, but the temptation was there. In any case, I would have turned up to work without any incentive, as would the majority who had been offering the club for services for years.

The oldest glider, the T21b (or 'the Barge', as it is affectionately known), was designed in the 30s for training ATC cadets. It had been built in considerable numbers. It is a parasol-winged, side-by-side two-seater. Its open cockpit offers two skimpy celluloid windscreens, bent in arcs to stiffen them mainly, but making a small concession to streamlining, too. These screens varied between yellow and brown dependent upon their age.

Lacking either air-brakes, or wheel brakes, it had wheel at about the point of balance, and a long skid to provide deceleration after touching down. These were an essential 'spare' item, as a rough landing, or even allowing the machine to pitch forward after touchdown, usually broke the skid.

Built of clear pine, with a skin of canvas, shrunk to the structure with red cellulose, this cellulose 'dope' now weathered to a matt surface, lent it a raffish gaiety, like of well-worn fairground equipment. To see it parked next to the Blanic, resembled a racing yacht moored next to a narrow boat, but its antique deep chord wing section provided good slow-flying characteristics, that helped make it a safe and forgiving training machine.

That said, its hefty drag burdened it with a steep glide angle, and lack of penetration flying upwind. Now that we give too much value to appearance, I am bound to say that taut canvas skin strained over the fuselage made it look like an old dry cow with its bony pelvis sticking out. Thirty years of being stuffed into the ground by cack-handed pupils, had given it the look of a once-loved rocking horse, now battered and neglected.

The Blanik, combined rugged aluminium stressed-skin construction with elegance of line, is a Czech designed and built tandem-seat training machine showing military parentage, in design and construction. Its polished duralumin skin is decorated with navy decals. The large blown-Perspex canopy offers both good visibility and low drag, while its aerofoil shape offers some extra lift to offset its drag.

Being designed as a sailplane, it good achieve altitudes at which oxygen might be required, and could meet (in thunder clouds) such violent up-currents next to equally fierce down-currents, that could break a wing off, so you would need a parachute before venturing into such a cloud. To allow two people to bail out the hinge-pins between the canopy and the cockpit coaming take the form of one long door bolt. Releasing this bolt will cause the canopy to be sucked off, so the crew can release their harness, and make swift exit.

The day finally arrived for my first launch. I sat in the Barge while Bert told me how he would handle the launch from the point when he gave the order to the winch driver, 'All out.' He would gently pick the tail up to reduce the strain on the cable, taking care to avoid the skid from touching the ground (which would cause a cable break).

He would adjust the angle of climb to get the most height off the launch. Having done so, he would then dip the nose to slacken the cable prior to releasing it, to avoid it twanging back in loops. The winch driver would then wind the cable back fast enough to be pulling against the drogue, so that it was taut enough to wind tidily on to the winch drum.

He then passed the time by telling me amusing stories about Samlesbury airfield, near Blackburn, where the management kindly offered the club free access at the weekend, when they never used it. The managing director had been a famous Typhoon pilot who developed his own way of downing V1 'buzz bombs' by tapping a wing tip with his wingtip, causing it to stabilise in a spiral dive, over farmland.

"I remember one afternoon, when the great man was admiring the roses in his garden, which ended at the airfield boundary. There was sufficient wind to 'Kite' gliders on the launch. Instead of releasing at the end of the climb, the pilot allows his glider to drift downwind, and the winch driver then pulls him higher. It is possible to do this repeatedly, so that the pilot actually releases at twice the altitude he would otherwise have achieved.

"Unfortunately, the winch driver lost his concentration, allowing the drogue to drop beyond the airfield perimeter. By the time the winch man stated to reel it in, he had about a thousand feet of cable draped across the ground. By the time he woke up and reeled it in, it lay across the MDs garden. Imagine his surprise when some of his precious roses disappeared over the fence at thirty to forty miles an hour!"

The field telephone at the launch point tinkled erratically as the winch driver cranked its handle. Bert rolled his eyes in mock despair. "Here comes a further delay." Sure enough, the signaller sent the next two on the flying list trudging to the winch to assist. "There is just enough wind for you to practise balancing the glider," said Bert. "Remember, you will need full movement of the ailerons, because your 'airspeed' is so low. Yes, you can have airspeed when stationary, it is obviously the headwind we are facing."

This proved to be easy, and Bert soon asked the wing man to pick up the wing and resume control. "It was a signaller who really offended the MD. He had borrowed a light aircraft from an employee, and returned to the airfield as the signaller was preparing to launch one of our gliders. The duty pilot asked the signaller to send 'await permission to land'.

"The signaller, un-tutored soul, gave him a flashing red with the aldis lamp, unaware that this means 'Airfield not available for landing,' which was bound to offend the man who was not only in charge of it, but allowing us to use it free of charge!"

"Right, Bert. We are getting 'ready' from the winch." Bert fastened his harness. "Carry on with your pre-flight checks, and let's get this show on the road." I checked the control column and rudder bar for 'full and free movement' by describing a full circle with the stick, while pressing each pedal back against the stops, checking visually the correct response from rudder, elevators, and ailerons. I then checked both my harness and Bert's

"What is the next check?" "Hatches, which we lack." "Carry on." "Instruments." I tapped the altimeter, and zeroed it. This now registered, not 'height above sea-level, but 'height above airfield'. I set the trim to neutral, and Bert reminded me that most other gliders had both canopies and brakes to be checked. Two weary peasants approached, dragging the drogue and ring end of the cable. "Cable on!" I bellowed, just in case they had forgotten what they were there for.

They had just brought it from the tractor to the glider, only to be chivvied by an adolescent Captain

Bligh. I toyed with the idea of threatening them with 'a taste of the rope's end, if they didn't step lively', but this might have seemed 'over the top'. One of the surly brutes clipped the ting on the end of its shock-absorbing rope to the rear of the two Ottfur hooks, and looked ready to shuffle away.

"Check for release under tension!" I demanded. He stooped to drag the cable forward and down, and I pulled the yellow release knob. He had to grovel in the mud to reconnect. "Check the overrun!" I ordered. He pulled the cable straight down, and it released cleanly. I shouted, "Cable on!" and Bert smiled his approval. I had a good look around for anything moving on the field, or above it, that might endanger our launch.

"Good man," said Bert. "I'll take over. All clear. I have control for during the launch and climb-out, and will hand over to you at about seven hundred feet, to maintain the same angle of climb. I will then tell you when to release. **Take up slack!**"

The signaller passed this on to the winch driver, and the cable slithered across the grass to twang taut, producing a resonance in the airframe as if we were inside a very large cello. **"All out!"** The signaller switched from dashes to frantic dots, and the winch exhaust stack spewed black smoke as the throttle opened, it dispersed in our direction, indicating that we were facing dead into wind.

Bert eased us off the ground cautiously, to avoid pitching on to the nose skid. The clattering of the wheel (there is usually mud to make it out of balance) died to a rumble. Bert held her close to the ground to pick up speed and ease the load on the cable, before rotating into the climb. The wings hummed with the energy of the wind as it converted the kinetic energy of the tow into lift and drag vectors.

Air swished over the cockpit, and all the different sounds rose in pitch, as the controls lost their sloppy feel as we settled to best climbing speed and taut response to the controls. I was following Bert's movements on the controls with the lightest touch I could manage.

The movements became ever smaller. He watched my face as he eased the stick back, simultaneously achieving increased speed and improved rate of climb, which felt unnatural, as if one was riding a bike uphill, and found it accelerating as the slope steepened! I realised that he was checking if I felt nervous at his efforts to achieve the highest possible altitude off the launch.

"Go for a high one!" I squeaked, as if he needed instruction from me. A contemptuous glance was his only response. It was quiet up here. The winch motor was the loudest sound but there was enough disturbed airflow over the cockpit to make shouting necessary.

"You have control. Don't allow the nose to drop, maintain firm back pressure on the stick." The altimeter registered eight hundred feet over the airfield, and I reached for the release, only to have my hand knocked away. "We don't want to lower the nose and release. We'll get at least another hundred feet." The exhaust note of the winch dropped as the altimeter registered nine hundred feet, and the winch driver throttled back. "Now you may release."

I administered the correct double-tug on the release knob. "Now zoom off your excess speed to gain extra height. Remember, speed is money to spend, but height is money in the bank." I gently raised the nose with thumb and forefinger, using the cross bar on the pitot head as an 'artificial horizon' while I adjusted the trim tab to achieve minimum sink speed.

The altimeter showed 960 feet. I looked back to the landing area. It seemed fantastic to see long familiar landmarks from a completely new vantage point. "As there is no chance of soaring, we won't proceed any further upwind. You can practise turns, and then we will make deliberately high approach, so I can show you how we deal with that situation without benefit of air-brakes.

"Follow me on the controls while we turn 180 degrees to the right. I look above me and to the rear before initiating the turn. Only then do I apply gentle pressure to the right rudder and aileron co-ordinating hand and foot until the angle between the pitot head and the horizon show that we are correctly banked. I then centralise the controls.

"I know that we are correctly established in the turn, because the nine inches of wool tied to the pitot head is blowing straight towards me, proof that we are neither slipping nor skidding. In either case, the glider is suffering extra drag by presenting more than its minimum profile. Bear in mind that part of the lift vector is helping to keep us in the turn, so this must be replaced by slight back pressure on the stick to maintain our rate of descent."

This was a copy-book example of instruction, but I rather wished he had kept it for later, as I was struggling to cope with all the sensory data. Only later did I realise that all he had told me reinforced what I could feel through the controls, which helped me to remember. As for telling me later, we would always be sat in the cockpit while the glider was manhandled back to the launch point (It needed ballasting with our weight, to make it easier for the retrieve crew).

The instructor debriefed the pupil and made his entry in the pupil's flying log. To spend longer with any pupil would reduce the number of launches, which would be very unpopular. Furthermore, if I thought that I was clever to have mugged up the theory of flight, etc., it didn't stop me from attempting to release too early, when I had only just been told that he would tell me when to release!

"Back on the stick, Ralph, or we'll end up in a spiral dive. Right, now straighten up!" I reversed stick and rudder, then allowed them to spring back to least-load position, restoring us to the approach speed. "We're still too high," as I intended. "Look around, and then perform a 360-degree turn to the left."

I snapped a glance over my left shoulder, and picked out a tree on the horizon to straighten up on, and then looked around and below before initiating the turn, with a bit of back-pressure. I was too diffident. The glider wallowed round in a big circle as I pushed and pulled, when I should have snapped into the turn, and then centralised the controls.

"That was ragged, but slightly better than your first attempt. We are now approaching the far boundary, so we need to check our height visually, then turn on to our crosswind leg, where we will estimate the wind at ground level by the angle of drift, then rattle through the pre-landing checks. As I intended, we are still too high, so take note of the appearance of trees and buildings. Every time you see the same conditions, you're either landing in a stronger wind, or else too high.

"Give me a ninety-degree left turn, and make it a tight one to lose some more height." I diffidently applied stick and rudder. "**No!** I want you to stand it on its ear." I felt the controls twitch violently as he steepened the turn. The rudder hit it left stop as the stick hit my right thigh, before the stick came hard back to tighten the turn. "Ease back on the stick to tighten the turn, and use a bit of right rudder to hold the nose up. We call this 'applying top rudder'.

"This is your first experience of using 'crossed controls', and you are about to meet the second. Right, we are straightened up on crosswind leg, and you have control. You are best able to judge the air velocity for landing by how much we have to crab into wind to judge our headwind for finals. Once turned on finals our options rapidly diminish. We look for other aircraft in the circuit, that we might have to defer to, then for vehicles or aircraft on the ground, and then where we expect to touch down.

"Now for the side-slip." He set up the glider for a rate two turn, and then crossed the controls until he had full left aileron, balanced by a bootful of right rudder. This steepened our descent as if we were parachuting onto the ground, the slipstream mainly hitting Bert's side around our skimpy windscreens. "I'll straighten her up, and then hand over to you." He tweaked the nose up, and allowed the controls to centralise. "I'll hand over to you." The glider lined up into wind, with the ASI climbing up from under-reading to the required 55kts. "Back slightly on the stick. Remember we are landing uphill, and look ahead, you will touch down before the only grass you can focus on. Hold off, as long as you can." We had passed the launch point, and could clearly hear conversations there, despite the swish of the Barge's passing.

I seemed to have a lot of speed to lose, having forgotten that I was holding off in a shallow climb, prior to landing uphill. "That was great stuff. Remember to ease back on the stick just before touchdown, to keep the skid off the ground." Even as he spoke, the port wing started to drop, and I felt his intervention as the column hit my right thigh and the rudder pedal knocked my left foot. "You have control." I held the skid off the ground as the wheel rumbled across the rough ground with the stick fully back, feeding vibrations into the airframe with the usual sound effects of being in an alpine chalet, bombarded by an avalanche.

I kept the wings level, and the noise abated as our forward motion did, until the skid touched the ground, soon dissipating remaining momentum.

Silence reigned. "Sit tight, while I turn a wingtip into wind." He got out, and turned the wingtip into wind, before resuming his seat. The retrieve crew from the launch point arrived to drag it back there. "Stay put, while I debrief you. Their task is easier with us as ballast. The two at the tail-plane lead the way, and without our help, they would be lifting most of the weight.

"That was not bad for a first launch. We expect someone of your age to progress rapidly away from initial slowness and indecision. You had anticipated cable breaks on take-off, which was good. But anticipating my next instruction, by trying to release prematurely, when I had just told you that I would tell you when to do it, was plain daft, and would have cost us the extra hundred and fifty feet that we achieved."

Creaks issued from our harness anchor points, as they took the load of two of the crew using our shoulder straps to drag the glider. The two at the tail shared a horizontal tube, parallel to the elevator, that was the designer's only concession to ground handling.

The fifth member of the crew steered the machine while holding one wing tip between thumb and forefinger, owing to the length of each wing providing so much leverage. You can nudge the tail right or left, despite two men each grasping that handle with both hands.

I was taking this in during my debriefing, enjoying the grunts of effort from the under-class. "Plan your flight thoroughly, by all means, but be ready to snatch every opportunity that presents itself, however briefly.

"I noticed that you anticipated the beginner's fault of overcorrecting, by leaving the glider to fly itself. This is why you couldn't establish the glider in a stable turn. You should be able to snap into the turn, and just as positively centralise the controls while applying light back pressure to hold the nose up.

"Fly positively! Establish the glider in a turn quickly, and centralise in the turn applying slight back pressure. Never fiddle around with the controls while turning. All that is required until you roll-out on your next heading is to hold the nose up enough to maintain your air speed.

"Remember the two circumstances that require crossed controls. In a tight turn, you tighten the turn by using back pressure to raise the elevators, and balance that with 'top rudder' to use the side of the fuselage on the inside of the turn as an aerofoil, to replace the 'lift' vector that is now holding you in the turn.

"What was the other use that I demonstrated to you?" "The side slip, which is vital on machines lacking air-brakes." "Good. You will remember that I told you to ignore the altimeter on crosswind leg, well this is equally so. Ignore the altimeter, in all situations that find you with less than 600 feet between you and the ground, because it only tells you what your altitude was, say, thirty seconds ago.

"We call this 'instrument lag'. Regularly assessing one's height on the approach will help you to make an instant judgement that will gradually improve. We trust that the size of our airstrip will allow for quite a wide safety margin. Remember, you will have already assessed the head wind on your crosswind leg, by the crab angle between your heading and your track over the ground.

"On finals you should have both wingtips within your peripheral vision in view, to avoid the 'dropped' wing that you failed to respond to today. That would have caused a 'ground loop' with inevitable serious damage to the outside wing. "Have you heard about ground loops?" "Yes, but I don't know what it means."

"It always starts with a wing dropping. The nearer you are to the stall, the less responsive the controls will be, so it demands instantly applying full opposite aileron to pick the wing up again and quickly keeping the wings level.

"Should the wing tip strike the ground, the braking effect (as you noticed during our retrieval) is magnified by the leverage of fifteen feet of wing, causing pivot around the wingtip, at which point centripetal force grounds the opposite tip, and the gliders remaining momentum crumples the end of that wing." "That sounds expensive." "It would be, and would take a long time to repair."

By now, we were approaching the launch point.

"It also puts your touchdown spot in the centre of your field of view. In still air **only,** the only spot with blades of grass not blurred. As you will never be required to land downwind, in all other conditions, you will touch down **before** that point. However, whenever you land in this direction, you will be landing uphill, which will further shorten your landing run.

"The other serious effect of landing in strong headwinds is that owing to 'wind shear' you will risk stalling on the approach unless you maintain airspeed by lowering the nose progressively as the glider reacts to gradually reducing airspeed. Of the out landings caused by insufficient height to cross the threshold, most are caused by misjudging the altitude. This a very serious error, as it usually results in an emergency landing in a much smaller field, usually resulting in colliding with the fence, hedge, a tree, or even a wall, whatever the field boundary consists of.

"However, back to the approach, where you are looking ahead for the focussing point. Don't be mesmerised by that patch of sharp grass, or you will crash land. You should be rounding out, especially when about to land uphill."

By now, we were nearing the launch point, and the next pupil was preparing to get in. "Give me your log book, and I'll record your flight." As he scribbled he added a final comment. "It seems only fair to warn you that we will continue to suffer a poor launch rate until all the piano wire cable has been used. If you want to progress quickly, you may need to get some time in at another club, or you might still be a pupil next year."

I didn't reply. I knew that that was not possible. It took a long time for all that instruction to be digested, let alone the actual experience. I was also overwhelmed by all the stuff that I had failed to anticipate. How I left my stomach behind when Bert pulled the stick on the launch, causing us to actually accelerate, and steepened the climb simultaneously! He was checking my reaction to this, so it wasn't done to scare me. Also, I had imagined that all my reading would help a lot, but it didn't.

I knew that aerial views flattened the landscape, but was still surprised when it happened. I was surprised to react to it all as a spectator, but Bert was not going to allow this. It would be wasting his time and mine, because I was there to be instructed. I was required to heed his words, maintain a lookout, and constantly plan for 'worst-case scenarios' regarding cable breaks and the like.

For instance, this could result in landing straight ahead, then reaching the point of no return, after which landing beyond the boundary, after which, achieving sufficient height to permit returning to the airfield. All that was required of me now, was to re-join the circuit at the right height to plan a good approach.

At this point I couldn't judge when I might expect to make a good landing, as well! While my instructors will make sure I am not allowed to cock up a landing for some time to come, every time one of them catches me looking 'fat, dumb, and happy', they will scream, "Where to now, if the cable breaks?"

They will not accept, "How about Tewitts' Field?" as a valid answer. I will never go solo until they are satisfied with my answer. I remember that Mum gave me a big hug when she heard I had finally been given a launch. I did vaguely wonder why this might please her. It was a big deal for me though, because I can remember nothing more of that week. That found me sitting in the Barge next to Dixie Dean, instructor and club safety officer.

In my impertinent way, I assumed that his beard was to give the stamp of authority to his slight stature. I was soon to learn that his temper was on a short fuse, like a terrier eager to pick a fight with every bigger dog. "It looks like another snarl-up at the winch. We have three spools of piano wire left, after which we'll be using braided cable. Can you splice piano wire?" "Yes. I did a spell of cable retrieving, and learnt do it then." "Hard cheese. You'll soon have to learn how to use the crimping pliers to close the nipples on the linked eyes of the braided cable, to stop the ends unravelling." "I was told that it was quicker and easier." "I guess so. You must always be wary of the cable when it is under tension. You are many times more likely to suffer injury from it than from a glider, either while in one, or on the ground. Oh, no! Not again!"

The field telephone rang in its usual tinny and haphazard way, as if it was being cranked by a drunk, using his toes. The duty officer at the launch point sent the next four pupils to help at the winch. "That suggests a further thirty-minute delay before you get your launch. You are a newcomer. What do you think is the most likely cause of an accident in our present set-up?"

"You couldn't have chosen a worse person to ask. When I talk to fellow pupil pilots, every one of them complains about the launch rate. This is bound to lead to accidents, because we will all be too long completing our tuition. I don't know at what age you learnt to ride a bike, but much longer would it have taken if you only got access to a bike at weekends, for an average time of nine minutes a week. Would you still be learning? Have you ever considered that every week the CFI flies for more time than an ab initio pilot will achieve in a year."

"I know you have been generous with your time since joining; otherwise you could expect the bollocking of your life for that load of bullshit. Would you be happy with a CFI who never flew more than the average pupil? Or if we trained pupils in the same way Glider Pilot Regiment were trained in two weeks during WW2?

"They wrote off umpteen gliders, and accepted a heavy casualty rate in achieving such intensive training. I read of one who went solo following two out landings due to under-shootings that wrote off two gliders. Anticipating that he might be rejected, he was surprised when his instructor passed him for solo. He could only assume that his instructor didn't dare fly with him again!

"Anyway, you should worry, living on the doorstep as you do. You can always be first on the flying list, even if you sign in your pyjamas! As you know, the average distance that members drive to get here is about forty to fifty miles.

"Our solo pilots have pitched a strong case for stopping ab initio training until they have all been cleared for solo on this slope-soaring site. To do so would instantly earn the club more per launch, and utilise all our single-seaters in short order, even at the present abysmal launch rate! What do you think of that?"

"Had that judgement been made when the club moved here, most of the recent members would have left you to get on with it until you recommenced ab initio training. I believe quite a few of your solo pilots have never attended since you moved, clearly proving that they were happy to let others labour on their behalf."

"My final word. When you are here, our relationship is that of pupil and instructor. It doesn't allow time for questioning what I tell you. When we are in the clubhouse, your opinion is as good as mine. Do you accept that?" "Yes, of course. May I ask what led you to take the safety officer task?"

"My uncle, Jack Aked, asked me to take it on, following a climbing accident that involved me. A couple of climbing friends and I arranged an ice-climbing expedition in the Alps. That holiday gave me the most visually beautiful experience of my life. As we crossed a glacier in brilliant sunshine we saw an ice cave. We stood in the entrance where stalagmites of ice created dozens of rainbows, painting the snow. I don't know how long we stood, silently. Then the cave collapsed, without warning. One friend died instantly, and the other is still in a wheelchair. I carried on climbing until Lorna's pregnancy, when it seemed selfish to inflict further stress on her.

"Jack founded this club, and was the original CFI, having served as an instructor in the RAF. He suggested that if I joined the club, once I had gained experience of gliding, I should be more strongly motivated to take responsibility as Safety Officer than any other member. That was his great gift, that and his belief that every disaster presents a new opportunity, as you will understand when you get to know our committee members, every one is a round peg in a round hole. They have each spent long hours dealing with problems from civil engineering to legal matters, to our advantage."

He had given me much food for thought, and it took me a long time to digest all that he had told me. The winch sprang instantly to mind. Those that gave their time to designing and building it had built from scrap for peanuts, knowing that by doing so, they were now the only members who knew it well enough to service and repair it for the rest of its useful life, or the end of their membership.

To remind me why I was sat next to him woolgathering, he sounded me out on theory of flight and navigation, checking whether I had sought academic sources of supplementing the lectures delivered by the instructors. These occurred whenever bad weather limited flying and groundwork. When he found I was quite well read on relevant matters, he visibly thawed a little. "I'll let you do as much of the flying as I can, we might even catch a thermal today, but if not, we will work on your turns."

Eventually, the tractor with Steve up, crept back from the winch to deliver the cable. I sped through the cable and pre-flight checks, and we were finally ready to go. I shouted, **"Take up slack!"** and watched the cable writhe about. As soon as it twanged taut, I shouted, **"All out!"** and we were off.

Once again I kept the skid off the ground with light back pressure, until we reached 65kts and I could rotate into the climb. As black smoke blew towards us from the winch, I re-trimmed to get the best climbing speed. It must have been blowing about 20kts, because I was surprised to find we were 1,000 feet above the airfield, and still climbing strongly. On hearing the winch driver throttle back, I dipped the nose to take the tension off the cable prior to releasing. I reached towards release, making eye contact with Dixie. He raised a thumb, so I released.

The right wing instantly dipped, and Dixie cried, "I've got her!" whipping us round in a steep left turn. "We've blundered into a thermal, as you released." The green ball flew up in the variometer, and he re-trimmed to fly more slowly while in the thermal. As soon as the red ball rose, he dipped the nose to fly faster in the sinking air.

"It's further to our left." We must have been near our release point, as the thermal tracked downwind at

20kts, and Dixie kept us in the core of the lift until the altimeter showed 1,200 feet. "We've got enough height for a quick look at the bowl. The south end, nearest to us, should be working. And we will have a tail wind as we re-join the circuit. Get closer to the hill and head north of Parlick. Be ready to break off and return if we hit sinking air."

The altimeter had unwound two hundred feet before we reached slope lift and the green ball rose again, I trimmed back to fly more slowly along my first beat, edging in cautiously until the wing tip was about twenty feet clear of the ridge.

I would need to turn away from the hill at the end of each beat, to avoid the danger of being blown too close (or much worse) out of the slope lift and descending towards the very rough and very close top of the bowl!

Seagulls eyed the Barge with disdain. Each seemed to stifle a yawn before effortlessly out-climbing us. Big deal! If I had a variometer built into my inner ear, as they have, (not to mention the same number of flying hours) I would show them a thing or two! I made one return beat, then suggested that the lift was getting too weak for me to sustain our altitude.

"You must fly faster through any sinking air."

"Whenever we do break off to re-join the circuit, give the winch a wide berth. If a launch commences, it will bear ten o'clock from us, and climbing steeply. We can't afford to waste altitude making life easier for others, until we are 'home and dry' ourselves."

Progressing downwind, we were tracking rapidly towards the circuit, but the altitude was unwinding.

"You might have to turn early onto base leg. You must constantly adjust your circuit pattern, as changing circumstances demand."

It was with relief that I banked towards the winch. I eased the nose up as I realised that we were approaching the downwind boundary too fast and too low. In my nervousness, I turned early onto base leg, rattling through my pre-landing checks like a chipmunk on helium. While the sands of time were fast running out, Dixie reclined, hands behind his neck, grinning at me before he took control. "I've got her. I'm turning ten degrees into wind, because our speed is far too high. I'll still need to side slip our turn onto finals, then I'll pass her back to you for the landing." He then side-slipped the hundred-degree turn onto finals. "You have her!"

I managed to relax as I focussed on the spot just beyond where I expected to touch down. Remembering the twenty-knot wind, I kept lowering the nose to allow for wind shear, bringing my touchdown spot twenty yards nearer still. Keeping the wing tips in the periphery of my vision, I held off as long as possible.

There was the usual racket from the wheel, as it clod-hopped over the tussocky pasture. I gradually applied back-pressure to the stick, holding the skid off the ground. I realised that I felt drained of energy. The port wing sank slowly to the ground. Not a bad landing, I thought, but a misjudged approach. "Watch your circuit planning! It's a common symptom of panic to arrive on finals at the wrong height, and too fast."

At the end of the day's flying, with the gliders stowed away, I learned that we were to be invited to attend holiday weeks at this new slope-soaring site, using our facilities to raise cash. Sure enough, I opened my next club newsletter to find that Britannia College GC would spend a week with us in August.

They hoped to explore the possibilities of including us in cross-country ventures. That is, to find how many other soaring sites could be reached from ours. Volunteers were required to operate he winch, the tractor, a retrieve crew, and duty pilot. Their own CFI would be in charge. It was hoped that a couple of these weeks could be arranged each year.

Indeed the Duke of Lancaster's own Yeomanry operated tented sports holidays every year, centred on climbing and hill-walking for the benefit of youth clubs, mainly those in inner-city areas. We were to provide the instructors, winch driver, and duty pilot, and they would provide tentage and catering.

I thought this was a great idea, because we had some loans, which had to be serviced, as opposed to the grants which we also received. I have always hated being asked to sell books of raffle tickets. The club was registered as a limited company, and it seemed unprofessional to me, to rely on a 'begging bowl' when we could sell our services instead.

Next Monday, flying and finance were put on the back burner, because our 'mock' exams loomed near, as they started at the end of the Easter Term. Once these were completed, Miss Rossi wanted us to take a break from coursework before seriously getting down to revision. She wanted each of us to complete a poem, short story, or even a play as a peace of creative writing.

I had decided to write an imaginative piece based on an essay completed for Mr Bradshaw, to milk research that I had already completed. To 'recycle data', I see as nothing but good time-management. After all, many artists and authors commonly revisit earlier work, if they can see it in a new light.

It was inspired by what Mr Bradshaw had described as 'history by empathy', which I saw as finding what was the best technology at any point in time, and assuming that people we now regard as being both well-educated and energetic would have used the best technology available to them to achieve their aims.

I focussed it on a Viking sailor who left Ireland to settle in 'Rheged', after I read about the discovery of the remains of a crude forge on the north east coast of America, dating from the 9th century AD. To explain the evidence of Iron Age technology in a Stone Age environment, it was assumed that a longship had been beached for repairs, and 'bog nodules' had been collected from a swamp to be reduced in a forge to iron, and used to make nails. So all that technology, plus the skills to work wood and repair sails, was present in a small crew at the end of a long voyage. How about that? Remember, they had landed in native Indian country, still living in the Stone Age! I had only the title so far. It was to be 'In Arnwulf's Footsteps.'

CHAPTER 6

In Arnwulf's Footsteps

"Are you sure you were right to 'press on', Grandpa?" He answered tersely, without breaking the rhythm of his pace. "It stands to reason. T'nearest garage to where **tha** ditched the Land Rover is in Wray, five miles farther from home, and won't open until the morrow. 'Appen we'd get help in Lowgill, but that would demand retracing our steps."

"If they couldn't pull us out with a tractor, they would at least let us use their phone."

His reply was sharper, contemptuous of my suggestion. "They'd take us for townies, if we expect them to turn out at all hours of the night to un-ditch us. Every few weeks they'd get such folk bangin' on their door, expectin' to be wet-nursed just because they own a car. **Tha's** ditched our transport, and now **tha** mun walk! It will be time to ask for help when we reach Higher Woodhouse Farm, the first dwelling t'other side o't fell. I aim to ring Alec from there, and meet him in Newton, two miles beyond. He can drive there in the time it will us to walk. Doing it **your** way he'd be over an hour finding Lowgill, by the time he's gone through Caton and with no folk abroad to ask directions. I'd be hard-put to find it meself, in't dark, hidden up a clough as it is.

"Ony road, tha came to follow the Salter Fell track, and follow it thou shall! What would Alec say to find that we've but covered half the eleven-mile distance we set out to explore?"

This was a convincing argument, mainly because Dad always met adversity by 'pressing on', although it committed him to leaving his Land Rover in a ditch overnight, for anyone to pick it clean.

He cheered up, having won the argument. "We're but two miles from t'watershed, and then it'll be downhill all the way, for the final two miles to Higher Woodhouse Farm."

This sounded promising. Might he settle for being collected from there, rather than walking to Newton? I realised that water was coming through the eye-holes of my boots. "Grandad, why is it so much wetter now? Both my feet are wet."

Because of the gentler gradient either side of the watershed, it can't drain away fast enough. He was probably cold and tiring, too, and starting to get worried. We'd both be glad to reach shelter, and the chance to tell Mum and Dad our situation.

The light was fading, and the temperature was falling. I could feel my warmth draining away as we splashed onwards. "Think of t'Roman legions as passed this way. Not quite where we are, their causeway (part of their road from Ribchester) forks northwards for Ingleborough about a mile south of us. Just the causeway alone must have taken months of heavy work. They didn't have engineers in their armies. Their legions were expected not just to fight, but to build causeways, roads, fords, and defence works, as required. You can bet your boots, they only built where they intended to stay long-term!

"Think of those poor foot-sloggers, leaving the Mediterranean, to tramp our moors in sandals and leather kilts! At least we don't march laden with bronze shields and helmets, and a short sword."

I heard a sound that raised the hair on the back of my neck. "Quiet, Granddad, I can hear them now!" as he tried to contain his laughter. I strained to hear the slightly muffled sound. It was a slow, steady footfall, softer than the sound of nailed boots on a hard surface. If it was a legion, five to six thousand well-drilled men moved as one, slow and regular as a metronome, eating the miles between ne camp and the next, while defying anyone to bar their way.

"I can't hear owt!" "It's there; right enough, with no other sound to mask it!" "Nay, Ralph, you're listening to the pulse in your ear. You young'ns aren't used to silence." "Please stop for a moment, so I can hear it." There was not so much as a boulder to sit on, nothing but sodden turf and mud, but he took off his coat, and spread it on the ground.

He took a pen-knife from his pocket, and opened both blades. Then he lay on his coat, and plunged the bigger blade into the ground, clamping the smaller blade in his teeth. Clearly, he could hear better by bone-conduction. "You're not wrong, young Ralph. I can hear men marching, and they're getting closer!"

"I should never have asked you to bring me here!" "Why ever not? I'm glad to be wanted. Many a long month has passed since any thought of **me** entered your head. Quiet for a moment while I check their progress." He clamped the blade in his teeth for the latest bulletin. "This time, they are moving away from us. That can only mean they have taken the causeway towards Ingleborough."

"Everywhere will be closed. No chance of a 'Mississippi Mud' or 'Death by Chocolate' at this hour." He put his knife back in his pocket, and put on his dripping wet coat. How many other adults would have trusted a schoolboy's opinion to the extent of suffering so much discomfort when already tired, cold, and exhausted? "Well, we won't be seein' them, whether or not there be owt to see! Let's press on, there's nowt but a cock-stride to go, now."

I felt very grateful for his presence, but couldn't help thinking that even if it was a cock ostrich; it would have to take many strides to reach the farm we were making for.

We sloshed onwards over the muddy turf until we arrived at the sheep-wire fence that defined the county boundary between Lancashire and Yorkshire North Riding, where we opted to cross the little beck of Shooter's Clough, rather than make a long detour up the higher ground of Lamb Hill on our left.

This had been a major obstacle for motorcyclists on the Lancashire Constabulary training course, and angle-iron pegs driven into the slippery banks of the beck testified to the passing of four-wheel drive vehicles. Damn the lot of them! We reached the far side with mud over the top of our boots, thanks to them!

It was a great relief to reach drier ground. Where our boots had squelched at every step, they now clanked on limestone chippings. We increased our pace, so that we gradually warmed up. The last orange light drained away behind the bleak height of Wolfstone Crag,

Pale moonlight lit the far side of Stock's reservoir, shining beneath the gloomy conifers of Gisburn Forest. It had been planted by the Forestry Commission after WW1. Then the track descended to our right above the ruins of House of Croasdale, until we could no longer see the reservoir.

The surface changed again, to weathered concrete, probably laid prior to the building of that feature, and long since broken into large slabs by frost and ground-heave. We negotiated two wooden gates across the track, and then – thank God! Higher Woodhouse Farm appeared on our left.

Despite our sodden clothing and mud-covered boots, Mrs Wood ushered us into her kitchen, and told Granddad to take his boots off to ring home from her phone in the hall. She listened to what was said, and when he asked to be met in Newton. She took the phone from him and spoke to Mum. "I insist that they must stay in my kitchen until collected, as they are in no state to continue."

I was glad to note that Granddad submitted to her bullying, which proved Mrs Wood's view must be correct! It would only take Dad a couple of minutes to drive from Newton, and would save us from hypothermia. I was telling Mrs Wood, over a large mug of sweet tea, that we were both due for a severe ear-bashing about abandoning his vehicle, but this drew a strange response from Granddad. "It will all seem different in the morning, when what your dad and I think will no longer matter. Hey, Ralph lad! Arnside were really bonny, weren't it? I seldom saw a prettier place, and it has plenty of visitors, to prove it. You don't expect crowds in a place between a swamp to the east, and coastal quicksands and a tidal bore to the west." He laughed ghoulishly. "If it ever **did** get crowded, one wet place or another would soon thin 'em out a bit!"

"Grandad! Talk about damning with faint praise! It is beautiful. I've always loved limestone country, but it must be very unusual to find heavily wooded limestone pavement with native deer as a bonus. I love where we live, but that was much lusher, and the light must be more intense with all that extra light reflected off the sea.

The Aga was going full blast, and the warmth of that and the hot tea acted like an anaesthetic to my weary body. I must have dozed off, only wakening briefly to see Granddad stuffing my boots (which he must have sluiced under the tap in the yard) then I stretched briefly in my Windsor chair, and I was out like a light again.

In my mind, I pressed on, down the Roman Road, which veered off forty-five degrees west of the Newton road, heading for Gamble Hole Farm. This name commemorates a German mining engineers who, in Elizabethan times, was contracted by the landowner to check the vein of lead ore beneath for the presence of silver. Suspecting that he wasn't going to get paid, he dug decoy workings at random, and told the landowner that he would have to pay first, before getting a sample of ore. No money was forthcoming, so the German left, and the source of silver was never found. No-one since has found any silver. The simplest solution must be that there wasn't any to find, but why spoil a good story?

That was what I was thinking of as I approached the bottom of the valley. Surely the Hodder should be visible by now? The difference was that what I knew to be pasture. It was heavily wooded with mature oak, mainly. I knew I was near Boarsden Farm, because the limestone reef pinnacle shone white in the moonlight. I recalled that the Nowells, who have farmed there for hundreds of years, take their name from that feature.

It was then that I realised that a camp fire lit a clearing, in which men in grey cloaks were setting up camp, with their pack ponies tethered and panniers were stacked. Instead of turning back, as in a dream, I approached with no sense of fear. There must have been about ten small shaggy ponies eating hungrily from their nose bags.

This would be the halfway point of a journey between fording the Wenning, and fording the Ribble, so it must have been a regular camp for jaggers. They had previously built a semicircle of turf walls, each of which was open to the fire. They were each one using spears for joists to support old sails as a roof.

Four large men in grey cloaks, pinned at the shoulder with brooches, while others prepared food.

All were wearing leather skull-caps, such as welders protect their scalps with. On the other side, the ponies were tethered, with wicker panniers stacked where they were lit by the fire.

I reckoned that we were within two or three hundred yards of the Hodder, about halfway between the Wenning and the Ribble, a perfect site as a staging post, as there was firewood and water in easy reach, and it was the lowest point of their journey, and therefore the least cold and wet! Being convinced that these were definitely not Boy Scouts, or film makers, it seemed best to make my presence known before I might provoke a fatal response from any of them.

I shouted, "Hello the camp!" before striding into the firelight. I was curious about the contents of the panniers. Although some bore oil-cloth bags, presumably salt, others were less full, and lumpier. A broad bear of a man with a black beard, hurriedly crossed himself as he slid his sheath knife closer to his right hand.

"Yet another strange being abroad tonight. Tell us you name." This was no Viking. He had an Irish accent. "Ralph Swindlehurst. My father farms some ten miles west of here." "Then ten miles of trackless wilderness separate you from home. Where is your mount?" "I am on foot, and not after one of your ponies. My father is on his way to meet me." "Then you chose well, because while we are here, Arnwulf's camp is the safest place to meet. My name is Miles, and I'm in charge in Arnwulf's absence."

The others didn't agree with this assertion, judging by the derisive laughter that it evoked. Undeterred, Miles continued. "Arnwulf is my brother-in-law. They married in Ireland, before deciding to settle in Rheged. He needed his ship's company, because of their various skills, but would never have come without the best blacksmith in Ireland, to make the wide variety of tools necessary to establish a new settlement.

"Have a cup of wine with us, and enjoy the crack until Arnwulf returns." As he had expected, this brought about a change in attitude in the others, as those who had been loudest in their derision decided that Miles was now their best friend, as they dug cups from their belongings, and crowded around him. He drank his cup first, before refilling it and then one for me, before his new friends got any.

He then launched into a long list of tools he had made since arriving. Axes, shovels, chains, turfing spades, hammers, and pry-bars were needed to clear stones and tree stumps for bothies and vegetable cultivation. Any shelter less basic than a bothy required a saw, chisels, a hammer, a maul, nails, and a thatch-knife! Ponies are useful to the carpenter for raising timbers with a block and tackle, but they need tack for such work.

"Every hour that I work requires the labour of others to provide me with timber for charcoal. Arnwulf and his crew wanted to make the salt production their priority, as they were more interested in travelling and trading than settlement, so Maeve had to keep chivvying them to get her house built.

"So making the salt pans, and sealing them with puddled clay was the first priority, and I was always short of labour. It took me a while to get started with tool-making. As summer ended and the temperature fell, paddling in sea water to spread a barrow load of clay into a thin layer to prevent seepage from the salt pans became strangely unpopular, so that I no longer struggled for wood cutters or charcoal-making teams."

I stifled a yawn at this point, as I was still worn out with my long hike in wet clothes. Good raconteur that he was, Miles changed the subject to what they had found different since landing in Rheged. He was a staunch supporter of the Celtic Church, as taught by St Patrick and others, and deeply resented the Germanic influence taught by Wilfrid and Hilda. This was mainly rooted, it seemed to me, in the Northumbrian invasion of Ireland in the 8th century, but they were certainly opportunistic.

"These people admired the political power that was as exerted by the Church of Rome. They would have worshipped Old Nick himself if he carried the same clout. They envied, but were unable to equal, Celtic Art, music, and craftsmanship. All of which were at their best in Erin, the westernmost outpost of the Celtic race.

"These new converts were whelped by that same Northumbrian Ecfrith, who led the treacherous invasion of Ireland in the 8th century. At the Synod of Whitby, with the help of those Angles, Saxons, and Jutes of the same blood, easily outvoted the very Celtic Christians who had inspired St Boniface to take Christianity to them."

Who had said, 'If an Irishman sees a dripping tap, it reminds him of the Flood?' I decided to staunch his marathon whinge. "Pardon me for interrupting, but you have seen many things, and learnt many things in your travels. I have long wondered how 'Beatrix Fell' came by its name, because despite Beatrice being a fairly common forename, a storyteller named 'Beatrix Potter' is the only person I've heard of to use that name."

"Sure, there is no mystery about it, other than how you don't know your own neighbours! Because it is farmed by an English man named Beotric. He is one of your neighbours, if what you told us is true!"

"I have never knowingly lied to you. If that is so, I know nothing of it. Indeed your jagging has been a better education than my schooling has. I learn something new every day. We only know him as 'Gimpy' because of his limp."

This seemed to please him, but once more, his storytelling skills alerted him to my dislike of lengthy religious rants, which launched him into an amusing anecdote, guaranteed to entertain.

"My only claim to fame is that, aided by this crew, I persuaded an Anglo-Saxon priest to dedicate a church to a non-existent Danish martyr. That was the church of St Alkelda at Giggleswick. We had been 'leading' lime there for mortar, making mortar lime putty, and lime-wash as a gift to a church that was still only half-built.

"We do a good trade with other Nordic settlers from Ireland. I had made candle sconces to light the interior, and door furniture in the form of hinges, door latches, and studs to decorate the oak door.

"To the best of my knowledge, this visit to accept our gifts was all he had done, and he had certainly never even got his hands dirty. He was only there to suggest that it be dedicated to St. Wilfrid, despite the fact that all the real work had been done by those who had previously been devotees of Odin."

Determined that this big-mouth would never saddle us with Wilfrid, I launched into myth-making mode. I looked around to seek inspiration, and as luck would have it, two fat 'house fraus' waddled past, from the direction of the 'Ebbing and Flowing Well', which not only tops up the spring up via a natural siphon, but is carbonated while underground.

Naturally this astonishes all those unburdened by technology, earning it an undeserved reputation for magical powers. They shuffled past him, but in his innocence he failed to realise that they had sought help for some feminine problem from what he would consider to be witchcraft. In a flash, inspiration came to me. "St Alkelda was martyred near this very spot, by a Danish heathen."

He should have known that to Vikings, it was called 'Ölkeld', because of its fizz. "Let's have a show of hands of those in favour of 'Alkelda', as opposed to 'Wilfrid'." The vote was almost unanimous, and as all of his opponents shared a threatening appearance, he agreed without demur. It still bears that same dedication, no-one having yet discovered that she was invented by an Irish blacksmith!"

"Miles does run-on a bit doesn't he?" The speaker, who I saw for the first time, was the largest of the Norsemen, and distinguished by a heavy silver torque. I could only guess that he had stayed out of sight, scouting around for a possible mount of mine. If so, he had done so, and sat next to me, without my ever seeing him or hearing him. He must have been exceptionally fast, and light on his feet for such a burly figure. Dad would have been impressed. "So,

Ralph, you find us finally joined together in the religion of Christ, but still racially divided."

"You are dead right! Miles considers himself more artistic and a better craftsman owing to his Celtic origins, and then describes his lie about 'St Alkelda' as being typically British!"

"My name is Arnwulf, as you must have guessed. I let Miles be my mouthpiece, because he has the 'gift of the gab'. In that skill, and in working iron, he excels me. I excel his skills in seamanship, shepherding, battle tactics, and mainly as a judge of women and horses. In fact, the best thing I see in him is that in embracing Christianity he surrendered his standing as a magi, which he had among all heathen Celts because that was their attitude to blacksmiths.

"Everyone else you see here is one of my ship's company, a team in which every member is both a seaman and able to make and mend every part of the boat, from sails to rope and even nails. So every individual has a part to play, but until we have all the shelter and implements that we need in building our settlement more of the team will be working to assist Miles than doing my bidding.

"Clearly, most of my proudest achievements will remain in the past, when I used my navigational skills to round some headland on an eastern shore just in time to ride the flood tide towards the nearest settlement. Then my longship would ghost out of the haar with the dawn sun behind it, and we would each have lifted a mount before our victims even knew of our presence. When I still sacrificed to Odin, this was my greatest pride."

He fixed me with his pale eyes, and I believed every word he said. "You, by contrast, look to be a clerkly young man, recklessly roaming in the dark with neither weapon nor mount. Your speech seems full of book-learning, but when both Miles and I spoke of Christianity, it failed to evoke any response from you! I don't like your attitude. Both of us prefer heathen pagans to Godless clerics!

"Of the two of us, I see you as being more like Miles, but lacking both his strength and his skills, just the gift of the gab. He can spin a yarn that will hold the attention of those around a camp fire, weaving magic out of common words. Such a skill could bring you wealth (If you worked a market stall) but might cost you the trust of the very people that you admire.

"Rightly or wrongly, I still judge men mainly by the military virtues." "What are they?" "You are well aware that I refer to stoicism, courage, and loyalty." "May I ask you a question?"

"Of course, and I will answer it as best I can." "I noticed that those panniers not filled with salt, appear to be scrap iron in oilcloth. I imagined that jaggers would be glad to sell for cash, rather than carry scrap."

"Then you don't understand trading, so your father will never make a farmer of you. We are lucky to be settled near a source of iron ore at Red Rake, but you don't grasp that digging ore and smelting it is both expensive and time consuming.

"The first thing to learn, is to trade for whatever will increase your capital! I pay my crew 'in kind' because they only seek whatever they can drink, eat, or wear, whereas my expenditure on such things I regard as spending my capital, and thus needs restraint!

"Many a proud man has beggared himself to buy a fine stallion, which would be a luxury to me. But to the owner of brood mares, it would represent a valuable investment that would soon pay for itself! If we relied entirely on our iron ore, the whole crew would be engaged in labouring for Miles, cutting wood, charcoal burning, mining and smelting ore. We live to travel, not to labour on Miles' behalf, and burn all the timber that is easily accessible to us!"

I seemed to be irritating him with my questions, and could remember no more of my dream.

CHAPTER 7

The Wild Colonial Boy Drops In

I looked carefully about me, and saw the Ka 6 porpoising away from Fairsnape, in the direction of Forton. The Swallow was working the slope, which the Blanik had just left, to return to the circuit. As usual, once I was ready to take off, there was some problem at the winch. I spoke to my instructor, Leslie, but his attention was elsewhere, so I got no reply.

I followed his gaze, and had just managed to focus on the Swallow as it turned out from the slope at the end of its beat and the sun caught its silver wings. "What's up, Leslie?" I asked, but it soon became clear.

"It's one of our solo pilots, just cleared for this site. This is probably his first attempt at slope soaring, and while he had his back to the slope, the wind has carried him out of the lift and he is now facing into wind with insufficient groundspeed to get back into rising air. We are about to witness an out-landing in a desperately unsuitable situation."

He climbed out to confer with the CFI, who was already speaking to the engineer, while the duty pilot collected those who had rigged the Swallow that morning, and were now faced with de-rigging it on rough, trackless ground, and then manhandling it for at least a mile along the top of the ridge, and then down a steep bracken-clad slope to the nearest rough track that a Land Rover and glider trailer could cope with. Leslie asked the duty plot to abort the launch, and notify the winch driver. I set off for the path up Parlick, but Leslie called me back.

"You'll only get under people's feet. Leave the de-rigging to those well practiced at it." He button-holed the CFI. "John Allen will have reached Forton by now, and he's got VHF radio in the Ka 6. We can call him up from one of the syndicate gliders, and ask him to see if mountain rescue, or the ambulance service should be alerted." Den assented, and Leslie found a syndicate team to ask them to contact John Allen.

The sun flashed from the white fibreglass wings of the Ka 6. Its wing-tips were springing in bubbling lift, as it sped back from Forton. For a moment its gleaming whiteness with blue shadows modelling subtle curves, created a magic sculpture that appeared translucent against the blue sky as if carved from smoked crystal. It approached as at about ninety knots, before popping the air brakes for a slow pass over the Swallow, into wind. The guy on the ground must have given him the OK sign. I imagined the bearded features of John Allen speaking into a hand mike before returning whence he had been thermalling.

Twenty minutes passed before a light aircraft appeared and the Swallow was inspected once again. It appeared to be a Piper cub, and as soon as its pilot had spotted our field, it joined the circuit to land. This seemed a good time to get a hot lunch, while all the grown-ups were busy. The guy from the light aircraft had the same priority, and he got there first. He was a tall guy, with a long, horsey face. He wore a khaki flying suit, and a green baseball cap with the deer emblem of John Deere tractors.

He had not only got there before me, but clearly already eaten He was now giving Rita (the CFI's wife) the benefit of his assessment. "I'll go another bowl of that, Rita. You might be interested to know that my dad plied his camel-train between the railhead at Alice Springs, and Birdsville, along the Birdsville Track. This was just how he liked his grub, stiff with vegemite and monosodium glutamate.

"'I need enough salt in me tucker to sweat off the odd pint of lager,' he'd say. I bet if you boiled it down for another ten minutes or so, it do as a salt-lick for sheep. What are the white bits floatin' in it? Is it all loaded with symbolism, like a Japanese garden?"

"Look at the blackboard, you thick colonial twit! This is spaghetti bolognese, and the white bits are spaghetti!"

"What? Together with **canned** baked beans and **canned** minced beef? Baked beans don't belong in spag. bolog. I imagine that you could be lynched for selling this in Bologna. And I had been hoping that the white bits were witchetty grubs. At least they would have been fresh!"

"If you find it uneatable, why are you asking for more?"

"No way! 'Uneatable' is an alien concept, down under. My dad always insisted that we ate whatever came to hand. He justified this by asserting that only a drunk would chunter on undiluted grog!"

I finally caught Rita's eye. "I'll take a bowl of that, too Rita, if you please. Did Rita happen to mention that she is married to the CFI? I'm Ralph. Would you care to share a table with me?"

He favoured me with a courtly bow, sweeping his cap off as he did so. "Tim Clancy, Your Excellency. Rita, I hope your hubby realises how lucky he is. This grub was cooked with authentic Italian passion which obviously matters far more to him than what he eats!"

We sat down at the far end of the clubhouse. "Do tell, I'm dying to know why a polished diplomat, such as yourself, should be clad like an Albanian night-shite shifter!"

"The Chyppen paparazzi tend to hound one when not travelling incognito. I consider myself no more self-effacing than other landed gentry. You however, could enthral an audience (even at the Glasgow Empire) with you definitive portrayal of a red-necked Ocker!"

"Rippah! Was I really that good? I had done little more than offer praise where praise was due. You look young and innocent. Are you a pupil pilot?"

"I'm afraid so. You must be the custodian of the Piper Cub. Are you an antiquarian, or have you just borrowed it from the Shuttleworth Collection?"

"Watch it, laddy boy! You are speaking of the woman I love. She's a Super Cub, not yet a teeny-bopper, having been bought new! So, you're the man to put me right on the set-up here. I made the mistake of reporting to the farmhouse after landing, and the lady who came to the door directed me to the clubhouse here. Is she the landowner, or what?"

"That's my mum. She was until recently. The gliding club were enjoying free facilities at the English Electric airfield at Samlesbury, but it was useless for gliders, being too close to the Ribble estuary to offer much unstable air, a good source of thermals. They sought a hill-soaring site, and found they could get a Sports Council grant to help purchase a suitable site, because the grant depended on security of tenure, and not available to tenants of such a site.

"This site needs draining, and as long as it retains agricultural use (it is pasturing some of my sheep) it gets a grant big enough to pay for all the material needed, plus the (second-hand) machinery required.

"So that is the present situation. All I can inherit is the house and the flock, most of which is grazing our share of open fell that the club soars."

"I am really sorry to hear about your dad. That must have been a terrible blow. I didn't expect to get such a detailed exposition, showing such grasp of the details. Your mum might think that you've told me much more than you needed to, but what you said will remain strictly between the two of us.

"To try to repay for what must be still be a painful experience for you, may I show you round the Super Cub? Learning to fly is a doddle at your age, and as I hold an instructor's rating, I'm willing to help further your flying ambition in any way I can. Let's go and have a look at my machine, and you will learn most if you watch me complete a pre-flight check."

"Thanks, that would be great." As we walked to where Tim had picketed his aircraft, he talked excitedly about the superiority of 'tail draggers' over the more modern light aircraft that use the tricycle undercarriage.

"Most of these are designed to make a light aircraft as much like an (American) car as possible, with the stick and rudder linked by bungee cord for the benefit of those unable to co-ordinate the two. The ailerons usually provide inadequate control in the rolling plane, and the elevators are usually too small for complete control in the pitching plane.

"They are extremely stable, where enthusiasts prefer responsiveness. Because of its low wing-loading and responsive controls the Super Cub is very popular with the Civil Air Guard, largely deployed in what we call mountain rescue tasks. Strong air currents and sudden gusts require quick thinking and plenty of response available."

He had only paused to draw breath. "Granted, if you let her 'balloon' after a rough touchdown, she'll need a burst of throttle at the top of the rebound before you touch down again, more gently. That results from having the main wheels **in front of** the centre of gravity. Trikes have the two main wheels **behind** their centre of gravity, so they pitch nose-down after a rough touchdown. If they do so too often, they rupture the oil seals in the front oleo strut, which involves an expensive new unit.

"The use of a control yoke in place of a control column may offer familiarity to car drivers, but I believe they should not think they are driving a car! Inadequate ailerons reduce the chance of aileron-drag leading to a ground loop, but ground loops require quick responses and response from the controls. Differential aileron controls aim to avoid loss of lift when using ailerons on the approach, which is great, up to the point when the leverage exerted by the 'up' aileron causes a strong yaw to that side, which demands a very quick response!"

I was baffled. Yes, I had read enough to follow the points he was making, but what use was all this to a schoolboy who was not yet earning, and wouldn't earn much when he left school? Did he hope to sell me one?

Once more, he had only paused for breath. "You'll learn more by just watching me do the pre-flight check than asking random question." I hadn't managed to staunch his verbal diarrhoea so far, so fat chance of me achieving even one random question!

"We always start with the port aileron, and work clockwise from there." Suiting deeds to words, he removed the aileron lock, which consisted of two squash balls threaded together with shock cord, and threaded between aileron and wing. Each bears an orange bunting streamer to make it more visible. (I imagined **myself** thinking, *So **that's** why I'm in a ground loop! I left the aileron locks in place!*) He moved to the port landing wheel.

"I'm checking marks on both the wheel and the tyre, to see if the tyre is 'creeping' on the wheel." The next stop was the pitot head, covered with an orange canvas sheath. It consists of two forward-facing tubes which are the main sensors for the air-speed indicator, and the altimeter. He next opened the port engine cowling to check the oil level.

"Here's a job you could do for me. My hand pump is double-acting, and moves a pint on each stroke. Each tank has a capacity of eighteen US gallons which translates as fifteen imperial gallons. Knowing that each is half-full, how many strokes dare you make before checking whether the tank is full?"

"I can do that." I pulled an old envelope out of my pocket, and found my ball pen. "Let's see. Each tank has about seven gallons in it, and will take about that much again. If I put six gallon in each at a pint a stroke, and then six gallons will be six times eight, or forty-eight strokes before I check it."

"Right! I don't want to see any evidence of spillage when I get back, at the price I have to pay in the UK." "Some guy with a Land Rover collected the drum for me." "Why doesn't **that** surprise me?" "Of course. I am rather imposing on you and I'll be back ASAP." "That's OK. I don't suppose you'll stop talking, but at least I won't be there to hear you." He reappeared with the Land Rover, and hopped out briskly, with a wooden pallet for a stillage, and a sand bag to break the fall of the drum when he rolled it out. He placed the pallet under the port tank, rolled the drum to drop it on the sandbag, and we both rolled the drum to the pallet on which we upended it. He produced a spanner and removed the bung, before mounting his hand pump on the threads for the bung, and tightening it in place.

He jumped back in the Land Rover. "Thanks

Ralph! Must rush, I've got a client waiting."

I pumped furiously as the Land Rover bumped across the rough pasture. Was I being subjected to some kind of test, like when some old dosser invited Arthur to pull the sword out of the stone? On the other hand, if I ever see myself as 'the once and future king' I'll know that I'm ripe for the 'funny farm'. Maybe, after all, I was being shown a possible future career. In which case, forget it. I know what I want my future to be, whatever obstacles might stand in the way.

When he returned, he gave me a whole fiver! Better still, he told me to write off for an official log book, as required by the Ministry of Aviation for those aspiring to become pilot-in-charge of a light aircraft in the UK! The log book I already had was issued by the British Gliding Association, to save official involvement in gliding administration.

CHAPTER 8

Powered Flight

You may remember my approval when the newsletter revealed that visits from other clubs would be arranged, to raise capital for the club, mainly with the intention of replacing some very elderly and infirm gliders. I therefore looked forward to the arrival of a party of members from the Imperial College GC, consisting of their own CFI, who would be responsible for them. The group consisted mainly of private and syndicate owners, only interested in cross-country ventures who sought aero-tows in preference to winch launches.

However, some other of their members hoped to use our solo machines or even our trainers. When their week arrived, two of their private owners got aero-tows, having set Sutton Bank (the field used by the Yorkshire GC) as their intended destination. Tim had offered his services for aero-tows, and was contracted to them for the week. The following

Monday, Tim took a call from the two successful pilots, asking for a tow back to Tewitts' Field.

He invited me to watch him prepare for the task. He rang Air Traffic Control at Broughton (this is the Broughton near Preston) and asked for the forecast wind velocity, and visibility at 3,000 feet, from Tewitts' Field to Sutton Bank. He was given 210°/25kts, with ten miles visibility.

He laid out his ICAO 1/25,000 airchart for the North of England on the kitchen table, and ruled a thick line with a carpenter's pencil between the two airfields, marking this line with two arrows, to show it represented the Required Track over the ground. With his (war surplus) Douglas Protractor he measured the True Course to bear 70° from Tewitts' Field. Using the 1/25,000 scale on his navigational ruler, he read the distance off as 56nm.

He then used the protractor to enter the wind vector on the map, that is, by a line bearing 210°, and of a length proportional to its force, that is 25 miles on the scale previously used. He marked this vector with three arrows, identifying it as the wind vector.

He then used the ruler to draw line joining the end of the wind vector to the destination. The length of this line represented true air speed, completing the vector triangle. The enclosed angle at the destination gives us the crab angle, that is the angle one must head into wind, in order to achieve the Required Track over the ground. He marked this line to identify it as True Heading.

He stared hard at me, obviously wondering how much of this had been understood. "Now to find how much you have taken in about the vector triangle. An easy one first. Where is our starting point?" "Tewitts' Field." "Yes, stay with that. How will the forecast wind affect our journey?" "Let me think. It represents a tail wind from our right, so it will shorten our flight, and having set the gyro compass to True North, we must head 70° plus the crab angle to make good the Required Track."

"Right, clever clogs, a harder one. Look at the huge vector triangle, defacing a large proportion of my chart with thick pencil lines. Can you find any evidence of previous marking?"

"None at all. You showed me the best way of visualising the vector triangle, but evidently use some other method, confined to adults. If I had to guess, you probably use a Ouija board, or possibly read chickens' entrails."

"My God! I have I have an undiscovered genius at imparting knowledge. I bet I could train your mutt to juggle, if I had a couple of hours to spare! What ground speed does the True Heading vector represent?" "You said your Super Cub cruises at 85kts, for what that's worth." "Then 85kts it is, you faithless agricultural Pom." "The True Heading vector is longer than the True Course one. We can read the ground speed directly off the 1/25,000 scale on your ruler." "**Very good!** I make that 104kts. Off the top of your head, what will our ETA be?"

I thought long and hard, having surprised myself so far, I didn't want to fall at the last fence. "It must take close to half an hour to fly 56nm at 104kts. I suppose you want that in minutes, which would be 15, plus 56 over 104 by 60." "Here's a calculator."

"Thanks. The ETA will be 15.32. Good God! Sutton Bank is only 32 minutes' flying time away?" "Exactly right! Meet the Jeppesen Computer! Note that it is merely a circular slide-rule with delusions of grandeur. Commercial pilots would probably look down on it, preferring some expensive electronic instrument, but the great danger with such things is punching numbers in never is the complete answer. All too often people fail to visualise the vector triangle, and get the wrong answer.

"If I may make another point, you were amazed at how quickly we can fly to Sutton Bank, but having covered the distance far quicker than is possible by road travel, one forgets that you are a mere pedestrian until you take off again.

"Suppose one of our two clients decided to do a bit of local flying, and lost track of the time, causing us to wait for him. Sutton Bank is miles from anywhere. (YGC members could rightly say that goes double for Tewitts' Field!) So it is probably like being in the forces. Nothing to do, and nowhere to go. Cock-ups are a regular occurrence, and you can expect to spend hours a day waiting for something else to happen."

"I'm so glad you made that point! I'm well aware that my peer group are all suckers for novelty, and I see that in myself very often. I bet large numbers of us make a false start, pursuing careers that have nothing except novelty to commend them."

"That's certainly what I think. Don't be surprised if you ever catch me selling my last aircraft to capitalise a well-equipped camel train. And your dad, wherever he may be, will be boasting about your flying exploits to anyone who'll listen."

"Yeah. Now, joke over and back to business. You had no difficulty in relating the forecast wind to how it would affect our return trip to Sutton bank. You had no difficulty in finding the ground speed by measuring the length of the true heading vector. It is unhelpful to over-praise pupils, but you wouldn't believe how thick some pupils can be. I've had pupils who couldn't show me on a map our location, and how can you start a journey elsewhere without knowing where you are now?

"I was on a field in Norfolk, having been told to prepare a pupil for his triangular cross-country flight, before entering him for a PPL test. I was getting such vague answers from him that I took him in the office where we had the ICAO 1/25,000 chart for southern England pinned to the wall.

"I said, 'Show me our present location.' After long deliberation he pointed to a spot in Southern Ireland. Needless to say, I told the CFI that he was months away from attempting any cross-country flight, and that he would be a danger to himself and others if he ventured out of sight of the airfield.

"Back to business. There are two reasons for drawing the vector triangle on the chart. Firstly, it is definitely the easiest way for the pupil to visualise himself at cruise altitude over the airfield, setting course and relating the effect of the forecast wind on your true course. I should inform you that you don't need to measure the distance from the chart.

"The BGA have published a list of every approved gliding site in the UK, which lists the bearing and distance from any chosen site to all the others. Use it, it is more accurate. The calculations can all be solved with that circular slide-rule called the Jeppesen Computer. It has a rotating wind rose with a square grid, on which we can make pencilled crosses to represent direction and velocity. For light aircraft, or gliders, it is most convenient to let each square represent 10kts, or 10kph, or 10mph, supposing we have been given a forecast wind 90°/25kts.

"The bearing of the wind is set on the rose, represented by a **small** pencil cross two and a half squares outwards from the centre, when the rose has been set to 90°. It can then be applied to any given course. If applied to a course of 90°, we can instantly grasp the this will be a headwind with no drift component, but will reduce our ground speed outbound, and if we choose to follow the reciprocal track back to where we started, it will **add** 25kts to our ground speed.

"Suppose with that same wind, we set course for a destination bearing 180° from our starting point. Then having set our true course to 180° on the rose, and drawn a line from the cross to the centre of the rose, it gives us a heading of 162° to make good a track of 180°. This gives us a crab angle of 18°, which can be found on the black scale, which shows our effective true air speed as 81kts.

"This demonstrates that even a moderate beam wind can slow us by 4kts. This becomes important when deciding which leg to fly first on your triangular cross-country. Usually, pupils are most nervous about landing at the biggest airfield, so make sure you land there in the most favourable conditions. The forecast will be most accurate for the first leg, and will slowly change from what you were given. If it looks good for the biggest field, reduce your anxiety by ticking that one off first, even if that doesn't offer the lowest distance for touching base at all three."

"Hold it there, Tim. I think that is all I can take in for now, and I would benefit from working through lots of different examples to get familiar with the navigation process."

"That's fine, I've completed my flight log calculations, and we've got half an hour in hand, so grab your gear, and let's saunter over to the Cub. The tanks are full, so there's no rush."

I grabbed my haversack, which contained camera and notebook, which I transferred to my jacket for the flight, leaving sandwiches and cans of lemonade to be stowed in the Cub's locker. It was a relief to be out in the sunshine again. Tim removed the port aileron lock, then the pitot head cover, and stowed them in the locker with the two tow-lines he would use already in. I included my haversack. He completed his pre-flight checks, removing the other aileron lock, and climbed in, fastening his harness. "We'll taxi over to the take-off point, and check the engine there, when it has warmed up."

I climbed in, and the main disadvantage of tail-draggers struck me. As we started to take off, the nearest ground I could see in front of me was a limited view to each side of the engine cowling, so that the whole of the take-off run was obscured for the 90° segment centred on our take-off path. I was aware that this blind spot would disappear as soon as Tim picked the tail up, but until then I hoped my flock had not been stampeded towards me by marauding Indians, or even by my mum, which was more likely. The pilot would always be sat behind me, where he could see even less!

As Tim completed his engine checks, I offered a feeble joke (even for a schoolboy). "In a flick, when the jet-jockey is set to go, he might say, 'Let's kick a tyre and light the fire!' They seem to have omitted rather a lot, don't they?"

"Too right! Why don't you include it in your compendium entitled 'A golden treasury of Yankee understatements'? I reckon you could list them all on the back of a match box."

As he spoke, he set the mixture to 'rich', carburettor heat to 'off', cabin heat to 'off' fuel cock from 'off' to 'port tank'. "Ready to start up now. Ignition on, trimmer fully aft, all clear ahead. (I've been clocking either side of the engine, and above it, so I'm not just hoping for the best!)" The engine cranked over slowly, pausing at each compression stroke, before it coughed and fired up. Tim shouted above the noise, "Always watch the oil pressure when it starts up, because if the oil is too low, you could do a lot of damage in a short time."

He parked at 90° to his take-off, to be sure nothing was moving on the ground or in the air that might endanger us. He ran the motor up to 1,700rpm to check the twin magnetos for 'mag. drop'. They are switched off one by one to make sure we still have 'twin spark' ignition. Both the oil pressure gauge and the ammeter showed satisfactory readings.

He checked the rudder and elevators for full and

free movement, and then moved the control column to describe the widest possible circle, for the same reason. He finally checked that the ailerons moved up when the stick was moved towards them. (In the services, following any work by an airframe or engine fitter, results in that person accompanying the test flight, in the hope that any mistake might be their last one!)

"Right, let's go. The time is fourteen fifty. We have full and free movement of the controls, trim fully nose-up, mixture rich, fuel switched to port tank, and sufficient for our flight. Flaps full on, oil pressure normal, hatches." He checked his door, then reached across to make sure mine was fastened, and the harness fastened. Again, he checked both.

"All clear on the runway, all clear in the air, let's go!" He raised his thumb to the signaller, who gave him a green on the aldis light. He eased the throttle forwards, and released the left heel brake until the Super Cub was lined up, into wind according to the wind sock. He held her on both the heel brakes until the rpm responded to full throttle by registering full-power rpm. The aircraft roared and shook on full song before he released the brakes, and let her go.

After about forty yards he was able to pick the tail up for the speed to build in 'ground effect', (where it sticks to the ground) before rotating. At 800 feet, he dipped the nose while retracting the flaps, to allow for the reduced lift. "We get our best rate of climb flying at 66kts with an engine speed of 2,300 revs. We have to leave the airfield at the departure time I gave ATC at Barton, at 3,000 in order to be able to check our forecast wind at the first check point which is always ten minutes outbound.

"If you arrive there earlier or later, you must recalculate the wind vector, because your ETA, and other check points en route, must all be recalculated. Obviously, collecting these two gliders needn't matter to fifteen to twenty minutes, but that will only be your situation when you have hundreds of flying hours. You will never fly accurately until you can do dead reckoning in your head.

"For the same reason, never just goof about if you have submitted a flight plan. They take a dim view if you don't turn up on the radar when they are expecting you, and they won't consider pausing for photography as a reasonable excuse!" After two lazy circles climbing to cruise altitude, he levelled off, crossing the centre of the field dead on 1500hrs. He punched the stopwatch on his clipboard to start recording elapsed time, re-trimmed to cruise speed and power, set the gyro compass to head 075° magnetic, and started peering ahead to find the ten-minute marker he had selected.

Ingleborough, Pen y Ghent, and Great Whernside were visible to the left of our track. Looking back, the afternoon sun glittered on the Irish Sea, through the haze. The Pennine hills appeared strangely flattened, beneath us, their colours greyed by haze, and cloud shadows hard to distinguish from woodland. Water features are always easiest to find. "Can you hold her on the gyro compass?" "I'd like to try." "It demands accurate flying. Short periods losing or gaining height play havoc with the cruise speed we need to maintain, as do short diversions to either side of our required track. Every minute flying off-course adds to the distance we will cover, and as we come to our markers, it might appear that our forecast wind was incorrect, when in reality, we are chasing errors caused by inaccurate flying."

He watched me for a while, going cross-eyed staring at the gyro compass. "Use a distant landmark (making sure it isn't a cloud) and you will be more relaxed, and watching where you are going, which can't be bad! There aren't many light aircraft pootling about over the Pennines, but quite a number of helicopters, which can appear very quickly from lower altitudes, which might scratch my paintwork badly, or even leave nasty dents where they bounced off!"

I looked across Stocks reservoir and Gisburn Forest for the first checkpoint to the first town on our track, Long Preston. I was soon shifting my gaze to Grassington. "Here she goes, Kirkby Malham, our first check dead on the nose at 15.10!"

"We were lucky," said Tim. "There's no need to recalculate. I'll take her. You can look around and use your camera, but we are approaching Dishforth, and if any training aircraft take off or land, remember that you form a young farmer-sized blind spot right in front of me."

"On the other hand, you'll never feel lonely while immersed in the rich odour of sheep!"

By the time I had exposed a few frames, Tim was banking clear of the soarable slope at Sutton Bank, with Tim's clients parked near the take-off point. He joined the circuit downwind out of everybody's way. "We are dead on time, and the signaller has given me a green."

We were soon descending with half-flap, then

bumping over the rough ground to park next to his clients. Having reported to the duty pilot, Tim took the two tow-lines from his locker, and I retrieved my haversack, to make sure we refreshed ourselves with sandwiches and lemonade before returning. It hadn't cost me any effort, but I was hungry just the same! I laid out our modest rations while Tim laid out the two tow-lines, a short one for the more experienced sailplane pilot, the longer one offered a more relaxing ride for his mate.

Tim briefed them both while I wondered why I felt tired after a half-hour flight as a passenger. Tim had packed so much into it, involving me in the navigation and communicating with Air Traffic Control. Tim had made a note of two farms which he thought might benefit from crop-spraying. I thought that considering that his crop-spraying gear was still in Norfolk, fitting his spraying tackle and removing it after only two small jobs made the game not worth the candle, but he probably planned to pay his mum to visit and get her to do it!

On Monday, my exam results arrived. I had far exceeded my expectations, despite having done less revision than I had planned to. Indeed, having failed physics in the mock exam, I had not revised any of the coursework. Thanks to getting the right questions, I got a decent pass, but only by virtue of some mechanics I had picked up (how the hand fuel pump worked). That evening, Mr Bradshaw rang to ask about my results, and to invite me to tea with him during the break. He met me at the door, and his first question was, "Can you remember our conversation following your father's funeral, Ralph?"

"Very clearly. You made quite an impression. I'm sure that I have you to thank for my results. I'm only sorry that I didn't do more revision."

"You got away with it, this time. Had you failed to learn how to apply your gifts, revision would not have helped. You obviously haven't realised that your new interest has been time well spent. Nothing would have pleased Alec more than to see you making new friends and involving yourself so willingly in new activities. While you remember him as a father, and a farmer, he had chosen a military career. All that you have learnt, about navigation, and aspects of flying, he would have 'got', as you would say.

"He never wanted to discuss soldiering with you, because he thought people should avoid it, unless strongly motivated. You could say the same about nursing, or teaching, or the theatre. That is why I believe that he wouldn't wish to see you struggle endlessly to keep the farm afloat, at the expense of your education, lest you wind up jobless and bankrupt, with no prospects.

"I realise how hurt you felt by your mother's decision to sell the dairy herd, but I believe that was done truly with your well-being in mind."

"Unfortunately, it didn't end there. It would be extremely difficult to live there and farm, but I believe that it would still be possible."

"Right then, make the most of your small hill flock, and the bantams. No doubt she would take them on should you attend university, but you couldn't cope with a dairy herd as well. Neither would it be reasonable to expect her to sacrifice her career to yours."

"I hadn't expected to get into the nuts and bolts of my life after school, but now that you have raised the issue, I believe I share Dad's strength as a stock man. The hill sheep flock will increase, and they attract Hill Sheep Subsidy. They are heafed to the stretch of fell that comes with the farm, so they will never be worth much, but I understand them, and they can contribute to the farm's turnover.

"The only relevance of the bantams, is that they are pedigree, and the demand for them proves my ability as a judge of stock. I would try and rent pasture locally, and take an agricultural mortgage secured by the house to start a pedigree sheep flock, preferably Lleyn sheep.

"In that situation, I don't think I could benefit from a degree, and could ill afford whatever it cost. I can only see it as putting my life on hold for three years, but I'm well aware of the importance of keeping closer family ties, and keeping in touch with my peers through Young Farmers."

"Come and eat, now, and I'll keep to more general topics. You may be surprised to find that I broadly agree with your attitude to university, considering all that you have learnt since we last spoke. I don't see flying having an important role in your future, and I'm sure that goes for you, too, but is hasn't stopped you learning a lot about it. That demonstrates the belief that you are prepared to spend effort learning stuff, for interest rather than profit."

True to his word, we enjoyed our meal, and stuck to general conversation.

He had a parting shot when he saw me out after

the meal. "As Alec would say, 'get stuck in' to your A-Levels. Everyone you know is behind you in your efforts."

I felt grateful, and embarrassed. "It is very kind of you to say so. Thank you for all your encouragement, and I've enjoyed having tea with you."

CHAPTER 9

The Barge Sails Back to Avalon

Next Saturday, I was talking to Mum about Mr Bradshaw, when the sound of several cars starting up outside the house interrupted our discussion. I ran outside to find what was happening, and bumped into Steve, who was sweating and breathless. "It's the Barge! Their CFI took a pupil up, and crashed it in the Bowl. He and his pupil appear to be unhurt."

"I'll take you as near as I can get in the Land Rover. Hang on, while I tell Tim what I intend to do."

Tim listened to what I had to say, and made his own contribution. "I'll take my camera, and get some close-ups to establish exactly where the Barge finished up, and help estimate the damage. It will almost certainly be a write-off, and the current value could only be a few hundred pounds, so that's all the club can expect to get. It will cost around another thousand pounds to find any two-seater suitable for a hill-soaring site. Go and ask how you can help, and let me know if I should take the photos. Don't get in the way."

I felt a tumult of emotions, mainly anger directed against our guests, their CFI in particular. Admittedly, one of our own solo pilots had landed out on top of Parlick, having just been cleared to fly solo at Cock Hill, but no damage had resulted. As for the Barge, it had been designed to teach ATC pupils to fly from RAF sites, probably most frequently depending on car-tows. At the end of WW2, they were offered for sale by the Air Ministry to BGA clubs **only** for £5, in crated form.

The intention was to hive off gliding clubs from the legislation controlling light aircraft flying in UK airspace. So they were happy to leave airframe maintenance, and even certifying new designs as being safe to fly, with the proviso that any laxity in infringing Air Law, or notifications for pilots, might result in regulation of gliding clubs reverting to the Air Ministry. I am sure that all new ab initio pupils regarded the Barge as a bit of a joke, but it was safe, slow, and definitely cost-effective.

Even so, its steep glide angle really made it unsuited to hill-soaring sites. So it took a while for the thing to appeal to me. It was obviously as obsolete as a penny-farthing bike, but then, it was almost as cheap. I now realised how deep my attachment had become, although I followed my dad's attitude about machinery and electronics, they are less important than animals, let alone people.

I saw Den, the CFI, running to catch Colin, the club engineer, and stopped him. "Tim has offered to take some aerial close-up photos of the Barge if that would help." "Thanks. It would." "Can I get you and Colin as close as possible in our Land Rover?" He conferred briefly with Colin. "Thanks. Just don't try to impress us, because we'd rather climb a bit further than end up upside-down in a ditch."

He obviously didn't realise how tactless this was! Tim had waited for a reply, with his camera hung around his neck so I waved to him, and raised my hand with my forefinger touching my thumb, to signal 'OK'. I watched to make sure he headed for his aircraft. I asked, "Should Steve accompany us?"

He had obviously anticipated this question, because he replied instantly. "Thanks for your help, but the two of you must stay out of earshot while we establish the facts. Your help will certainly be useful if either, or both of them require help descending a very steep path."

I accepted that he was under great pressure, but I got he and Colin to the narrow footpath to the top of Parlick before he had even established the best route to take, because I had frequently climbed it, and he was unaware of its presence. Having parked across the slope, and facing slightly downhill to make it easier to move off, we all had a long hot scramble through fly-infested bracken to reach a viewpoint looking north west towards the crash site, which was slightly lower.

We were now clear of the bracken, in a 20mph breeze to refresh us and disperse the flies. The two occupants had not spotted us, and were walking round the wreck, with no obvious sign of injury.

What really touched us all on the raw, was the sight

of Ken, the CFI, handing his camera to his pupil to get a shot of him posing like a big-game hunter with his chest stuck out, and one foot on the stove-in cockpit. Den spoke first. "Knowing Ken, he will have concocted some story that absolves him of any blame!"

Colin raised his hand to shut him up, and spoke to us. "You two stay right here, until summoned. If we hear any rumours in the clubhouse about what happens next, you two are for the high jump."

"Yes," said Den, "and that goes double for me!" I went through the motions by moving farther away, and then kept walking towards the bowl to be downwind, where it was possible to catch part of what was said. I managed to catch all of what Colin said. It was rather like attending any French-language film, when anything you don't understand is probably something particularly filthy, leaving you substituting the sexiest words you know for anything you failed to grasp.

There you have it. Don't trust what Steve and I **thought** we heard. It was bad enough, but what was actually said might have been innocuous enough not to be interesting! I'll start with Colin's briefing to Den, which is true!

"I'll get straight down to taking photographs to establish the first contact with the ground, and measuring the depth and length of the groove, and its bearing. This would typically be a wing-tip, causing the fuselage to pivot around until the nose skid hits the ground hard, tracing a curve as it digs in. It is usually followed by the opposite wing tip hitting the ground by centripetal force, which usually breaks that wing spar where it has two support struts.

"Of course, Tim's aerial shots will be a useful backup, but the BGA go a bundle on marks on the ground. They will want great detail about the state of the glider **before** it leaves the crash site, as some interested party might claim that most of the damage occurred during de-rigging, and manhandling the wings and fuselage downhill to the nearest spot where it can be loaded on a trailer."

We heard most of Den's reply, complimenting Colin for dotting every 'i' and crossing every 't'. I suggested to Steve that should we be needed, they would look for us where they left us, so a strategic withdrawal was required. We sneaked back towards the footpath up Parlick, singing 'Tiptoe Through the Tulips', safe in the knowledge that we were downwind of them, and out of earshot.

From when we left our listening post to creep back, the conversation was roughly as follows. Den said, "Well Kenneth, at least both of you escaped injury." "Yes. Frightfully sorry about the T21, but no doubt your insurers will see you right."

There was a long pause, as everyone watched Colin taking measurements and making notes. Then Den, choking on his bile, replied, "Of course, the insurance is our problem. Our aim now, is to provide answers to their questions. Was there any sort of malfunction?"

"No, we were halfway round our outward 180° turn at the end of the beat when we suddenly lost slope lift. Sometimes a thermal pops off from one's hill slope, swallowing the uphill wind. She dropped the port wing, which struck the ground, which leapt up and clobbered us, crumpling the nose. Of course, these things are very forgiving, and it was the crumpling of the wooden structure that left us unhurt. The cockpit floor is stove-in, and the outward roll resulting from the ground-loop fractured the starboard wing where it is braced by two struts to the bottom of the fuselage."

By then Colin had re-joined them. "I agree with your assessment of the damage. As Den and I made our way here, we agreed that this was not the time to apportion blame. I'm sure that you will agree that this is definitely a write-off."

There was an embarrassing (and chilly) wait for enough skilled members to arrive for Colin to organise de-rigging. It took an hour to remove the wings in such an awkward situation, by which time we were thoroughly chilled, thanks to our ignorance of rigging and de-rigging.

The length of the wings offers such enormous leverage, that it is extremely difficult to move a wing root by a thousandth of an inch, or two, by raising or lowering the wingtip, which is almost thirty feet away. If any party involved is stood on a steep muddy slope, it becomes almost impossible to align the two steel sockets on the wing root either side of the steel socket behind the top of the cockpit.

Once the task was completed, Steve and I moved as one to grab the tail handle on the Barge, which consists of a steel tube just in front of the tail plane. You need ballast in the cockpit so Ken put his pupil in, and Colin advised Ken to get in as well. "We might ask you to get out for the steeper sections."

We guessed that whoever provided ballast was in

for a bumpy ride, and how sad it would be if Ken and his pupil managed to race us to the bottom of Parlick! As usual, helpers each side of the cockpit checked the descent of the fuselage, by each holding a harness shoulder strap. Steve and I needed to warm our chilled bodies by setting a cracking pace downhill.

This soon drew attention to us. Den shouted, "Slow down, you mad young buggers! Things are bad enough, without reaching the bottom as a pile of kindling." Actually, it would have been really good as kindling, consisting as it did of a clear pine frame, covered with taut canvas soaked in many coats of cellulose lacquer.

Colin was right, of course. The Barge never flew again. The Britannia Club dispersed that Sunday, so our CFI had to complete an accident report for the BGA before dear Kenneth made himself scarce. The money from our insurers fell £600 short of any practical replacement for the Barge. Sentiment apart, it would have been throwing good money after bad to fossick around for a similar machine. We were using it because it had cost peanuts, and was there to be used. We needed a two-seater with better penetration, which suggested a tandem two-seater like our Blanik, but they cost serious money.

Bill Scull, the senior CFI at BGA, wrote to ask permission to use Tewitts' Field to explore the soaring potential of the new site, using a Falke self-launching glider, which he thought might well be the future for glider training. Indeed, they were being made under license at Kirby Moreside.

CHAPTER 10

Enter Chet the Jet!

———— ⨳ ————

Tim stayed on after towing the same two clients back to their home site, to meet his American expat friend who lived and worked near Shannon Airport in the Republic. It was in a black mood that I took a broom to the clubhouse, and commenced to tidy up and wash whatever pots, glasses, and cutlery had been left from the weekend.

After a while, I heard a light plane land, and then taxi near the hangar. Then I heard Tim's voice, deep in conversation with a stranger who had a shriller and louder voice. It also sounded over familiar. I almost recognised it, but only from American cop shows, not in real life. I saw him getting typecast as the police informer, the smart-arse who always knows what is 'going down' before the bad guys have finished planning it. In fact, he got right up my nose before I even clapped eyes on him.

Evidently Tim expected to find the clubhouse to be empty, and was bringing him in for a coffee, with the intention of talking business. This wasn't so bad, considering that the only alternative was to take him into our kitchen, because Tim was sleeping in our house while Mum visited her sister. If I'd found them in the house, I would really have blown my top!

I had started sweeping along the wall with the entrance in it, so the voices suddenly got really close. "So this widow of yours lives right here on the airfield? You can just log in and get laid? That's cool!" I was forced to leap behind the door with my brush, to avoid being struck by the door as it opened.

I introduced myself by booting our visitor up the backside with enough clout to send him head first across a small table and onto the floor. Quick as a flash, he rolled onto his hands and knees to launch himself at me. I stood, relaxed and smiling, ready to smack him down again, but Tim reached him first, and pinned his forearm to the floor with his boot.

My excitement gave way to shame. I felt sorry for humiliating him. His baseball cap dangled from his ponytail, and as he replaced the cap, I saw the legend 'Da Nang' embroidered in gold thread above oak leaves. Tim was clearly the instigator of this impertinent insult to my mum, and the other guy had done no more than respond to a laddish boast with a laddish response. It was standard school-room behaviour

Once I knew both of them better, I always preferred Chet's attitude to that of Tim, who was a real teacher's pet, until he wasn't getting his own way, when his selfish side could be relied on to come to the fore.

Judging from the cap, this guy had seen things that we should thank God not to have seen. Tim used the pause to make introductions. "Helen's name is Swindlehurst. Chet Berrigan, meet her son, Ralph Swindlehurst. You just asked to get punched out, Chet. You were lucky I got to you before he did!"

I interrupted angrily. "Typical Tim! You made bullets for him to fire, and then you blame everything on him! I'm just beginning to find out what you are **really** like, and you are certainly not fit company for my mother, who is on her way back as we speak. It would be completely wrong for me to conceal this from her, because she needs to open her eyes to your true nature."

"You are wrong, Ralph." He tried to assert control again. "My only fault lay in asking Chet to visit without telling him that I stayed here **in her absence** while she visited her sister."

"If that was **all** you said, it would never have led to Chet's insulting comment about 'just logging in, and getting laid'. Those were the words used, are you now going to call **him** a liar?" Chet stared him down, and looked pretty angry himself. "I think Chet and I can see who the liar is." He made a further attempt to justify his presence in the clubhouse, and get rid of the kid, so the grown-ups could talk business. "Anyway, Ralph, I'm going to make coffee for Chet and I, so please make yourself scarce while we talk business."

I still wanted to clean up, so I gave them twenty minutes, and returned. I had cooled off, and Chet greeted me with a big smile.

"Hey, Ralph! I was only intending to wind Tim up! He isn't a very good liar, is he? There was no intention on my part to insult either you or your mother, and I respect you for your reaction. My mother would expect me to react in the same way! In short, I deserved to get decked. It was a case of 'failing to engage brain before operating mouth'. So much for that. Tim tells me that for a little folding money, you collect his avgas, and set it up on a stillage, is that right?"

I was completely taken aback by his verbal judo, letting my verbal attack launch me past him and three rows back in the auditorium. Did he really hold no grudge against me for my pedal assault? Had I found an infallible way of 'making friends and influencing people'? It could be fun!

"From what little I've seen of you, I'd rather do it for you than for **him**! However, might I presume to offer advice to my elder and better?" "Sure, go right ahead." "Then use your residence in the Republic to shed all that machismo crap, and kiss the Blarney Stone." "Sure, the red imprint of an English boot on my buttocks makes me an honorary Rebel already. Next time we meet, I'll come on like I'm auditioning for Finian's Rainbow!"

"Then why not order a couple of drums, and I'll collect them? I'll carry proof of identity, and that's our Land Rover, so tell them the registration and it will always be collected by me, in that Land Rover. Just give me a buzz when you want me to spring into action, and Bob's your uncle!" "Does the avgas vendor have to use a matching password?" "Tell him, or preferably her, to bare one bosom, and reply, 'And Fanny's my aunt,' I will then uncock my pistol, and apply the safety catch." "You would be a shoo-in for the CIA, except they don't bother with safety catches, preferring to accept the accidental discharge of firearms that usually results."

"I presume we will be using Good Old Tim's hand pump on your avgas?" "Sure, why not? How well you know me, already. By the bye, I'm flattered that I give you a buzz." "As long as your dollars root me to this reservation, so shall your scalp remain rooted to your tiny pointed skull." "I'll smoke a calumet with you to that, Geronimo. We bush pilots fly by the seat of the arse, and mine is too delicate an instrument to be subjected to regular kicking."

Tim turned up at that moment, and produced a large hankie. "I just **love** happy endings. They make me want to link hands and dance with the fairies." "Then don't let us stop you." "Wait! I want to borrow the 'ute first to see Chet off, and tell Helen I'll be back shortly." "In that case, bugger the fairies, they'll just have to wait."

Mum drove up as I reached the house, and I put the kettle on and passed on Tim's message. I added that he had let her down in her absence, and she responded angrily to what I told her, and told me that I was quite wrong to take it out on Chet, and that she preferred to fight her own battles. I decided that I had missed her enough to offer fruit cake with her tea (well, she made it!).

I also told her that Tim's meeting with Chet was obviously connected with the business loan he was seeking, which was why I wanted her to hear about his bad behaviour before boosting his ego too much about the progress of his business plan, such as it was. "You were right to do so. He's too damned casual to handle hefty loans, which I intend to make absolutely clear to him."

We heard Chet's 172 complete engine checks and take off, and then our returning landie. Tim walked in briskly, trying to hide his excitement. Mum glared at him. "OK, spit it out, and then we can tell you what a clever boy you are, just for a little peace and quiet." She left him in no doubt that he was in disgrace.

"Well, I've had an interview in Douglas with Bank of America, and they are prepared to make a dollar loan available to me at that branch (due to Bank of England requirements) subject to several conditions. They have already checked my credit status, both back home and in the UK."

"Let's hear the conditions."

"I must send an airframe fitter to the White Eagle factory in Poland, and he needs to be cleared by them for airframe inspections and repair and maintenance. When I find a specialist for engine repair and maintenance, they will need to send someone to the factory, probably just for a week, as there are fewer differences between aero engines than between airframes.

"I must also carry a stock of spares, but I might persuade the firm at Squires Gate who does most of the aircraft maintenance to finance the required spares. That seems to be up for horse trading. Thanks to restrictive UK Currency Laws, I can't bring dollars into the country, but that won't stop me tendering dollar cheques in Poland, which they prefer to Sterling anyway."

"You obviously see this as a 'one man and a dog' setup, so aren't you worried about carrying an airframe fitter? I bet they don't come cheap! Or have you persuaded your mum to qualify?"

"That would be the ideal solution. She could have a hutch in the hangar, and rent out her bungalow, and I wouldn't need to hire security for the business. I would throw in all the fish and chips she could eat. Oh, and Blackpool rock and candyfloss too, if she plays hard to get!"

"My solution, and it is far less attractive, is to parlay rented hangar space, available from the aircraft maintenance people, in return for both financing my spares, and offering me engine maintenance availability. It isn't like a deal with your local garage, because ninety per cent of the work arising from compulsory checks (like MOTs) requires following the elapse of engine hours or flying hours, both of which are recorded by sealed units on the aircraft, which might be examined at any time!

"Just as every business requires regular stock-taking, that can include elapsed engine hours per aircraft, plus elapsed flying hours, which flag up the proximity of which aircraft will be getting nearer being unusable for a week or more, and incurring a wodge of dosh from the coffers, to put it technically. In short, your maintenance provider always knows how soon you will require his services, and roughly at what cost to you."

Mum said, "I must say, I am impressed to find that

you actually have what seems to be a decent business plan. Do you mind if I probe further?"

"Ask what you like. It helps me remove any glitches. Might I impose on you to type this up, to further impress accountant-type people?"

"OK. Your efforts so far deserve some reward, but don't push your luck!"

"Ask whatever you like! It will help me work through my business plan, and invariably a fresh pair of eyes spots some possibility that one has never even considered. There is currently some excitement in French private flying circles, about – you guessed it – the White Eagle!

"You may not know that private flying is actively encouraged in France, as it is in America, and strongly discouraged in this country. It seems to be some weird Puritan throwback, when people consider fox hunting, or country house parties, or gliding, or light aircraft in general, as if whatever I don't want, or can't have, should be barred to other people. This attitude was portrayed by George Orwell in '1984', the final injunction was, "Everything not forbidden is now compulsory." What about homosexual behaviour? It would have started a civil war in Oz, for a start."

"I'm not sure whether or not what you just said was intended as 'Pom-bashing', or not. Can you get back to the point?"

"Sure. That was taken up in a British mag. which quoted Sterling prices for the White Eagle comparing very favourably with Piper and Cessna prices, and stating that as a military spotting aircraft (as the Auster was, converted from the Taylorcraft), the White Eagle would be preferred to those American Trikes.

"Indeed, you might describe trikes as 'light aircraft for American motorists'. Such machines should sell like hotcakes in the UK, if bought with US dollars. I could match that price, and still take twenty-five per cent profit! You would have to satisfy buyers that the design, build quality, and sales backup were good, then they would strongly undercut American products, which seem to be all that is available here."

"Here comes a googly. You start with a showroom full of really shiny new aeroplanes, preferably with coloured lights on the dashboard, and at the month end, the till is bulging with small change, and the showroom looks like a museum of light aviation between the World Wars, with a few Vickers Vimy twin-engined, open-cockpit biplane bombers, and a lot of 'Pou de Ciel' home-built, single-cylinder microlights. Do you at that point seek early retirement?"

"In that case **only**, definitely **yes!** And it would serve me right! Obviously, I couldn't carry second-hand stock, so I wouldn't buy anything in that wouldn't sell quickly at auction. No doubt there would be many occasions when I succeed in persuading the client to sell privately, and sign them up to pay 'on the drip' as Scousers say."

"And now a bouncer. Tell me how much your profit on one sale represents as a percentage of a fitters annual salary."

"Off the top of my head, about twenty per cent, until Mum gets her airframe fitter's ticket, when it will drop to less than five per cent."

"Well then, any shopkeeper will tell you five sales a

year will go to that item. This is your cue to list all other annual expenses, so as to find your net annual profit. This is probably the most vital information any lender will require, and there are a lot of other things, too."

"I would have thought that the fact that I am getting a living already, and this will be additional income, was the most important."

"Yeah. Ralph told me that you spotted two opportunities for crop-spraying on your return from Sutton Bank. He said he couldn't see that ever happening, because you spotted two small fields, only.

"Flying back to Norfolk, fitting the spraying gear, doing the jobs, flying back to Norfolk, cleaning out the gear, removing it, and flying back wouldn't put one pound in your piggy bank. From where I stand, you are losing money as we speak, I described your agency set-up as 'a one man and a dog' operation. You haven't **got** a dog. Your banker will be in no doubt that all your eggs are in one basket, and anything you don't do yourself, isn't going to get done at all."

"So I played your googly and your bouncer. Have you shot your bolt now?"

"No. I wouldn't have said this a year ago, but he has opened my eyes since. I actually quoted Ralph's opinion of something you said. I shall ask him for any suggestion, and furthermore, I guarantee a practical suggestion from him.

"One nugget from my own financial experience, I now offer you as a free gift. My income, like yours, is in pounds Sterling. It would **scare me to death** to have a dollar loan, because year on year, it will require

THERE WAS A WILD COLONIAL BOY

ever greater repayments to meet the same number of dollars that they require from you.

"I think you will have hoped that growing sales might strengthen your position with the White Eagle people to the point that they will accept Sterling payment, or at least, Euros. The danger is, that your ever-increasing repayments on the dollar loan might stop you ever benefitting from growing sales.

"The point is, is there chance of the pound strengthening against the dollar during the life of your loan? If not, you have written a blank cheque for the total cost of the loan in pounds Sterling. If that doesn't scare you, it ought to!"

"That may be so for Poms, but I'm an Ocker!" He leant forward to ruffle her hair. "Come off it, Helen, why try to hide your excitement?"

"Because you represent a bad risk, which makes me suspect **their** motivation. If it all ends in tears, they aren't going to lose by it."

"Why should it end in tears?"

"Because of your carelessness. You offered Chet and his mate a discount on purchasing a new plane, didn't you?" "I did." "Discounts are for those who pay the whole purchase price up-front, thick-head, and you agreed to give them credit terms."

"That's too bad. I can't go back on it now." "Your business plan is not credit-worthy, but they went ahead anyway." "What's wrong with my business plan?" "The money they lent is mainly in the form of new aircraft, kept in rented property. You could leave the UK in hours, taking your capital with you, and owing rent." "**Yeah!** How about that? On that happy thought, I'm taking you out for a slap-up lunch, somewhere decent. Champagne will be served." Helen blushed as she ran her fingers through her hair. Time for me to contribute. **"Leave right now,** Mum, while you are winning. You can cut him down to size while enjoying his largesse, rather than persuade him first, and then only get a half of shandy and a packet of crisps."

I rewarded myself by eating my burger watching a rubbish Western on the box, with a can of beer. The club newsletter came through the letterbox, and I read it right away. I was sad to find that the 'social season' was upon us. 'Bring your friends on the first Saturday in October to our 'Beer & Bangers Evening". I believe that when they were really scraping the barrel, they had been known to offer 'A Noggin & A Natter'.

CHAPTER 11

Only the Brave Deserve the Fair

———⟨❈⟩———

Harold Dukinfield greeted me as I entered the clubhouse. His wife was with him, and their guests, a married couple, with their ravishing teenage daughter. "Get Ralph one in, as well, Norman. What will it be, Ralph?"

"A half of bitter, please, Harold." "Meet Leah and Neville Breslau, Ralph, not forgetting Rachel, of course." "Heaven forbid," I croaked hoarsely. Her mother laughed pleasantly. It must be par for the course for young men to be gobsmacked by her daughter. Rachel was really something special. I judged her to possibly be a year younger than me, but about ten years ahead of me in sophistication, social poise, and self-confidence. She had shiny black hair, professionally cut in a Vidal Sassoon bob, and a face with a Grecian profile, an olive complexion, and large brown eyes with long curling lashes.

She was tall, with a slim, athletic build. She wore a scarlet roll-neck sweater, with a dark green skirt, worn with a black shiny belt and matching shoes with Cuban heels. She was definitely not overdressed for a 'Beer & Bangers Evening' in a converted barn!

The party eyed me expectantly, as if I was a spaniel puppy that might trip over one of its ears sometime soon. I obliged them by doing so. I failed to notice that Harold was addressing me, only catching the words, "I thought Neville might like to meet Norman, as Neville was an observer in Fleet Air Arm Swordfish, and Norman flew a Spitfire from Italy, in the ground-attack role."

"How about that, Harold? Rachel, was it a burning lust for bangers and mash that finally dragged you here, to mix with the utter dregs of society in rural squalor?" "Wow! That must be what they described as 'a rhetorical question' in English Lang. I suppose the attraction was, to watch young lads make fools of themselves (preferably on a competitive basis) and this looks like a good start." "There are few others present, and most of them are married or 'spoken for' even if they don't admit to it." "Why don't you give your tongue a rest? You could creep away and look up more long words in the dictionary. I like the look of that tall guy with shoulder-length hair in the far corner. He looks pleasantly normal to me, by comparison." "What discernment Madame displays! He is that rare human, a successful athlete with outstanding academic achievements! He won a scholarship to Cambridge, and has several cups won in inter public school track events. "Best of all, he is so modest that his National Front pals convinced him that his success is entirely due to his pure Aryan breeding, and nothing to brag about!"

Rachel hooted with laughter. "You really had me going for a moment there. One does not suspect an honest son of the soil like yourself to indulge in genuine malicious bitchery. Pin your ears back. You are going to exert yourself on our behalf. We need to eat from a table, so organise one and lay it for six. We would like a generous portion each, and drinks. I would like a Coke on ice, and make sure it is the last drink served, because I don't like it flat. Keep one eye on that far corner, in case that guy takes exception to your National Front gag. From what you said, I guess he could be upon you in about five strides!"

Her mother spoke up. "Really, Rachel! Take no notice, Ralph love. She is turning into a bossy little madam."

Harold smiled at her. "If the lads swarm round her like bees around a honey pot, you can't blame her for turning it to her advantage." "It's not a problem, Mrs Breslau, I've nothing better to do, and living on the doorstep as I do, I often come here and do a bit of skivvying. It isn't a problem so long as my schoolmates don't know!" I eavesdropped on Neville and Norman's conversation at the bar. I was always interested in WW2 anecdotes, as they were very rare. Nearly every veteran I ever met from either Great War, never speaks of it. However, Neville's tale was of pride coming before a fall, rather than involvement in a heroic incident.

"The pilot of our Swordfish was hell-bent on buzzing the troopship with all the nurses on board, so we made a low wave-skimming pass, to give them a thrill. There we were, leering up at them, all teeth and Brylcreem, when the wooden prop struck a wave. As usual, this broke the engine bearers of the radial engine, causing it to fall off.

"Once this happened, the plane might float for weeks, relieved of the weight. In combat, it might be necessary to sink it, if it might otherwise risk recovery by the enemy. Of course, Bert insisted that it was engine failure that brought us down, but the old man must have known as well as we did, that an engine that isn't running when it ditches, never breaks off!"

I missed the rest of the conversation, while dishing up the food and taking it to the table.

Norman shouted me when the drinks were ready. This round was going to cost more than I could afford, but I share the common fault of being stingy with the poor, and only generous to those better off than me. However, Neville saved the day by paying for the round. Norman had poured Rachel's Coke last, as requested, and her Dad collected her to eat her meal while it was hot.

Regretting my earlier childish behaviour, I kept up a more subdued conversation with Rachel. I asked what subjects she was taking.

"I want to take maths, chemistry, and botany at A-Level, with a view to working in horticultural research. Just practical studies, as in 'making blades of grass grow where one grew before'. I'm expected to do my stint in a kibbutz, in Neville and Leah's footsteps, and I've set my heart on work experience at the Kimberley Institute near Kununurra in the Kimberleys, but," she dropped her voice, "they don't know about it yet."

"Give over! I can't see you mucking out livestock!"
"Hardly surprising, considering that you know
nothing about me. I really want to know if Israel is all
that special. I suspect that its greatest advocates are
the ones who return slightly disillusioned. I guess the
more you con yourself into believing that Israel is
your cultural and historical birthright, the more it is
bound to disappoint your excessive investment in it."

"That is my own problem. One of my ancestors in
the 11ᵗʰ century was a lay brother at a Cistercian
monastery who was tasked with creating winter
pasture for wild deer, so that they jumped a ditch
downhill form the forest with empty bellies, and ate
their fill, only to find that that they couldn't jump the
same ditch uphill!

"When the forest sprouted new grass in the spring,
he would be sent back to drive them through a gate
back into the forest. "He was succeeded by
generations of hill sheep farmers, whose flocks were
not constrained by boundary fences, but 'heafed to
the fell', that is the older ewes knew which was their
pasture, and where to lead the flock to shelter when
floods or drifting snow threatened.

"Over the generations, the sheep farmers become
'heafed to the fell' too. So to land-owning gentry in
the area, we are the Palestinian Arabs to their Israelis.
I reckon to many of them, we are nothing but a
nuisance and have no electoral clout. The weird thing
is, that we stand shoulder to shoulder, whether C of
E, Catholic, or free-thinker, and protect each other in
times of religious persecution.

"So, your dream of 'two blades of grass growing where one grew before' almost sounds like a **threat** to me. Where a kibbutz feeds fifty people on what had been dry scrub getting a bare livelihood for a handful of Arabs with a few goats, I wonder if that justifies you taking it off them? I know **some** land was bought, which is fair enough, but I guess that most of it wasn't.

"If I was looking down from a thousand feet above Tewitts' Field, I believe I could name nearly every visible feature. Much of it belongs to Oxbridge colleges. They own it, but most of the pursers have never seen it. To my mind, **we** own it more than they do, and now I understand why the Irish always hated their absentee landlords."

"What brought that on? When Harold invited us, he never warned us about the threat of militant Islamists, for goodness' sake!" "Blame it on a surfeit of sausage, I will have to avoid them in future. I never intended to launch into a diatribe. Harold would consider it discourteous of me to do so." "Forget it. It was a bit of an eye-opener, in that I never saw anything but good in increasing the yield of crops. In future, I will take into account that in some areas grazing animals can get a livelihood where food crops for humans can never grow, and those grazing animals can feed humans." She made a 'peace' sign, crossing two fingers from each hand. "Pax! Can we skip the history lesson now, and change the subject?"

Chet, waiting to order from Norman, caught the end of his anecdote about how he came to be shot down six times by German ground fire. "Hey, man! I thought I'd had **my** share of that, I'd like a rum and Coke, and maybe you gentlemen would care to join me?"

"Thank you, sir. I'll put a half in my pot, a pint for Neville, and your 'Cuba Libre'. In Vietnam, were you?" "Believing that every disaster presents an opportunity, I volunteered for duty in the US Army. I was after a helicopter rating, without having to pay for it. I imagined the conflict might end before it involved in me, but the Pentagon must have already arrived at the same conclusion. I had no sooner learned to fly a Cessna 150, than I found myself flying one at the sharp end. My buddy illuminated targets with a laser beam for B52s safely cruising in the stratosphere beyond the range of ground-fire, and they dropped smart bombs that rode down the laser beam to the target. The B52s were safe from retaliation, but **we** weren't."

"You are taking me back, lad," said Neville. "I always remember that Bert flew straight at the flak. I thought he was after a medal, but he explained that he had to keep the engine between him and the bad guys, because our plane was built of steel tubing covered with fabric, like your Cessna."

Chet decided to liven things up with a little religious bigotry. "I had one aid that you lacked, Neville. My mom gave me a St Christopher medallion." "The hell she did! The Jewish board of Deputies tried to get them outlawed under the Geneva Convention on the grounds that they make Goys feel invincible, and more likely to attack Jews, and launch the next Crusade!"

"Yeah? Who needs such protection? We Latino Goys are ready to rumble at the snap of a finger!" So saying, Chet stepped between the tables, and gave us the Jets' dance from 'West Side Story'. To my embarrassment, Rachel got up, placed a rose from the table between her teeth, and joined in, heels stomping and fingers clicking. Chet started singing, to the tune of Wayne Fontana's song 'I've got a thirty-eight in a forty-five frame'.

He used the words, "We favour switch-blades, or a zip-gun over amulet or talisman." They finished their dance and sat down to general applause. Neville brought Rachel down to earth, out of fatherly duty. "You may not scare the Sharks, but you'd reduce Leonard Bernstein to tears. Best get the drinks in, Norman, to postpone the pogrom." I was thoughtlessly included in the round, with another half. How much had I downed by now? I sipped my beer while scheming haw to see Rachel again. I couldn't imagine any affluent father wanting his daughter to associate with me, even if we shared the same faith.

He might be impressed if he knew that I was getting flying lessons by doing chores for Tim and Chet, but Rachel certainly wouldn't! My only strong card was Mum, and I thought they might like her, but doubted if she would like them! "Hey, Rachel, the pair of you looked great dancing. I'm so hopeless at dancing that I'm ashamed to be seen on the dance floor. Listen, this used to be our barn, and we still live in the farm house." She showed a flicker of interest. "I left Mum on her own. Why don't you come and have coffee with us?"

"That would be nice, but I don't want to leave Leah in the midst of a WW2 re-enactment. I can see she has had her fill of it." Without hesitation I replied, "You'll both be more than welcome! Mrs Breslau,

168

would you care to meet my mother and have a coffee with us? Our house is right next to the car park." Mum was going to kill me for this. To my surprise, there was a favourable response. "Do you mind, Neville? Ralph lives in that lovely house next to the car park, and he's invited Rachel and I to have a coffee with his mother." "How long will you be? We should be making tracks before long." "Give us half an hour then, and come and collect us. You can blacken Hitler's character without my help, can't you?" "Great!" I said. "Just give me five minutes to warn Mum. She can whip off her head-scarf and pinny and dimp her Woodbine, and she'll be ready to receive royalty!"

"Wait till I tell her that you portray her as Andy Capp's missus! I feel for her, looking for an evening of respite from your company, only for you to descend on her bringing strangers."

I flew back to the house, my ardour already cooling. It really was downright cheek on my part, but I could always count on my mum to rise to the occasion. "Darling Mother! You always understood how the best of my bantams 'fill the eye' when I see them." "What brings you home at this hour to rant about banties? Have you discovered girls?"

"As ever, my thoughts are transparent to you. I've just met this fantastic girl, somewhat spoiled by wealthy parents. She's arty, and very bossy. She hopes to do horticultural research, after a short time in a kibbutz first. That's all I know. Your role is to impersonate a lady of leisure, more used to drifting round the garden with secateurs in a trug, than negotiating the rock-bottom price for a field of mangold wurzels for our breeding yows. Keep it ethereal, if you can.

"Play it with plenty of authority, however, while trying to break them down under interrogation, and don't serve the coffee in cracked mugs! I hope to wheedle some future outing with Rachel, so don't bang on about what sound breeding stock we are, and how my genes are greatly in demand, please?"

"They **aren't,** to the best of my knowledge. Are you confusing yourself with your prize cockerel? You do have a lot in common. By the way, my usually taciturn little man. Did you concoct the whole of that speech between the clubhouse and our kitchen? If so, you've really got it bad, and your tiny mind is functioning much faster than it used to. This girl must be spectacular, but it was a master stroke to include her mum, because that's how she will look in twenty years."

"Well if that goes for me too, I'll be beating all the guys off with a stick." "If you show off, like you are doing now, I can show them pictures of your infancy that will have them in stitches." When I returned with my guests, we were soon chatting away like old friends. Mum kicked off the conversation. "Does your husband share Harold Dukinfield's interest in flying?"

"Oh yes, we've a Cessna 172, hangared at Squires Gate. Neville runs a caravan dealership, and during the holiday season the local roads are often gridlocked. It's not unusual for us to deliver caravans overnight, and Neville picks up a lot of second-hand 'vans from classified ads. He trawls the ads for those near small airfields, and rings the vendor to ask if he will collect us. I often hope he won't buy, because I know it will take **me** the rest of the day towing it back! If he can pick up enough business that way in a tax year, they allow a proportion of the Cessna's expenses as business use."

"How interesting. Ralph has bartered his time collecting avgas, and setting it up here for a few hours' tuition on a Super Cub with Tim Clancy." "The problem I have with it is the noise scrambles my brain. One hour's flying can be quite tiring, but you do cover about three times the distance that you would in a car. One can usually take a direct route rather than zig-zag by road, and cover ninety miles in an hour, rather than thirty or forty.

"We choose our destinations for a Bank Holiday or a weekend for those inaccessible by road, or Grand Prix venues that have their own landing ground. Douglas is a popular destination for us, and the Channel Islands, the Western Isles, and Orkney. Of course, anyone can manage without a light aircraft, but few families could manage without a car. Where do you fly from, Ralph?"

"As luck would have it, right here. I'm a gliding club member, but if that was all, I'd definitely be lucky to solo next year. I'm getting regular dual circuits in Tim's Super Cub, and hope to go solo at a week's gliding course near Marlborough next year.

"If so, I'll be on the flying list to be checked out for slope soaring here at the club, and should not have a problem getting a solo launch every time I put my name on the list. I've only flown one dual, cross-country powered flight, to Sutton Bank and back, and found the communication with ATC, let alone solving the vector triangle, quite intimidating. It was very interesting though, as Tim returned with two sailplanes on the hook."

"Don't tell Neville! He'll feel compelled to climb Sutton Bank with two caravans in tow. We know Sutton Bank well, as it is one of the few main road ascents that is barred to caravans. Did you start on gliders?"

"It was all I could afford. When Dad died, Mum was offered her management job back, at the creamery in Chyppen. The dairy herd was Dad's last farming venture, and required an agricultural mortgage, so Mum sold the herd, plus as much of the dairy equipment as we could, and part of the flock to pay off the mortgage.

"The gliding club contacted the local NFU to buy a field within reach of the Bowl, nearly a mile north of Parlick. They could get a Sports Council grant towards this, and an agricultural drainage grant, both dependent on security of tenure, so renting a field was not an option.

"Tewitts' Field is owned by the club, but the house is ours, and I rent the grazing rights from the club, which commits the club to keeping it stock-proof. Not an ideal situation, but I can manage what remains without falling behind at school, and Mum is back in the job she wanted. I always intended to farm here, and should I do so I would definitely need to rent or buy some decent pasture, and increase the flock. So, as you see, gliding just dropped into my lap, but probably has no place in my future."

"I'd love to do a bit of aerial sight-seeing in a

glider, to avoid the engine noise. It's as bad as trying to converse in the cab of a tractor. I help Neville with the map-reading, which should be much easier than in a car, but destroys my ability to concentrate. Isn't that so, Rachel?"

"Like all my mates, I don't find noise such a problem. I'd go along with you for a passenger ride, but definitely not in an open cockpit, in this climate." "Well then, I believe you could get a ride in a Blanik like ours, off an aero-tow at Walney Island, Barrow, which you can probably see from cruise altitude, having taken off from Squire's Gate. The aero-tow mostly ends on the slope lift at Black Combe, so you would be very unfortunate to be up for less than an hour, and as it is a tandem two-seater, you would be sat right at the front of a five-foot long canopy, in front of the pilot."

On reflection, I would hate it if Rachel caught the gliding bug, and spent her way to solo while I trudged about in the mud. Of course, apart from such thoughts being merely expressions of envy, our paths were unlikely to cross again, because she was not yet independent, and once she was, she might not even share the same continent with me.

Back to reality. Our autumn term ended on a memorable note. Miss Rossi had been right. This was her swansong before returning to the States, and she had boldly chosen Auden's 'Ascent of F6'. We didn't really get it, but she sweated blood until she extracted the performance she wanted from each of us. Judging by the response of the audience, our parents, she could not have chosen better. From the first reading, and through every subsequent rehearsal, we thought the plot rather mawkish, and the dialogue even more so.

At the dress rehearsal, we finally flung British reticence aside to give full rein to the poetry. Heartened by our performance, we stormed into the opening night holding nothing back. We were stunned by the audience's total silence in response to the most moving passages.

It had tugged at adult heartstrings, where we, lacking experience of loss and sacrifice, had thought it melodramatic. Encouraged by our success, we attended the end of term dance in a mood of achievement and brimming confidence.

Our school dances were never up to much, but it seemed to me that now we all knew each other much better, anything was possible. In a rare mood of confidence, I commenced to 'put myself about' but must have danced mostly with Jane.

This led me to more false assumptions. Because each time I asked for a dance she agreed, I assumed that she must fancy me, just a little, but was shy about it. The fact that I felt immature in her presence held me back, and encouraged me to dance with other girls too, but when I looked into her big brown eyes, magnified by her glasses, I was intoxicated by her presence.

How long had this been going on? It suddenly seemed that she had been 'there for me' for a year, at least. She obviously didn't wish to risk spoiling everything by confessing to her hopeless passion. How grateful she would be to find that she was in with a chance of enjoying my company on a regular basis?

Of course, the truth was that if she had ever

helped me it was no more than she would have done for any other dumb helpless creature. My fantasy was encouraged by the evidence that while I was 'leading' her, fewer collisions resulted from our 'Brownian' movement around the dance floor. (Pardon my physics. Brownian motion is exhibited by small particles in liquid moving apparently at random, due to more molecules striking it first from one direction, and then from a different one.)

I expect I looked besotted, and Jane looked bored. Sonia passed us, and grasped the situation in a flash. A malicious intervention was clearly required. "**Hey, Jane**! Has he finally got the message?" Thus encouraged, I steered her into the darkest corner, and nuzzled behind her ear, scented with lavender. "Thanks, Jane, for a wonderful evening. This has been the best dance I ever attended." "That's OK. I needed the exercise," was her enigmatic reply. "You know what puzzles me most about you, Ralph?" "No. Do tell." "Even given miles of empty sky around you when gliding, surely you must have suffered several multiple collisions already? Do you just bounce off each other like bumper cars at a fairground?"

I laughed in what was intended to be a masterful way. "You mustn't worry your little head on my behalf! It puzzles me, too, but I guess the other idiots give me a wide berth." "That figures. You seem completely manic this evening. Have you forgotten your medication?" "None has been prescribed. If I'm high, your presence is responsible. Hey, that's Nat King Cole, may I have the next dance with you, too?" It was 'When I Fall in Love', a cue to chat her up. "You can't realise how much it meant to me to realise how you have been 'there for me' ever since Dad died." "**Really?** Was this song your cue to remind me of my **alleged** attachment?"

This wasn't going in the right direction. That should have cut me down to size, but I rashly persisted.

"Sorry, but that role-playing stuff came when I needed it. It brought me out of my silent daydreams and involved me with my classmates. It seemed to involve me more with you, than with the others." "I agree that you have been more fluent since then. Even lucid, occasionally. That's why I'm surprised that this guy's rich tone of voice, and a good arrangement, blinds you to the egocentric message. Wait for the last verse." We danced on, she, still as close to me, I, chastened but unrepentant. "Now, listen!" **"And the moment that I feel that you feel that way too, is when I'll fall in love with you!"** "Get it, Ralph? The unspoken alternative could only be, 'If **you** are not in love with **me**, stop wasting my time!'"

I was angry enough to respond rudely. "I'm sorry to have wasted your time. I had hoped we might meet over the Christmas break." "What for? We've known each other for years, and this is the first time you have even spoken to me. Clearly you haven't been interested in me, why expect that I would be interested in you?" I think she regretted this snub, as her final words were, "As long as we've got that clear, there's no harm in going out, just as friends."

CHAPTER 12

A Christmas of Re-alignment

One Thursday, I turned out by prior arrangement to deliver Tim's next drum of avgas, and set it up on a stillage. I had just upended it and was mounting his hand pump, when I heard him land. He strode towards me, hands in pockets. "Top 'em up, Ralph, I'll be in the house." When I joined them, Tim seemed to be getting the rough side of Mum's tongue just as I had recently experienced from Jane.

"Sometimes you take me too much for granted. I am **not** your mother! You always seem to bludge others to take on your responsibilities. Not **this** year, though. **I've** volunteered you to sing with St Bart's choir. As the first practise is tonight, you are too late to back out."

If we hoped for an ill-tempered response, we were disappointed. "'**Bludging**'," he hooted. "I'll have you speaking pure 'Strine' by the New Year! Of course,

I'm less fluent than my dad was. One English tourist asked me if he was a Greek New Chum, having been unable to grasp a word he said. Did I ever mention that he used to **gouge opals** in Coober Pedy?" "Was that before or after he tracked and then retrieved live missiles at Woomera?"

"If that was intended as sarcasm, poor old Dad cashed in his chips before such opportunities existed. Had he been spared, he might well have sounded out the military attachés, at the Russian and Chinese Embassies, for their best offer. Had he got a good sale, he would definitely have slipped a sweetener to the local Abos, because they would be the biggest threat to his security."

"He would have been ahead of his time regarding Fair Trade then, you reckon?" "Yes, as on many other issues! However, you must really avoid trying to deliver repartee after 'Children's Hour' finishes, because you are totally brain-fagged by then." "As ever, you overstate your assertion by omitting the disclaimer **'in my opinion'**." "This suggests that you are **the** senior world authority on all the subjects that you rant about, which is not borne out by any evidence." "That's not you speaking, it is the notorious 'Mr Bradshaw'?" "Gosh, yes! It was a 'put-down' worthy of him, wasn't it? Make a note of it for the benefit of my biographer. Your memories of **me** might prove to be the most, or possibly **only** memorable part of your own life!"

Mum shut us up. "Girls, please! Spare me from your bitching. I wanted to tell Tim about St Bart's augmented church choir." "Right, Helen, you got it! Ralph, can you cope with a small clerical task on my behalf, if I cross your palm with silver?" "Almost certainly, yes." "Here's a tenner for Christmas cards and stamps, with a list of prospects. Each one bears a name, address, and friend who gave me their name. Tell them I'll contact them over the next few weeks, when I find myself in their area." "Mum wasn't wrong about you, was she? I will, of course, keep the change." The choir master got off on the right tack by picking 'Wild Colonia Boy' for all to warm up with an Irish whinge about an Oz version of 'Robin Hood' just to break the ice. He even offered to provide a coal scuttle, in case Tim wanted to dress up for the role.

"Thanks, but no thanks. You are confusing **Jack Duggan** with **Ned Kelly**, the bushranger. But then you Brits always manage to instantly forget those you have shot or executed, which is why **we** sing about them, to keep their exploits alive."

Those choristers not pretending to weep copiously at this, demanded instant retribution from the choir master. One lady (ex-navy, possibly) suggested he needed a 'taste of the rope's end'.

I suspect that Tim kept the whole pantomime on the boil to make Mum regret ever involving him in the first place. However, he engaged with their more polished efforts till his nasal braying rose above their more harmonious sound, his voice competing in volume for what it lacked in quality. The choir seemed to gain some competitive edge that Christmas, due to an influx of young adults. So, it wasn't all down to Tim. Who would not enjoy raising their voice in praise amidst such good company as Chyppen always provides?

Christmas Day was really great that year. We had

invited Chet, as another expat, to join us, and Aunt Hazel drove over, just for the day. She had doted on me when I was a baby, and we had remained very close, sometimes ganging up on her older sister to get her back for her bossy attitude.

Tim and Chet did their share of the chores, which I assumed to be Chet's influence. The turkey had to be in the oven at 8am, according to Mum's timetable, so we had to rise early and get cracking, if only to allow everyone access to the bathroom. We were allowed to grab breakfast, before Mum shooed us out of the house on the pretext of gaining an appetite before a serious lunch. Tim suggested we climb Parlick. All was still, with mist clinging to the damp hill, and the church bells sounding strangely muffled and distant.

From Parlick's shoulder, we gazed westwards to the insignificant shallow cone of Beacon Fell. A seagull screamed, and in the distance someone was chopping wood. On our return, no sooner had we laid the table, than lunch was served.

We were all ravenous, and I must have drunk more than I intended, because Chet had assumed the role of butler, and as soon as a glass was emptied, Chet would be there refilling it. "I'll tell you what, Helen," he volunteered. "I attended a Thanksgiving dinner for American expats in Dublin, a couple of months back, and their turkey didn't taste as good as yours, despite being invented in the US of A!"

"I don't think they ever claimed to have **invented** them," said Hazel, "they just developed them (from vultures, I believe). Anyone for seconds?" "Whatever," said Chet. "I found the best way to appreciate America is from the other side of the Atlantic, and through the bottom of a glass."

Everyone complimented Mum on her tapioca-based Christmas pudding, except me. "It must be a Victorian recipe to have about half a bottle of 'lead and opium' mixture for fractious infants." "Drowsiness is **your** fault, Ralph, not mine. It results from too much to eat, and **far** too much to drink. Your next walk must be much longer, and after the washing up! I'll be with you." Chet pushed his chair back, and grabbed a tea-towel, flinging the dishcloth at Tim. "Get to the sink, where you belong, sport. Just as we Latins are legendary lovers, scions of Oz are superb scullions!"

I volunteered. "I'll come and join you Chet, I'm bound to learn something." "At least where to put everything," Chet replied.

I quite expected Mum and Hazel to want to watch the Queen's speech, but they both preferred to enjoy a walk while it wasn't raining, We started the same route as this morning, but past the path up to Parlick, staying on about the same contour as the road to reach the narrow valley of the Loud which leads up to the ruins of Wolfen Hall. Where it had been shrouded in mist, now the sky was clear and sunny. As we approached close country, it now offered a new vista at every turn. It was open oak woodland along both banks of the infant river, little more than a tumbling brook adding its music to the scene.

Handsome stone houses from the 17th century snuggled among the trees, likes hares in their forms. Chet was enchanted. "Say, Hazel, what did they smuggle here, so far from the coast?" "Catholic priests, if you can call it smuggling. Only the wealthier people dwelt in stone houses, and they were mostly conservative in their beliefs, and therefore Catholics. Their lives would have been forfeit had they been found." "Surely, that indicates quite a number of people at risk?" "This area was noted for religious tolerance. The C of E church had the same priest through the rule of both Catholic and Protestant monarchs, and John Wesley preached in his church." "And why should that happen here, rather than somewhere else?"

"My guess would be, because the Normans instituted deer parks, reserved for royalty, and those sent to hold castles, and defend them. Some hungry people had been known to be hanged for daring to pick berries in land subject to Forest Law.

"Local gentry also broke these laws to take timber and build manors for themselves, so I suppose not getting caught was all that mattered, in the end."

Suddenly, the valley widened, to reveal the chair factory, and after passing the old hives, we took a field path on our right, that avoided the road. Tim looked disgruntled, and as usual, let everyone know about it. "I'm used to climbing out of a new airfield, and seeing everything for twenty miles. Back home, that mostly includes only one dwelling.

"We've only been walking about half an hour, and every few minutes, some other feature sneaks into view. Granted, it's more picturesque than the back streets of Salford, but it still looks overdeveloped to me! The whole damn theme-park recalls 'the old woman that lived in a shoe'. Why the hell is everything smaller and older than it needs to be? Did no-one hereabout ever make a fresh start a mile away? Why do they just add a lean-to when they start a new enterprise, so they wind up with a jigsaw of small, cramped buildings?

"Generally, people start dividing farms up with each generation until there are too many small units to compete. Then, the more successful buy contagious farms where people have been forced to sell up. When you are clearly thriving in the midst of farms being sold off, you can afford to start with a clean sheet of paper and plan the flow of feedstuffs or fertiliser coming in, and crops or livestock being transported to market.

"Areas handling the most traffic need sealed roads and hard standing, and this makes it simple to keep the place clean and tidy. Barns, shippons, clipping sheds, and even cold stores may be needed later, and should be considered at the planning stage."

Mum wasn't having that. "You are talking rubbish. You have nothing older than Victorian buildings, and I'm sure most Australians cherish them and avoid tearing them down unnecessarily. If you were lucky enough to have stone buildings that have been dwelt in for hundreds of years, you would seek to adapt them, not bulldoze them to create space for a bungalow.

"Basically, you look at what we have, and you don't get it. Try this model to grasp. Did you listen to what Hazel had to say about the worst aspects of the feudal system introduced by the Normans? I instantly recognised it. This area is still populated by abos. That's the church congregation and the thousands in the churchyard. We have spent our lives hanging on to all that was familiar to our ancestors.

"Australian settlers were to the aborigines, what the Normans were to their English subjects. Of all the wildlife that existed there when settlement started (and the abos had lived there for forty thousand years), nearly half of it has gone due rats, cats, rabbits, and foxes. The abos, living hand-to-mouth, usually plant two cuttings if they uproot anything, and despite eating all sorts of plants, roots, and insects, they conserved every food source. They must look at you with your vast mines and grandiose hydroelectric schemes as vandals, unaware of what you destroy.

"You are really making me wonder just what **I'm** getting into. I wonder if being better looking is the only thing you've got that they haven't." "He does look pastier than your average abo, Mum, as if he just crawled from under a stone."

"I know that Ralph, but that goes for **you**, too."

Tim backpedalled. "I suppose the stone farmsteads **do** appeal, in a twee, English sort of way."

"Hey, man! Is that the way to speak to our host? Few states offer the political and religious freedom that Britain offers. No British ruler since Cromwell has felt it necessary to destroy what others worship.

"Neither nowadays, would they claim to know best how to run other countries. Dictators, however, think they **do** know best, which is why the Brits looked at Cromwell's reign, and the possibility of 'tumbledown Dick' succeeding him, and decided they preferred constitutional monarchy after all. I can't think of any other country where that has happened."

"Good God, Chet! Have you read a book since we

last met? Or are you hoping for something in the New Year's Honours List? Or perhaps it's because of the famous Latin charm, and all the soft soap that goes with it. Believe me, the 'Old Country' has lost touch with reality. In the **real** world, people choose to live where they work. If the available housing stock is gradually filled with the retired and second-home owners, then jobs are only open to commuters.

"The English village is on a downward slide then. The school shuts for lack of pupils, the post office falls in value, which is tied to the turnover, and the pub needs to be run as a 'gastropub' to get a living with a smaller footfall. The place may become gentrified to attract tourists, because most of the children born there must start a new life elsewhere. No longer an ecosystem, it is turning into a theme-park.

"In contrast, consider Chyppen a hundred years ago when the dairy and chair works knockers-up made their rounds, to rouse employees for the day's work. It would have sounded like bedlam, with the iron-tyred carts delivering churns of milk to the two dairies, clattering over the cobbles, to the accompaniment of at least a couple of hundred pairs of iron-clad wooden clogs worn by the work force.

"There were two blacksmiths hammering away, and every shopkeeper had staff to scream at. All production was a noisy business then, and if they could see their town as it is now they would find it almost as silent as the grave. Those guys were focussed on **work**, as we now seem to be focussed on 'leisure', another word for poverty, to the less wealthy most of the time. I would prefer the sound of kids in a playground, and could live with more noise, some smoke and dust even.

"Back home, it has been necessary on occasion to offer incentives for people to move to underdeveloped areas. In the Kimberleys in West Australia, Queensland, and Northern Territories they were offered tax relief to move there. That primed the pump for investment in 'infrastructure' roads, rail, and utilities. Once all that was done, there was no longer any need for the tax relief."

Aware that he was starting to sound like a party political broadcast, he switched to soap-box oratory. "Dereliction shall spread from silent factories, shabby suburbs, and neglected terraces of workers' cottages, to run-down market towns with more boarded-up shops than those still trading.

"Every rush and bracken-filled pasture bounded by tumbled dry-stone walls will have an 'improved' farmhouse, with a BMW on the drive and a converted barn. Who would want a barn conversion with views across wet, derelict pasture? Can your Women's Institute ever build Jerusalem there?" "Tim, Tim! Are we going to lose you?" She realised her mistake at once. He needed putting in his place, not pleading with.

Hazel jumped in to defend her sister. "You came here, as your forebears came to Australia, as an outsider. You and yours could find no virtue in Aboriginal culture, although we think nothing became extinct during their sole tenure. That ended with British settlement.

"Since then you've lost about twenty to twenty-five per cent of plants and animals. It seems downright bad manners to me, that you should treat every difference between what you did in Kununurra, and what we do here as being wrong on **our** part. Apart from that, if you have any true cause for complaint, it is bloody rude to launch an attack on Helen while enjoying her hospitality over Christmas!"

"I don't accept **your** opinion, as it's none of your business, and you only know half the story." Chet intervened. "That is the limit! Seriously, Tim! If you don't hold your tongue **right now**, I'm taking everyone out for a meal, and you can clear off before we return." Mum protested. "Thanks for standing up for me, Chet. You are a gentleman, but that **won't** be necessary. All may be revealed within the next few weeks." Hazel rewarded Chet with a hug. He returned it with feeling, saying, "I could be a child again, listening to my grandmother. Best not cry, though. I might have to join in." To my surprise, I felt quite scared by all this emotional catharsis. I needed to learn more, before Pandora's Box closed again, possibly for good. "Aunt Hazel, while the gloves are off, what was what was **Dad's** response to the proposition that Chyppen was a unique religious sanctuary?" Hazel looked to Mum for guidance. "Say what you please, Hazel. You have done so far."

"What you would expect, I guess. I certainly remember him telling you that different faiths must be supported and protected from interference. In general, he was prepared to compromise. He described it as having the strength to cleave to your own faith, but always being ready to stand up for other faiths. He called this 'bending to the wind', meaning 'never breaking' under pressure.

"Knowing how I loved academic study, he chided me for settling for teaching when I was capable of research, but this was so I could teach locally, compared with seeking more advanced work at Lancaster. Although Alec and Dad had much in common, Alec never seemed to fully agree with him.

"Whenever Dad sought agreement, Alec fended him off by saying that no-one outside the Paras could teach him about tribalism. I took this to mean that he might bear false witness to protect his own men, but not for anyone else. Dad thought to be accused of tribalism was comparing him with Hottentots, or Gypsies!"

"Once in a while, Alec might be in a pub when some stranger started extolling the virtues of a foreign country, He would interrupt to ask, 'Have you ever lived there?' If they said no, he would quote, 'What do they know of England, that only England know?'

"This led me to think that he preferred to score debating points off Dad or I to seeking agreement." Helen answered. "That is another sad result of his failure to discuss things more fully with people. As if he thought 'Sergeants don't do that. They **tell** people what to do.' He disliked argument, and also always played relentlessly to win, in the belief that to do anything less was to risk his men's lives needlessly.

"He was no male chauvinist. In business he deferred to me, and in managing the farm we were equal partners. It was his decision to buy himself out of the Army that changed him, and he had a long and bitter struggle between loyalties before deciding to leave the forces.

"The Colonel told the Padre to rein him in, but **that** backfired because Alec persuaded the Padre that the Anglo-French invasion of the Canal Zone was the result of collusion between the two of them and Israel. There was no way he would have dredged up those painful memories just to score debating points. "He rightly judged his actions as sacrificing a successful career to his beliefs. As far as I know, your beliefs, though well aired, have not yet demanded any sacrifice from you." "Talk about stating the obvious! I am well aware of that. It is probably the main difference between his job and mine, and is reflected in the pay."

I thought Mum's comment unfair to Hazel. "Thanks, Aunt Hazel. You've certainly opened my eyes to a number of things that I never previously understood. I apologise for raking this up, and as we have visitors, may we change the subject?"

"Amen to that," said Mum. "I wish people would mind their own business. The reason why you don't grasp all that is happening, is that you are not in full possession of all the facts, nor is this likely to change in the near future!"

I called Blue back, and put him on the lead. I was furious that Tim had caused an argument between the sisters, while a guest under our roof. I had certainly stirred up a hornet's nest, but was immature enough to believe that family secrets cause more trouble than openness. I gave my Aunt a hug. "All that you said was better brought into the open than hushed up. Please don't return home today. We need to put disagreement behind us before you and Mum part again."

She didn't reply at once, so I hugged her until she

did. Mum grabbed her and swung her around as if they were children again. "Chet can fly us somewhere, after all! I was just blaming myself for sowing discord n what had been intended as a family gathering. Let's go back and eat, then we can get a weather forecast and decide the best option for tomorrow. Some interest was also expressed about dinner this evening."

I was glad to note that Tim was far more considerate for the rest of the day. Chet, who had offended no-one, was chatting to Hazel. It seemed to me that Tim had latched onto me like some father figure before he had even met Mum, and much of my disappointment in him resulted from not keeping him at arm's length until I had got to know him.

As usual, my initial distrust had been replaced by equally unnecessary total acceptance. Obviously, it was Mum that attracted him, and I could hardly expect to ever be more than an impediment to his courtship. My attitude to Tim was now neutral, except as my mum's new partner. In all probability, two years hence when I started earning my living, it was unlikely that I would still have flying as an interest in common with him.

The warmth of the house welcomed us back. I rang Jane, to ask if we could meet the next day. After all the protests about having eaten enough already, everyone seemed interested in afternoon tea. Tim announced that he had booked what seemed like a really good place to dine on Boxing Day. "I included Hazel in the booking, in the hope that you would stay."

Ever the opportunist, I went for my chance. "I had a loose arrangement with Jane for Boxing Day. Is she included in your invitation?" "Ralph, you crafty little rat! I know you would never angle to be included, no way, but Jane is definitely included, even if we have to manage without you!" I may not trust him, but that wouldn't stop me from accepting his hospitality. I lost no time in passing on the good news to Jane. "Don't feel any compunction about accepting his hospitality when you don't know him, because he gave Mum (and my Aunt Hazel) a hard time over Christmas, and before we despatch him with blackberry leaf tea (as advocated in 'Cold Comfort Farm') we intend to plunder his wealth, so that he won't have died in vain." "Will that make me an accomplice after the fact?"

"Of course not! You are local, as we are, and these petty byelaws to prevent homicide are clearly only for the benefit of strangers. Besides, now I am approaching adulthood, it will be more urbane to dine at his expense, rather than run him through the guts with me rapier."

"You **are** coming on! Only last term, it would have been with a muck fork. Hang on, while I consult my mum." She soon returned. "What are the other ladies wearing?" I put Mum on, and she waved me away so that she could hang up when she finished. They worked out the timetable for their aerial tour of the Lakes backwards from last light. Chet suggested that the lakes seemed to radiate from Ambleside, and suggested that he should fly a 'daisy petal' pattern, up the centre of Windermere, and then go clockwise, south to the end of Coniston Water at Blawith, and then make for Nether Wastwater, and north east from there over Wastwater, and so on. He would break off at last light, for the short flight back.

As I now judged Tim and Chet, Chet was more caring and considerate, where Tim was pragmatic to the point that little concerned him much, beyond his own welfare. After lunch on Boxing Day, Hazel ran me over to Jane's parents'. It appeared that they had met previously, because her parting words were, "Don't stand any nonsense form Daphne!" I'm afraid this might have been better left unsaid, because it gave me a lot to worry about. Was I regarded by mothers as morally hazardous to their daughters? Possibly the Don Juan of Tewitts' Field? It certainly had unfortunate aspects. It would fit neatly into a 'News of the World' headline!

Her mum's words increased my anxiety. "I remember the sad news of your father's death in the papers, but not much after that until Miss Rossi made her presence felt in the school." "Oh yes, she was the first teacher since Mr Bradshaw started teaching us, to make such a strong impression. Outstanding stuff, for an American student teacher!" Jane seemed to be grimacing in the background, but I couldn't make out why.

As usual, I responded by retreating into fantasy. And also as usual, this has an unsettling affect owing to people assuming that you are 'taking the Mickey', to put it politely. "I seem to have spent the last ten years digging drains," I ventured. "Did you get to see 'I was a prisoner on the Chain Gang'? That could have been me.

"Of course, I went home every night, thank goodness, but I only got to sleep in the barn, because there was too much mud on my chains to clean up before I slept, so it was quicker to lie in the barn, covered with straw. You'd be surprised how clean it keeps you, and quite cosy, too."

Her father must have walked into the hall unnoticed, while this drivel was being uttered, and I must have jumped like a shot rabbit when he spoke. "That figures. Jane told us you had a fertile imagination for one built like a navvy." He extended his hand to me. "Call me Brian, and Daphne answers to her Christian name, too. You appear a little ill at ease, but now we've established that you aren't good enough for our daughter, we can all relax, can't we? What will you drink?" "I will try and hide my embarrassment in a half of bitter, please." "Good," said Jane. "I can have a shandy with the other half." She returned with the drinks, and perched on the side of my armchair. "Well, you certainly haven't got your mum to yourself **this** Christmas." "That's right. Last year was special for us. Dad couldn't be with us every year, but having bought himself out, that appeared to be a possibility in the future.

"I expected we would be propping each other up. Instead of which, our lives changed permanently, and it seems they will continue to change. To our surprise, we have enjoyed most of it, so far. This year our social lives, which ceased to exist when we took on the dairy herd, have increased a little. The herd were a twenty-four hour a day, seven days a week commitment." "So what is it like to have guests?"

"I don't really know what brought Tim, but he is a long way from home, and even from his digs in Norfolk, and welcome to join us. He asked if Chet could fly over from Shannon on business, and it seemed natural to include him. To be fair, he is a really nice guy, and certainly more considerate than Tim is." "So we have taken you away from your guests this afternoon?" "Not at all. Chet's Cessna 172 is a four-seater. I don't know why but my Aunt Hazel was always ready to let me sit on her knee at Primary School, but she never offers to nowadays. It suits me well enough. We get an extra day with Hazel, and to be fair to Chet, he's better company than Tim."

"Poor old you," said Jane, clutching my knee. "Cast aside in your teens, like an old sock. Bring your drink in the kitchen." "Right. Helen seems determined to grind down some of Tim's sharp corners, and as for me, I'll be proud to go out with you beside me!" I wondered if I would be rebuked for this small gallantry, but she slipped her arm round my neck and gave me a swift peck on the cheek. "There you are, you can say nice things when you aren't on the defensive." I shuddered slightly. "Hadn't we better join the others?" Coffee followed. I lingered over it as we sat side by side on the settee, very conscious of her warmth, and her scent in my nostrils.

Brian spoke up. "I thought you had planned to walk back to Tewitts' Field, but with a lively evening ahead of you, there isn't sufficient time left to do so. Why don't we have a shorter walk, and then I'll drive you both there?" That made sense, so we all took a short walk on Jeffrey Hill, and then Jane changed and put her coat on for the short drive home.

It was nearly four o'clock when we turned into our drive, and sure enough, last light brought the Cessna's return. I could just hear it, possibly above Grizedale Fell, with Tewitts' Field already in sight. Chet would be diving off height from that far out, assuming his altitude was around six thousand feet. As failing light drained the ruddy light from the scene, the shiny duralumin fuselage suddenly leapt out of the turquoise sky, blazing with orange light reflected off the sea to the west.

"How can he hover like that?" asked Daphne. "They are approaching us at 120mph, but the only apparent movement is their profile getting bigger, so their approach is scarcely discernible. Please don't think of dashing off. Now you have kindly brought us here, stay and have tea with us. Come in and make yourselves comfortable while I put the kettle on."

Brian wanted to watch Chet land, so I asked him to stay near the hedge, and stay there until Chet switched off his engine. Daphne enthused over Mum's interior decoration, and told me how lucky we were to own a home of such character. I agreed that it had been a source of pleasure to us since the dairy herd was sold off. Until then, it was Alec's workplace.

He had taken on an agricultural mortgage, and intended to work his socks off until it was paid off. He was just holding everything together until his investment bore fruit. All the improvements took place after he died; the dairy herd, the dairy equipment, and part of the flock were all sold off, and Mum was getting a salary from the dairy again.

"I hate to see a farm go out of use," said Jane. "He must have felt duty-bound to farm it, but it so seldom gets restored to productivity." "It could happen, but something will have to give," I said. "Had he known how little time he had left, I'm sure he would have opted for more shared time with us, and less work."

Daphne looked downcast. "It always seems such a waste, when a man dies in the prime of life, after surviving a dangerous livelihood." I felt that I owed it to him to tell her why the farm occupied him almost to the exclusion of all else. "He had intended to make the army his career, but having bought himself out, he felt a farming career could only be justified by passing on the farm in more profitable form than he inherited it.

"We no longer own the land, and to make the farm viable, we need to own or rent good pasture, continue to 'fold the hill flock on mangold' to get earlier to market than other people's hill lambs, and get a better price per head.

"On top of that, we would also need a pedigree flock, or else fatten bullocks for beef. All that would require borrowed money, more land, and keeping it fully stocked. It will take years, and the only alternative is to start re-developing it, and then sell up, which I would consider a personal failure.

"I would have left school to maintain the dairy herd, given the chance, but that would have been a very bad decision. It was only when faced with 'Theory of Flight' and the trigonometry required for the navigation part of the PPL, that I started catching up on maths and science subjects.

"I need those and English at least, to ever qualify for any decent job. The sound of an approaching Lycoming engine reminded me that the day-trippers were back. I then heard Brian start his car up to save them plodding across the soggy field. Daphne walked out to meet them, and Jane stood next to me in the empty room, and squeezed my hand.

"You are feeling very close to Alec just now, aren't you?" "I know it sounds silly, but I imagine him hanging around, chafing at the bit because of all the things he could be doing if he was still here." That comment was deep enough to kill further conversation. Fortunately, eight of us sat down for afternoon tea, and Brian and Daphne were clearly curious about Tim and Chet. Both were affable enough, without giving much away.

The 'remittance men', as Mum called them, were quite taken with Jane, and Chet wanted to know what music interested her, and Tim was exploring her gullibility with some of the more plausible legends about his father. Hazel could see what was happening, and was discussing education with Brian and Daphne. At a loose end, I did my usual trick of eavesdropping on other people's conversation.

Mum was discussing her job at the dairy, so I tuned out again, and switched to Tim and Chet. They were discussing Asian countries, but they could see that Brian wanted to join in, and shut him out. When Hong Kong was mentioned, Brian had been there, but Chet told him he had gone there for R&R while serving in Vietnam.

However, he had seen nothing of it, owing to taking the first ferry to Maçao for the casino. Once Daphne caught the name of an African commonwealth country, but they evaded her by sticking to the post-independence names. I soon realised that Chet had been slightly indoctrinated by Castro's regime, in that he showed a marked preference for ex-Portuguese colonies to commonwealth countries. He preferred Mozambique to Zimbabwe, and Goa to Bombay.

Tea over, Mum stood at the door to say Brian and Daphne off. "No, honestly, it was no trouble. Now you know the way, drop in whenever you ae passing outside working hours!" I joined her as they drove off. "Hey, Mum! Is it OK to call you Helen now?" "Well, now you have noticed girls, I suppose some development must be stirring to stop humanity becoming extinct." "Has that become **my** responsibility?" "Whoa there, boy! **You** needn't worry about it just yet. Come upstairs, Jane love, while Hazel and I change in my bedroom." "Ralph, take the remittance men in the kitchen, and do the pots for being unsociable with Brian and Daphne. There's just about room for you all to change in your bedroom."

Jane was wondering whether this was normal behaviour for widows, or whether this woman had always been a total ball-breaker. If so, had he jumped on his bike, when he would **otherwise** have taken the car? The more one thought about such things, the more complex they appeared, and beyond correction, anyway.

Unaware of Jane's embarrassing insights, I applied myself to the new problem of pretending to be interested in my appearance. I donned my best suit. I only ever had **one**, and that was like something out of the dressing-up cupboard. It must have been something Alec grew out of, when he was about my age. Whatever, I looked like 'the man from the Pru'.

The remainder of my wardrobe consisted of hand-me-down garments that had once served as a temporary protection against cow muck. The closest thing to defining me as a 'raunchy young stud' was my tweed hacking jacket, and some 'cavalry twill' trousers. In this guise, I could be an advert for the Fifty Shilling Tailor, a newly qualified teacher, or possibly a painfully innocent DC.

To put the cap on it, Tim and Chet reappeared in 'go-to-town' guise. Tim wore his 'Jackaroo strides', tightly-woven blue wool as tough as sailcloth. They went with a blue moleskin shirt, and brown suede desert boots and suede blouson. Chet was more 'biker style', in jeans with silver-mounted cowboy boots with a red roll-neck sweater, and black horsehide biker jacket.

This was definitely the first time I had felt the lack of clothes for special occasions, and I wondered whether they would ever be necessary. Not to be buried in, if I opted for cremation! It must have shown on my face, because Chet came to my rescue. Tim explained that his kit offered little more than a change of clothes, and could therefore offer nothing but a spongebag with which to cover my nakedness.

Chet had only come from Ireland, and had more locker space and three empty seats. He took me aside. "Hey, kid! Lighten up! You'll be earning real money soon enough. Meanwhile, you can strut your stuff in my embroidered Levi denim jacket. It fits real easy on me, so you might squeeze into it.

"My first Merchant Service voyage was Havana to N'York. I headed for 'Birdland' to catch Charlie Parker. I was so knocked out by the music that I never noticed my surroundings, until I realised that I was in a crowd of cool dudes and chicks in their weekend best, while I was dressed for the Welfare Queue! Next time I hit Birdland I had blown some of my dough on this Levi hand-embroidered jacket, and thought myself the height of fashion!"

I ran upstairs with him and donned the shirt, adding jeans and chukka boots. "Thanks Chet, that's great!" Embroidered, it certainly was! There was less denim in view than embroidery. An Aztec Thunderbird stretched from shoulder to shoulder, across the back, and embroidered roses covered the flaps of the patch pockets. It was certainly tight, in fact I should have been singing 'Spring is busting out all over!' I looked less well turned out than my fellow caballeros, but with a T-shirt beneath, it could be worn unbuttoned. It would pass at a pinch. We looked both overdressed, and ill-assorted, as if attending a fancy-dress ball.

Jane wore her hair up, with one of those 'little back dresses' in black velvet, with blue Lurex tights, and matching blue eyeshadow. She was an absolute knockout; her neck and shoulders smoothly curved, and she glowed with health.

Hazel had gone for the 'ethnic look' with a floral print Laura Ashley dress, with those crumpled peasant boots, without looking like a crumpled peasant, or even downtrodden. Helen wore her bare-shouldered shiny gold top, with black harem pants ending in cuffs at the ankle.

I couldn't tell you what I ate or drank that night, but I do remember that we all enjoyed ourselves hugely. I expect that we all regretted the ructions on Christmas Day, which nearly ruined the day for us. Maybe we had decided that we needed to work harder at avoiding a repetition. The sisters both had a lot to say about what Grandad believed, and whether Alec had rubbed him up the wrong way. As a counter-irritant, Tim rubbished the locality, and indeed Britain in general, to the annoyance of the rest of us.

As this was Tim's treat, Chet had offered to buy the drinks. Jane was included in every conversation, and I was tolerated whenever I ventured an opinion! No objection was raised by the landlord when asked if we may dance to the juke box in the games room, which I enjoyed more than the end of term dance because I had no delusions about Jane this time, and as we had no audience, I was less self-conscious. We had wined and dined well, and were high on good company.

All too soon, we were on our way to Longridge to drop Jane off. As Jane thanked everyone for a lovely evening, I strolled up the drive to ambush her. What I intended to be a lingering kiss was effortlessly parried, and a peck on the cheek resulted. "If it's excitement you're after, look elsewhere!"

For some reason, I still walked back to the car as if walking on air. "Tim, that was my best night out ever!" "In that case, you've led a very sheltered life," said Tim. This aroused general laughter. "I enjoyed it all so much, I couldn't keep it to myself!" "We all think that she is lovely, Ralph. She is too good for you!" said Mum. "She just now hinted at that probability," I replied. "Hang in there, man," said Chet. "You could play a convincing Lil Abner to her Daisy Mae."

Hazel carried on with that metaphor. "You'll soon find out, come Sadie Hawkins Day. Don't wait till then, though. Ring her up and arrange something for the New Year."

We drove through the moonlit fields, hedgerows, and roadside trees. It felt as though a lifetime had passed since school broke up for Christmas. My life had changed in a week. Mum had made it clear that she had her own life to lead. It would have been short-sighted of her not to have plans for her life at Tewitts' Field in my absence.

I would clearly stay put if I started work, but not if I entered tertiary education. From now on, this seemed an increasingly remote likelihood, because developing the farm would need a hefty loan, and I couldn't afford to accumulate further debt beforehand. I wasn't scared by the prospect of borrowing, because at least I need never anticipate borrowing for a home.

Even Hazel's choice of school was dependent on Mum and I, because we were her only living relatives, and had always met her on weekends, Bank Holidays, and school holidays. Once Helen had visited tropical Northern Australia, I bet she would want to live there, and no way could I see Tim settling **here!** Be that as it may, I would be stock-raising for my living, and there was no point in my promising regular visits to Oz, because they were never going to happen.

I placed Chet's Levi jacket on a hanger in the wardrobe, and put out my work clothes ready for tomorrow. I couldn't see myself getting to sleep any time soon. My brain had got the bit between its teeth, and I was likely to emulate Joe Stalin with my own five-year plan before I got a wink of sleep. Just for starters, my mind spewed out a list of people and animals who would depend on me for some aspect of their life.

Blue was **my** dog, not Mum's. Even the bantams were totally dependent on me, and the flock. I needed to contact the Westmorland farmer who 'folded our hill flock on mangolds', to confirm that Dad had booked his services, and our neighbour with the wagon adapted for sheep, to haul them up there.

Anxious to sleep, but not yet relaxed, I riffled through my more selfish concerns. After my next birthday I would be able to drive. Could I persuade Mum to get herself a newer car, and prise her loose from her present vintage landie? A few weasel words about how a Daimler, or a Rover at least, would more appropriate for one of Chyppens two cheese makers!

Of course, if I found that Jane was a sucker for suitors with legs like a billiard table, I could manage with my old bike, but otherwise, I needed wheels. Mum would knock all this on the head by telling me that she would always take me there, if asked.

This would hardly enhance the image of a young man about time. Don't suggest that I could secrete my beloved in the bantam shed, and meet there as often as I could manage to, because I would be too scared to ask her, and the bantams would lose all respect for me.

If Tim was ever invited to move in, he might anticipate that once I had secured my A-Levels, I would be 'in hall' at Lancaster except for vacations. In his shoes, I would be in no hurry to move before the fledgling had flown the nest. Nor would he expect Helen to join him while **my** future was uncertain.

My feelings for Jane were much deeper than my feelings for Rachel, but neither they nor their parents would never even have considered me as husband material. They might consider me as a suitable alternative to a hog roast, but little else. Considering that she is too good for me **right now**, by the time she qualifies, the gulf between us might be unbridgeable.

A flash of insight led me to wonder if Mum's job offer from the dairy, coinciding as it did with Dad's decision to buy himself out of the only career he ever wanted, sparked a moment's jealousy? As ever, she got what she wanted, while he sacrificed his career on a matter of principle.

I remembered having a similar insight when she told me that 'I wasn't the sharpest knife in the drawer', and I asked her if she had used the same phrase with him. Eventually, after three hours or so, I slept, to awake in a more positive state of mind, thinking, *Yes, after all, this was the best Christmas ever.*

After breakfast, I rang Jane to see if there was anything we might do together at the New Year. "I know there's a Young Farmers dance at Chyppen, but they can only dance under heavy sedation, so none of the lads turn up until the pubs close. It always smells like a brewery, and looks like a sleepwalkers' convention."

"I've just remembered that the gliding club are hosting a barn dance, in the clubhouse. Well actually, they just took out our cows and their stalls, installed lighting and toilets, and it only needed straw bales to sit on."

"It sounds delightfully informal. Does it have a roof?" "Yes, I can assure you of that. I also expect to know everyone present, and can guarantee the absence of both drunkenness and fighting. After all, you can get your fill of that at your local in Longbridge, whenever you want to rumble."

"You got it! I gratefully accept your invite to the Cotillion Ball in your cow shed. I must get off the phone now, having received dirty looks for the last ten minutes."

"Lovely. I'll look forward to that. Helen offered to collect you and return you. Don't forget, we can eat there." When we collected Jane, Brian and Daphne thanked Helen for getting her to the dance and back again. However, they had not been impressed by the progress made by our shippon in aspiring to be a clubhouse. It had not yet upped its game enough to demand the full-time services of a commissionaire.

I tried to get rid of their worries by explaining that I had attended every club function since I joined. That was a bonfire night, to which Helen had been invited on the grounds that she was going to be disturbed anyway, so at least she may as well attend as a guest. I always put this down to Jack Aked, always the most considerate of men.

Helen bore testimony to this. "Probably the worst pest was Ralph, chasing girls into the outer darkness to make them scream." Brian grinned as he knocked his pipe out on the fireplace. "We had feared something like a rugby-club thrash, all beer and bawdy songs. Having watched Jane playing hockey, she'll have no problem if Ralph is the worst she'll have to cope with."

"I had made similar false assumptions about my

fellow members. I imagined that they would be cut-price Bertie Woosters, and they turned out to be more like Heath Robinson. Their improvised telecommunication set-up consists of two war-surplus field telephones powered by a car battery, and augmented by two aldis lamps, each with its own car battery." "Daphne roared with laughter at this commonplace remark. She put her arm around me to say, "No offence, love but in your case, I expected Biggles, and got Wurzel Gummidge instead."

Just in time to hear this, Jane suddenly materialised. She wore a woollen lumberjack shirt, and a denim skirt, with black lisle tights, and her hair bunched above each ear. She was tapping one foot on the floor impatiently, and looked like a Yorkshire terrier, anxious to go walkies.

"I don't want to hustle you, Helen, but once men start gabbing they lose all track of time." "You're right there, Jane love. If they get on to their twinges, and funny turns, we might as well go back to bed. By the way, I've left a lump of coal in the porch, in case you don't burn it. In case the young master forgets, I'll expect you around one o'clock, and woe betide the pair of you if you aren't stood coal in hand when I open the door."

"Is everything sorted at the clubhouse?" Jane asked, as we drove homeward.

"Well, we did disturb a severe infestation of bird-eating spiders," I lied. "They must have arrived from the West Indies in a bunch of bananas. As you are the wrong sort of bird, they shouldn't bother you anyway."

We clattered over the cattle grid, and Mum dropped

us at the entrance before parking next to the house. They were testing the amps when I left, and the stone flags on the roof were rippling like pianola keys."

I squeezed her hand. "You look just as good as you did at the 'Craven Heifer'." She thanked me with a quick peck on the cheek. "Thanks. That's just what I needed before meeting a load of strangers." "Not strangers! Just enemies that you haven't sussed out yet."

We plunged in to join the dancing couples, anxious to break the ice, and get the party underway. Whenever we did stop to rest, few couples passed without exchanging a word. Dixie stopped by with Lorna. "I had hoped he would be 'another brand plucked from the burning' only to catch him 'womanising'. He'll never go solo now."

"Neither do I intend to postpone my social life until my State Pension offers some security," I replied. "Let's hope Dixie arrives at the same conclusion soon," said Lorna. "I had hoped that the arrival of a daughter might remind him of my presence. Do join us at our table. We are only taking a breather before re-joining the scrum." Dixie added his voice. "Yes, Jane please do! Then we can converse rather than just trade insults with him."

The evening really went with a bang. We spent most of the evening on our feet dancing, but we never sat without someone giving us the time of day, and having avoided such occasions in the past, I must say I did enjoy it, even if they only stopped to have a pop at me!

Jane collared Den when he stopped by with Rita to

have a word. "You must be the CFI he gripes about. I can't believe that you find him difficult to train. I don't, and Tim Clancy has him jumping through hoops like a circus dog!"

Rita gave a roar of approval. "The sooner we can get more ladies learning to fly, the sooner we will have some decent lady instructors! We all know these men who say that they can't understand women. They are wrong. It's **people** that they can't understand!"

"I've got to get a law degree first, Rita, but I may give that a throw when my present commitments have been achieved." "It's time we got our heads in the trough, Jane, before the best stuff has been trampled underfoot." The food was better than expected. Had Tim got a result by locking horns with Rita? By the time we had finished eating, midnight had struck, and we were all ready for 'Auld Lang Syne', then time to saunter back to the house to let the New Year in for Mum.

"I do hope you enjoyed the evening, Jane, I certainly did." "Of course I did! You seem to be surprised to be accepted by them. Why? You seem to like them, and apparently the feeling is mutual. Your CFI was quick to defuse my attempt to embarrass him, which suggests that he is less pompous than you suppose."

"Less than other CFIs, possibly. Other than hospital consultants, theirs is the profession most likely to claim Papal infallibility." "That sort of comment is childish rubbish, and only fit for the playground! An adult hearing it might reasonably wonder how many CFIs and consultants you have ever spoken to, and whether you have any inkling of the Catholic Church's current position on Papal infallibility."

I felt like a naughty schoolboy. "I stand corrected! No hard feelings." "I only said that because tonight, you were accepted as an adult in adult company." "I'm going to spend much more time on schoolwork this year. I shall give gliding a miss, because having put my name on the flying list, I am then committed to stay until the club machines are de-rigged and stowed in the hangar. I can get a little power-flying with Tim just for keeping the Super Cub's tanks full. No contest! Might one presume to ask for a quick hug, before we go in?" "That far, and no further!"

I gave her a quick hug, before ringing our door bell, then remembered the coal, and picked it up. When Helen answered, I asked, "Is your mummy in, love?" If looks could kill, that would have been the end of me. I hurriedly proffered the lump of coal, shouting, "Happy New Year!"

"Happy New Year! Come in, there's fruit cake and a glass of port for each of you to see the New Year in with. I'll have some wine and cake with you, before I run Jane home."

Jane gave me a sly look, before addressing Helen. "Let me be the first to tell you, Ralph has rashly proposed (no, not **that**, he's not yet certifiable) to drop gliding in favour of a few hours' dual with Tim, and spend more time with me, and revising!" "Can you assure me that no cruelty was involved in achieving this?" "Look for yourself. There's not a mark on him." "Amen to that, Jane. It's time he got his priorities right." "All I need to do now, is find some way of harnessing Mum's aggression to boost my career prospects." "Come on Jane, we won't keep your parents up any longer." "Goodnight Ralph, I enjoyed the dance and your friends were good company, too!" I went into the kitchen and raked the fire back into life, and brewed up for Mum and I. Maybe these hours of reverie before dying embers in our family home, might become a thing of the past quite soon.

Spring term started, and we returned to a different world, feeling like adults among children. Next term would bring our Intermediate Higher School Certificate. One needed to consider the possibility of failing HSC itself, in which case, a good result at intermediate level might suffice to gain university entrance, especially in the less popular science and maths-based disciplines.

That very effort to gain a good result might boost your confidence enough to improve your results in the second exam. I've always found late winter pretty miserable. For a start, I think that we haven't seen the worst of the winter until we've got through February. 'As the days lengthen, the cold strengthens.'

I let my gliding club friends struggle on without me (to be honest, there was little that needed doing). This gave me time to do all the organic chemistry preparations that the syllabus required. This afforded me extra revision time in my weaker subjects.

February always features amorous vixens screaming for a mate, sometimes loudly enough to disturb my sleep. The freezing dawns would soon lead to spring. March brought exciting news from Tim. I answered the phone to hear his voice. "G'day, Ralph. Is Helen in?" "I'm afraid not. Can I give her a message?" "There will be no need for one, if you can put me up tomorrow night and Saturday." "No problem. You'll have to land well up the field, because the first couple of hundred yards is waterlogged. I'll put your avgas on a stillage with the pump. You sound full of the joys of spring,"

"Yeah. As ever. I should have good news to share with you. Everything fine at your end?" "We are both well, but everything seems a bit dull after the festive season." "Then aren't you the lucky ones to have your Uncle Tim to let a little Australian sunshine into your drab Pommy lives?"

"Shall I pass that message to Helen?" "Heaven forbid! You can tell her that I come bearing steak and plonk, to save her the bother of butchering one of your jumbuks." "Just as you wish. It's the only part of food preparation that she really enjoys."

"I'm running short of change, so save the chat till I see you. Bye!" We never even heard him touch down. We were startled by his bursts of throttle as he taxied into the lee of the hangar, were his avgas was. He picketed the Super Cub where he could see it from one of our upstairs windows. The light was failing as I screwed his hand pump down tight against the lid of the drum. "Wotcha, Tim!"

"Hi, Ralph. See you up at the house." I filled both tanks, and trudged across the dew-wet pasture.

"Sit down, Ralph. I asked Tim to wait till you were here." "Well, Helen, we last discussed the White Eagle agency the day the Barge was written off. In a nutshell, I think I am now ready to set things in motion. Up to this point, all my planning has been on the basis of making sure every necessary requirement of my business plan is allowed for when I ask for the bank loan to be made available. At this point however, nothing is set in stone, so I want to run it past you to be sure that I haven't missed anything.

"Firstly, I can now meet the manufacturer's requirement for agencies outside Poland. They aren't that thrilled at the prospect of payment in GBP, but understand our limited legal options as an agency registered in the Isle of Man.

"Secondly, the aero engineers at Squires Gate who will rent me showroom space, will carry my requisite stock of spares, provided that I pay for them upfront. They will send an airframe fitter to Poland, provided that I pay him for every hour that he works on my behalf. "Incidentally, Chet and one of his buddies at Shannon each now want to lease an aircraft from me, having asked for discount on two aircraft to buy from me."

"Really? Now is the time to tell them that discount is reserved for purchasers, and 'you get no bread with one meatball'. Furthermore, leased UK-registered aircraft in the Republic are hostages to fortune until such time as they returned to UK jurisdiction.

"You should consider making it a business rule never to lease outside the UK. To do so would be to make yourself a target for con men, and it would only take one successful theft to bankrupt you! Ralph suggested to me that there is a huge market for leased light aircraft in UK flying clubs, where club fleets include Tiger Moths and Austers sold off by the Air Ministry at the end of the war. They were only available to aero clubs, crated, and at a price of £50 each.

"Any club with a waiting list of pupil pilots, and with fleets that need replacing, can lease new White Eagles, and some of the training can be conducted by members with an instructor's rating, at no cost to the club. If adjacent clubs don't follow suit, their pupil pilots will transfer their allegiance to the club with new aircraft, and instructors!"

"My God, Ralph! My instructional genius has transformed your common Pommy clay into a potential Dragon in 'Dragons' Den'." "Watch it, Ocker! Beneath that vacant stare, his parents' genes lurk."

"I am well aware of your valuable contribution, dear heart! I worship each and every one of your genes. By the way, concerning the White Eagles, I was considering getting one equipped for spraying, and maybe one for aero tows."

"Well forget it, then. You shouldn't have your fingers in too many pies. I would have thought that it would be very difficult to get a living from crop-spraying outside Australasia, and even there, it might be difficult to compete against helicopters." "For goodness' sake! I keep trying to simplify your new business, and you seem to bend all your energies towards involving yourself in unprofitable sideshows. Speaking of which, it would be worth listing all the features of this agency launch compared with relaunching in Oz! We don't want to find our feet here, only to be sand-bagged by differences in our new home."

"I can't do anything until I have a demonstrator to show customers." "Why don't you tell the makers that making one available to the flying magazines would focus the minds of potential customers? In fact, as there is no British product suitable for artillery spotting, there might be an opening for demonstrating one to the Army Air Corps. After all, there is already interest in the French civil market, and we have military links with France beyond NATO and the European Union.

CHAPTER 13

With Neville to Ronaldsway

Neville Breslau rang me one evening. "Can you make it to Squires Gate for 0800 on Saturday? If so, you will be welcome to join us for a brief shopping trip." "Will you excuse me while I ask Mum?" "Of course, and give her my regards!" I got a grudging acceptance from her, and asked Neville what I should wear. "Dress for walking, and loose heavy items should be in a bag to avoid possible injury to any passenger. We will take a taxi into town, but we expect to spend most of the day on our feet."

Helen thought that even accepting this invitation was disloyal to Jane. I said I needed to be piloted by someone other than Tim for once, and that I am sure Jane would think it ridiculous to behave as if we were engaged, particularly in view of her wish to gain a law degree before even considering any other major decision.

For my part, neither would I take on any major responsibility until I was convinced that I could achieve a hill-sheep farming career. Of course, this was hypocrisy, because of Rachel's off-the-clock nubility quotient, and the self-confidence and glamour bestowed by wealth.

We were going on the second Saturday in April, and I made a point of telling Jane about it, and taking her out on the Sunday. I was only a couple of weeks away from my seventeenth birthday, and had done sufficient driving, on and off-road, to feel confident about passing the test. I intended to book the test now, so as to complete it as soon as possible, so that it would no longer mean either using my bike, or asking Mum to drive me.

The day of our flight arrived, and I had completed my homework, packed some sandwiches, and got my camera (and sandwiches) in a small haversack. Mum had dug out a really good Grenfell jacket of Dad's. I would be expected to return with adequate gifts for the women in my life (**not** Blackpool rock!). Shopping would definitely be on the menu, and no doubt Rachel or Leah could point me in the right direction for some adequate 'smelly'.

Helen drove me to Squires Gate (none too willingly) and came to greet the Breslaus, and ask Leah for some good dress shops, while she was in Blackpool with time to kill. As usual for Blackpool, a stiff on-shore breeze seemed to blow straight through our clothes as we made for the hangar that Neville uses. I really needed my thickest cords, and that Grenfell jacket.

Neville hailed us as he returned from filing his

flight plan at the control tower. Having pushed the Cessna out onto the apron, we re-closed the hangar door, and gratefully climbed aboard and closed the doors. Having completed his pre-flight checks, he used his VHF radio to ask the tower for permission to move to the runway for take-off.

Despite being much-derided by Tim, I was soon thinking that I would find it almost impossible to find the end of the runway while taxiing a tail dragger, while struggling with a 90-degree blind spot directly ahead of me, and the tail wildly weather-cocking. By contrast, Neville had an almost 360-degree view of the airfield, and unimpeded steering by the steering yoke. The handling problems experienced by pilots of tail draggers often result in them being told to land and take off from a grass area parallel to one of the runways.

The sun emerged from behind a cloud as we stopped at the runway end for engine checks. We all donned our sunglasses. Neville asked the tower for permission to take off, having checked all round for both ground traffic on the airfield, and whether there was air traffic about to land or take off. Neville applied full throttle, and was holding the Cessna on the heel brakes, as Leah entered the time of take-off on her flight plan, on a clipboard with attached stopwatch.

Neville had elected to fly at 6,000 feet, in case of a loss of power during the sea-crossing. This meant that we must climb to that altitude before setting course for the lighthouse at Fleetwood, our first checkpoint to check the forecast wind, and the point at which we would set course for Ronaldsway.

It occurred to me that it would be extremely embarrassing to find that our forecast wind was inaccurate at this point, because without a radio compass, it would be extremely difficult to gauge the wind velocity while flying over the sea. If I found myself in that position, I think I would ask the tower to identify my blip on the radar (by asking me to turn onto a different course) and direct me to the required track made good. I asked Neville afterwards about radio compasses, and he said that if he ever thought they were in danger without one, he would get one!

Thanks to the twenty-knot headwind, Neville was soon able to rotate into the climb, and we went up like a lift, while he set the throttle and re-trimmed for best climbing speed. I looked around for Mum, and could see no sign of her. Three circuits of the airfield brought to our 6,000 feet cruising altitude, at which Leah started the stopwatch, and wrote down when our flight commenced. This altitude was recommended for crossing over the sea to Ronaldsway, although insufficient to permit us to reach landfall with a dead engine from the Point of No Return!

Neville leaned towards me to shout in my ear, "I've left the airfield at 6,000 feet in order to check the forecast wind at the first checkpoint, Fleetwood lighthouse. It would be a problem, if we had started our sea-crossing with an inaccurate wind vector. We would have to calculate the correction, and have no other checkpoint until we can see Ronaldsway. As Ronaldsway bears 280 degrees from Fleetwood lighthouse, the forecast w/v will bear ten degrees to port, reducing our ground speed to 90kts. We are close enough to the forecast to achieve the ETA on our flight plan."

I settled back to enjoy the ride. Before long, the whole Isle of Man became visible, and then Ronaldsway circuit. Neville called the tower to give our position and ETA. As soon as we landed, Neville parked near the avgas, and gave me his BP card to fill the tanks while he filed his inbound flight plan. On his return, I drew his attention to the White Eagle being refuelled, and made a note of the registration.

"You don't see many of those. Tim Clancy will be opening an agency for them at Squires Gate." He didn't seem thrilled. "Polish? You mean the country that specialises in horse-drawn farm implements? Does it boast a two-stroke motor from a Trabant that spews at more smoke than a space shuttle at take-off? I couldn't care less! Listen, Leah is getting down to some serious research about holiday accommodation for one of her pals, and needs our help.

"I'd be grateful if you would ride herd on Rachel for me? Make sure that she is back here at one, for lunch. Think you can manage that?" "That is a lot to expect. I will certainly keep track of the time, and sit on her if she tries to do a runner."

"That will serve admirably. We will then share a taxi into Douglas, for lunch, because we prefer it to Castletown. Rachel can show you around, and we'll meet up at the Peveril Square taxi rank. After lunch, we will be busy in Douglas all afternoon."

When we split up in town on the seafront, I asked Rachel if there was a pier, in the hope of postponing the shopping. Before we had turned off the promenade for the pier, there was a screech of brakes, and a red Porsche stopped beside us. The driver wound down his passenger window, and addressed Rachel.

"Haven't we met?" The driver had gold reflective sunglasses and collar-length fair hair. He had a loud public school accent, and removed his glasses to aid recognition. "Don't tell me! You were posing on a TVR for a photographer at the Northern Sports Car Show at Ripon!"

"As you can see, I am with someone." She added something that I failed to catch, nor did I catch his reply, which raised a laugh from her. That was all the encouragement he needed, and he leant across to open the passenger door. My arm blocked her entry as I tipped the passenger seat forward to dive onto the two occasional seats in the back. She glowered at me, then pushed the passenger seat back, and sat on it, slamming the door

"Cor! What will she do, mister? More than a ton, I'll bet." "A lot less, with you in the back." "But surely handling and acceleration are the whole point of the thing! You would hardly buy one as a passion wagon, would you? Because you would get more **bang** per buck from a van lined with fake fur and a six-speaker sound system. Wouldn't that be more **you?** Or do you find it more stylish to hire a hotel room, when required? Of course, that would be sailing too close to the wind, when your partner is a school girl." I nudged Rachel, and guffawed loudly.

"I think your remarks are quite offensive to Miss, er, er..." "Miss Danziger," I added helpfully. "Sharon, to her friends. I am her cousin Carl, known to one and all as Chutzpah Danziger." "Miss Danziger and I are already acquainted. She will now skip out of my car while you remove yourself. You've got just two minutes to get out, after which I shall remove you by force. You may not be aware that I am a Boxing Blue!" "In that case, may I have your autograph?"

Rachel climbed out, with me on her heels, to grip her elbow and hurry her to the pier. I leaned through the window. "Should you wish to renew your acquaintance, we Danzigers are in the phone book. Meanwhile, on any weekday you will find loads of raunchy young maidens spilling out of school at three thirty, any one of whom would be easier to lead astray than she is." We set off up the pier where his car could not follow.

"Why did you refer to me as a schoolgirl?" "Obviously, to shame him! You could pass muster anywhere as a well-to-do young socialite, but you are still a schoolgirl, and it is very dangerous to pretend to be over the age of consent. At what stage of becoming spoilt and wealthy did you lose touch with reality?" This was pretty rude, so I changed the subject. "What do you want to do until lunch?"

"I can show you some of my favourite spots around the harbour, and you can take some pictures of me." "Thanks, I would really like that. You can tell me what I'm doing wrong." During lunch, Neville told me that he had three caravans to look at, with a view to making an offer on them. He told me a bit about his business, a subject on which everyone has something of interest to say. "Would you like me to make myself scarce until your business is concluded?"

"No, just stay out of earshot while I discuss terms. I will explain that you are just here for the ride." I had found him terse when I was talking about the White Eagle, but that was just due to business on his mind, I expect. He let me pay for lunch, having been most generous to me at the Barn Dance.

Helen had enjoyed her day shopping in Blackpool, and when we got home we discussed my forthcoming gliding holiday at Southern Soaring, which Tim would pay for. I had made considerable preparation, down to reading up soaring lenticular clouds (fat chance!).

CHAPTER 14

Bellerephon Astride Winged Pegasus

I has received a brochure with a nice covering letter from CFI Peter Cotterell's business partner, Assistant CFI Steve Cunliffe. He suggested possible places to stay, and as one was a pub, 'The Plough' at Inkpen, that was the one that I chose. He also recommended that club membership would be more cost-effective than a course (possibly no-one else had asked for a course?).

I rang 'The Plough', and made a booking. Jane held me to my promise, and I took her to Manchester by coach, for a tour of the galleries, followed by a concert by the Hallé Orchestra. I really enjoyed the galleries, but the music was for Jane's benefit.

As I travelled south by train, and then a local bus,

my mind roamed through our Manchester trip, and onto other recent events. I piously resolved to be less selfish with my time in future. 'Shalbourne' appeared on a finger post, and I realised that I had almost reached my destination. I was soon climbing down with my rucksack outside 'The Plough' and it looked like a dump even before I had set foot inside. It seemed that it didn't offer much of a living for the landlord. Breweries with tied houses find it cheaper to hire a manager to run them. As a result, lack of ambition often leads to falling beer sales, which they can cure by letting the pub to a tenant, who usually restores the 'barrelage' consumed in the pub. Manager or not, this guy clearly had no plans to remedy that situation.

I booked in, and asked where the shops were, to be told that a PO was the only shop here. I asked for directions up to 'Southern Soaring', and went to see what the PO offered. As with the pub, not much! I bought a small sliced brown loaf, and half a pound of boiled ham, with a tube of mustard, and decided to plan my evening meal on my return.

The nearest thing to a ready-meal at the PO was a Fray Bentos pie in puff pastry, like beef steak cooked in sea water. I set off on a two-mile walk, and hoped that someone at the club might offer me a lift, now and then. I don't have a problem with walking, but if it was raining, I would need to turn up and hope for the best, and getting soaked is not a great prelude to hanging about for hours on a windy airstrips! It seemed worthwhile for the chance to learn the topography en route. It is always less stressful than doing all your reconnaissance while being taught to fly.

A sunny May morning had overdeveloped, leaving few breaks in the cloud cover. The road was almost deserted, until I reached the top. I traversed the scarp on a narrow land with overgrown hedges, and Inkpen came into view. The scarp was devoted to close-cropped chalk sheep pasture, full of tiny flowers.

I climbed slightly higher, and Shalbourne reappeared. Eventually, I reached the fork in the road where I had been told to bear left. A little further on, we approached the ridge top, which was mainly chalk and flint planted with barley. A breeze sprang up, which started to clear the overcast. There was no evidence of flying as yet. I knew that all the launches would by aero-tow, which I had not experienced, so this would kick off by the CFI checking the scarp for slope lift, and once the overcast had cleared, no doubt thermals would be popping off from east-to-south facing slopes.

After another ten minutes, an aero-engine started up, and a rather elderly silver Auster made an appearance, to climb all the way up to cloud base to check for thermal activity before looking along the scarp for slope lift.

I finally arrived at the farm; Southern Soaring's landlord provided two caravans that constituted their office and clubhouse, plus an Atcost farm building for a hangar.

The farmer was a horse racing enthusiast, and owned one of those 'push-me-pull-you' Cessna twins that provide safer water crossing ability without requiring a twin-engine rating for the private pilot. They have two booms, bridged by the elevator, and a stubby nacelle provides the passenger cabin with a 'pusher' engine behind it and a normal 'puller' engine in front. Should either engine fail on take-off, no 'asymmetric' thrust can result, hence no necessity for a twin-engine rating.

The smaller caravan proved to be the office, where I found Rob Cunningham in charge. The partners were both ex-RAF flying instructors. "The CFI is doing the daily weather check. We aren't using the winch at the moment, but we'll soon check you out on aero-tows.

"We only recommend aero-tows when soaring is envisaged, as it is obviously a lot more costly. However, we only used the winch when the scarp is soarable, because it is labour intensive, and the resulting three-minute flight a waste of pupils' time. Both are in use when our private owners want to exploit thermalling conditions, and the pupils are keen to soar the slope. Let's see your log book."

It didn't take him long. He tapped his teeth with a pencil. "We had a couple of Blackpool and Fylde lads at our previous site. Didn't they used to operate from English Electric at Samlesbury?" "They did immediately before I joined, yes. Shortly after my dad bought himself out of the army, he took an agricultural mortgage to finance a dairy enterprise on our hill sheep farm. Sadly, he died in a motorbike accident shortly afterwards, and Mum and I had more farm than we could manage.

"When the dust had settled, the club had bought our field, but not the farm, so that they had security of tenure for a grant from the sports council, and I rented the pasture, which, by keeping the land in agricultural use, enabled them to claim an agricultural

226

drainage grant. This covered the cost of materials and second-hand machinery, provided the members to do the labouring required.

"All this was a huge leap of faith from having free use at weekends of a working airfield with the main runway a mile long! The problem was, despite having a Blanik as well as the T21b, you couldn't soar there anyway, so they gambled everything on Tewitts' Field, almost a mile from a south-west facing bowl, offering the chance of stepping off the slope to catch passing thermals. I was told that the Ribble Estuary (in common with all others) seldom provides that unstable air that we need to provide thermal."

"We've been there, too. By now, we've got quite a chunk of capital tied up in our business, and having operated from a number of sites, we are always hoping that things will be more secure at the next change, but it's never long before a new threat heads in our direction. You might say that anything you would do without being paid to, will never guarantee an income."

"Gosh! That is worthy of Maynard Keynes! I **might** be able to make hill-sheep farming my career, but only by abandoning a degree course. However, regarding Tewitts' Field, it is nearly a mile distant from 'The Bowl' and **beneath** it, whereas as you have a much smaller (but much better drained) airstrip perched **on top** of your scarp.

"The club had many solo pilots when it moved, many of whom I have never seen. Now the hard work has been done, these guys want to get flying, but the committee doesn't intend to turn them loose until they have been checked out for the new site, preferably by the CFI. Ab initio pupils like myself could still be kicking our heels in a year's time, unless we get some hours in at clubs like yours."

"We'll soon remedy that, in a couple of weeks. Have you read-up aero-tow procedure?" "That and loads more beside. Meteorology, Air Law, Theory of Flight, 'On Being a Bird'." "OK, then I'll give you a briefing, and then we'll get a launch." I opted for an hour's flying, and the CFIs pushed the Blanik out of the hangar, the tow aircraft being out and warmed up already.

I carried out the pre-flight checks while the tug pilot (a recently released fighter pilot) ran out the tow line. Rob sat briefing me, to tell me that he would rotate into the climb, re-trim to best climb, and then hand over to me. For this short field, a shorter tow-line was necessary, which made life harder for both the tow pilot, and the glider pilot. The glider had to be flown as smoothly as possible.

Particularly near the ground, the tow pilot would be ready to jettison the tow-line in the event of the glider turning late, or wide. The other danger was to allow the line to snatch, dragging the towing machine to be suddenly brought close to the stall, dangerously low. He would jettison the line, and the glider pilot must immediately jettison his end, before it caught the ground and dragged it into a nosedive.

It was essential to bank the glider when the tow aircraft banked, because it was dangerous if the tow aircraft turned wider, which would tweak its tail outward. If any slack developed in the tow line, it would be snatched taut, catapulting the glider forward to cause another bow. The tow pilot would have to jettison the tow line, for fear of stalling him near the ground.

At 2,000 feet, the tow plane bumped through a thermal, and waggled his wings for us to slip the tow. I released and made a climbing turn to the right, zooming off towing speed right, and anticipating the tow aircraft diving left to return to the strip, so that I increased our separation. Rob took over to centre in the thermal, which petered out at 2,800 feet. I did thirty minutes of thermalling and some spin recoveries. We landed, and after a further briefing, I was told that I could attempt a solo aero-tow after lunch. I ate my sandwiches on my own behind the office, all wound up to go!

After a short fifteen-minute dual take-off, handling the take-off on my own, I could hardly believe it when, despite a strengthening wind, which would try to get under my port wing during take-off, I was given the go-ahead. I was walking on eggshells during the take-off, thinking how many wrong things I might do, and not much that would be right!

I only held the control column with thumb and forefinger because the whole take-off was done at higher speed than on a winch-launch, which made overcorrecting more likely.

Eventually, the tow aircraft bumped in a thermal, and waggled his wings. I did a climbing turn to the right, zooming off excess speed. I watched the tow aircraft turned left in a diving left turn on his return to the strip. I turned into the thermal, and the starboard wing rose, 'tipping me out'.

I reacted quickly with right stick and right rudder,

and up popped the port wing. This time I got in the centre of the lift, and established it in a slipping turn, that held me in the core of the lift, with my port wing tip describing a small circle over the ground, and then rode it to the top. I was almost at 3,000 feet this time, so the thermals were now stronger.

Since I cast off, I had been proceeding downwind at wind speed, like a balloon, and rather than drift downwind until I tired of thermalling, it seemed safer to keep as much altitude as possible, while flying upwind to the next thermal. I was fairly settled by now, and could see little difficulty in staying up as long as I wished. This seemed weird, because I expected thermals to attract gliders like wasps around a jam jar.

I had always felt that up to a point, I expected to be less nervous **without** an instructor. This might very quickly change if I ran into difficulties, in which case, Mummy wouldn't be there for me to run to! Anyway, I did more thermalling, then some loops for a change, and then some spin recoveries. After a while, having been airborne for an hour, and feeling somewhat blasé, I headed for the circuit. I couldn't believe that no-one else had arrived, even though it was a weekday.

This was definitely the way gliding **ought** to be! Flying had only resumed at Tewitts' Field on the 18th of March, after the club had last flown at Samlesbury on the 18th of October '72. Three days of gliding 'from home' had only given me five launches and added thirty minutes to my dual flying experience. This was clearly quite pointless, but still committed me to stay there till flying stopped, and all the gliders were de-rigged and returned to the hangar.

After the fourth thermal, I decided to return. I saw the tow pilot heading for the office. I made a long upwind approach, and turned crosswind to run through my pre-landing checks. I had plenty of time on finals, and kept a little height in hand, popping the air brakes as I crossed the threshold.

The 'swoosh' of the brakes alerted someone to my arrival. Peter Cotterel strode over to me as I picketed the Blanik's wing with a tire. "Had you planned this, or where you not aware that you have acquired a 'bronze leg' for duration on your first solo?"

"What is a Bronze Leg?" I asked, in all innocence. Apparently, once I had achieved the required gain of altitude from release, and distance achieved I would be awarded the Bronze Leg. One would never dare to boast of it, for fear of people counter claiming, **"Big deal! I've got a Brass arse!"**

As you can imagine, I felt on top of the world! This is very dangerous for teenage boys, as they are easily persuaded that they differ from others by virtue of superhuman powers. Who knows might I might yet accomplish to astound the other Lancs. Gliding Club members? I made a shorter (wasted?) twenty-minute solo in the Blanik, after which the weather steadily worsened.

Next day, after the usual first-light calm, blustery conditions resumed. The whole morning passed, with the weather too bad for me, but with a steady stream of private owners arriving with cross-country attempts in mind. The CFI told me that I would go on the aero-tow rota, if I felt happy coping with the combination of the short tow-line and the blustery conditions. One of the main problems was that my opinion of my own ability to cope was not worth having.

Clearly, any aero-tow, anywhere, was harder than a winch launch. The trick is, getting enough to make progress without taking unnecessary risks at the outset. I was feeling twitchy, and preferred my own company, which was no problem in the absence of other pupils! As at our own club, the private owner tend to be briefly matey until their sailplanes have been rigged, and pushed out to the take-off point, when you cease to be visible.

Eventually the CFI emerged from his office, to offer me the next launch, if I accepted the difficulties involved. My reaction was that he would not have made the offer had he felt me to be incapable of coping with it. I therefore expressed my confidence in coping, believing that I would feel less safe had I felt more confident! We all have to live our lives that way. If one is overcautious, it will limit one's ability to develop further skills. Once I had completed a ground check and climbed on board, he gave me a final briefing.

"As you know, our narrow airstrip only offers the two reciprocal take-off directions. Today, the tug pilot is compelled to take off ten degrees starboard of being into wind. You will take off well before he does, and drop the port wing very briefly, just to avoid a gust beneath your port wing endangering him. You have more wing span, making it very dangerous for him if you either let slack develop in the tow-line, or don't instantly follow him as soon as he banks.

"If you swing wide, he must instantly jettison the

tow line, and you must jettison before the line touches the ground. We know the Ottfur linkage is designed to release on the overrun, but should it fail to, it would pull you into a nosedive into the ground!" I rattled through my pre-flight checks, and gave him the 'cable on' signal, thinking that there was a lot to be said in favour of safer things, like flower-arranging. He dragged the cable end by its drogue, to snap the ring on, and gave the tug pilot the sign to 'take up slack'.

I watched the Auster creep forwards until the line twanged taut, and signalled 'All out!' The Blanik moved forwards, and was soon airborne. I flicked the stick towards the port wing, and instantly back again, while keeping the nose just beneath the horizon. I held the stick lightly between thumb and forefinger, giving the lightest touch of right rudder to keep aligned with the tug. I would have liked to have a glance at the ground, but as when driving in traffic in thick fog, I felt that I daren't take my eyes off the tug, even for a quick glance elsewhere.

While I was straining to avoid slack in the tow-line and straying out of station, the tug had found a thermal, and the pilot waggled his wings, so I released, and zoomed off excess speed in a climbing turn to the right, as he made his diving turn to the left, to descend back to the field. It was a shock to have had all my attention focussed on him for the last ten minutes or so, and then to imagine myself alone in the sky!

That was when I should have forgotten him, and centred in the thermal while I was close to it! Surely, I had only to look up to see the cloud sat above it! That is panic for you. It seems to leave you incapable of simple logic. I had been watching the silver Auster as a black silhouette against the sky, but there was overcast, and had I spotted it, it would not have benefitted by sunlight to offer a flash from tilting wings, just a grey shape against a dull grey background.

We had taken off from Inkpen Ridge, following it to its far end, where it aligned with Sheepless Hill, which had hatched the thermal in which I had cast off from the tug. The whole top of Sheepless Hill was occupied by a long field of barley, much larger than the airstrip that I had just left. I really liked the look of it!

I have just spelled out how easily I could get my bearings, and then quickly work out if I had enough height to return whence I came. I was over one ridge, and wanting to get to the far end of the nearest one, not in the middle of a vast flat plain where I was unlikely ever to find it again!

However, having taken a 'sick fancy' to Sheepless Hill, this seemed to be my next decision, that I must waste no more time making alternative choices, but make an easy decision which left me time to plan a circuit offering a long final approach that offered time to approach with height in hand, and a relaxed attitude in contrast to my initial panic!

As the CFI pointed out to me when debriefing me afterwards, there had never been any need to land out. So this was it, let's engage with the problem! I would approach downwind, and not too close to the ridge, because I needed enough space crosswind to complete pre-landing checks.

There was I, full of practical common sense, when

I was suddenly aware that I was about to pass the far end of the ridge, and should have been farther out, having turned crosswind. Close to the ridge as I was, I would have been in trouble but for the sudden appearance of a deep gully. I did a steep turn while the gulley made space for the port wing, and started my crosswind leg, gabbling my pre-landing checks like a ground squirrel on helium.

I turned less than 90°, to enable another steep turn over the far end of the ridge of 95° to align myself with the longest landing run. I took a deep breath, and finally settled on long finals fully relaxed. I popped the air brakes, and my beautiful Blanik greased onto the chalk and flint of the barley field. I opened the canopy, making a mental note never to admit to my steep turn in the gulley, as I gathered stones and flints to ballast my jacket, to picket the wing tip that that I swung into wind, first.

I realised that it might take me hours to find the landowner, and then make contact with Southern Sailplanes. I had been lucky to make my precautionary landing without damaging the Blanik, but I wasn't going to be very popular either with the partners, or with those private owners with cross-countries in mind, then finding themselves lumbered with rescuing thoughtless proles who left their toys out when going out to play.

I used to like the silent passage of gliders, thinking how commendable it is, but it results in you arriving unexpectedly on other people's property without anyone being aware of your presence! It might take the best part of an hour to find a road, let alone a dwelling. I had got there in twenty minutes, but it was another two hours before I could report my intrusion to the estate manager who was responsible for Sheepless Hill. I don't think he believed my story, but he let me ring Southern Sailplanes, and then drove me to the Blanik. He said no damage had resulted to the crop, but when I explained that that it would need a trailer, and that the Blanik would have to be de-rigged and manhandled on to the trailer, he decided that he had better stay put to see that no damage resulted.

It took a further two hours to get the trailer there with enough crew. It was a long time before we started the long, slow journey back. The first job was rigging the Blanik. Obviously, I must remain until no further work was necessary. Pete Cotterel addressed me. "I have to debrief you on your out-landing, and there is no time like the present. As you owe a drink to all your helpers, I suggest that we repair to 'The Plough', and I will save the interrogation until you have got the drinks in."

My heart sank, because I was cold (no jacket for four hours) worn out, and desperately tired. Things looked up when I had a pint in front of me. "When did your troubles start?"

"I had underestimated the difficulties that blustery wind would cause to our take-off. It reminded me of driving in traffic, in fog, when you daren't steal a glance at a traffic sign, or even the speedometer, for fear of colliding with someone not yet visible to you. I now realise that my priorities were wrong.

"Had I just centred in the thermal, clearly I could have stayed there without loss of height until it expired. More than enough time to spot the flash of the Auster's wings as it turned in the circuit, and note the strips bearing from that part of the scarp of Sheepless Hill that was hatching thermals." "So you were circling, looking for the next thermal. In what direction?" "Upwind." "Why?" "As a third-solo pilot, I expect you briefed the tug pilot to find a thermal upwind of our airstrip, to avoid my running out of altitude, and faced with a headwind to penetrate in order to return." "So, in other words, you blundered around, failing to find either the thermal or the air strip, until you felt that a precautionary landing was required?" "I assumed that the thermals would be hatching at roughly fifteen-minute intervals, and also that I needed to make a decision and act on it, while the safe option of landing **on** the ridge was still possible. Down below, the fields were small, wet, and the bigger ones seemed to have mature trees or a telephone wire on the approach."

"What was your altitude when you committed to landing on Sheepless Hill?" "One thousand feet." "Well, when I came looking for you in the Auster, I could see our air strip from that altitude, and you could have reached it in the Blanik."

"I never flew from there till yesterday, and for a third solo, the short tow line and blustery conditions were as much as I could cope with. When I was signalled to cast off, that was my first chance to look for the tug, or even glance at the ground. As soon as tug and glider separated, I would not expect to see the tug above the horizon, so what had been a silhouette against the sky until then, would have been a silver plane, looking grey against a hazy background under an overcast sky. In short, I had no way of knowing our strip was downwind. I was obviously in a panic, and I committed to Sheepless Hill, believing it was necessary to land on a long, safe field while that option was still open."

"I guess that covers everything. You need to do some dual with Rob in the Falke, to learn more about emergency and precautionary landings."

"Then may I take this opportunity to offer my thanks to all of you who turned out hoping for a day's cross-country attempts in your own sailplanes, and wound up spending hours clearing up my mess instead."

Next day, I went straight to the office and studied the handling notes for the Falke. Rob gave me a lengthy period of ground instruction on field landings. I told him that Bill Scull, the BGA's test pilot, had brought their Slingsby T61 (a Falke built under license by Slingsby sailplanes at Kirby Moorside) up to Salmesbury, to check out soaring areas that could be reached from Tewitts' Field.

In common with most instructors, Pete and Rob believed that powered gliders would revolutionise gliding instruction. One instructor, with one powered glider can prepare one ab initio pupil for the solo machines in three to four hours, and then they can be launched by the winches that the clubs already own, with the proviso that once they reach solo stage, they must be supported by a CFI, a winch driver, a recovery team of three, a tractor and a tractor driver, plus a pair of signallers and a duty pilot. That is your instructor, plus a rota to provide at least nine other bods for every day flown!

"At one time, we used to prepare pilots for field

landings by marking a reduced area of our existing landing strip. This is just inadequate, when you consider that such landings are nearly always in places not intended for such use, and therefore induce panic due to their lack of familiarity! The three main causes of damage resulting from field landings are: one, having left it too late to select a field you collide with the far hedge; two, your planning was OK, but lack of judgement was responsible; three, your planning and judgement were OK, but you had failed to spot soft ground, a shallow ditch, or even rabbit holes that damaged the glider by stopping it abruptly.

"So how are we to prepare? Well obviously, we make such preparations on every launch we ever experience! You make a winch launch, back home. What will you do if you experience a cable break before the point of no return? Release and land straight ahead. Past the PNR? Hop over the hedge and land straight ahead, etc. So this is what you should be doing as a matter of course.

"You can't identify every tiny obstacle during a hurried recce of the field seen from a partial circuit, and if you first spot a problem on finals, in a glider, you will be too late to avoid it! There is no substitute for eternal vigilance!"

Finally briefed and ready to fly, we found that the weather had changed. A design fault in the Falke had lumbered it with a wing section that lost much of its lift when dewed with rain! Even when taking off from a proper runway. What I didn't realise on the 2nd of May, was that it would be the 8th before we would fly!

"Do you know anything about the Falke?" "Yes, Bill Scull, who I think might be the test pilot for the

BGA, took one to Samlesbury when Lancs. Gliding Club were operating there. They wanted him to prospect for hill-soaring sites that could be reached from there.

"By chance, I saw him, without even knowing what a self-launching glider was. They tell me that the Falke has a laminar-flow wing section of such Teutonic perfection, that a dimpling of rainwater causes it to be capable of motoring down a mile of asphalt runway like a clockwork mouse, without actually taking off. The same feature could become quite an embarrassing feature in an airliner! I believe the motor is a Limbach modified VW flat-four air-cooled one."

"Stripped of your hyperbole and xenophobia, that is broadly true. Ours is the 60bhp Limbach version, quite a boost from its original 34bhp. The Super Falke followed, with a higher aspect wing, of Gottingen section like the Ka6 and Ka13, gaining a reduced stalling speed, but at the cost of performance. It was slimmed down to permit tandem seating, endowing it with far better penetration. It also has a 75bhp motor." "Ours has a lower minimum-sink speed, but poorer performance."

We had arrived at the hangar by now, and Rob opened up so I could help him to wheel it out like a new father. I couldn't resist taking the mickey in my facetious schoolboy way. "Whoever sold you **that**? Someone saw you coming, squire! It's frugal is it? So is a camel. OK for remote strips, so long as they are in a desert somewhere. In that case I might trade six camels for one."

"Don't you dare insult our Falke with your Arthur

Daley impressions. I'm glad you've bounced back from your setback, but I won't hear a word against self-launching gliders for dual tuition!"

"I did a lot of dual on an old Barge bought from the Air Ministry for £600." "Yes, but just consider what a Falke **doesn't** need. The Barge needs a skilled man on the winch, probably the most dangerous job on the airfield. It consumes diesel, but the dearest thing it eats is cable. Their needs to be a guy with a vehicle to retrieve the cable, three men to retrieve the gliders, and two signal men. You need a mob of unruly tribesmen assembled, before anything commences, and a wrong signal or a botched splice can bring everything to a halt again!"

"Ouch! How accurately you describe our standard procedure at Tewitts' Field. We would get as much exercise Morris dancing, and the accoutrements are cheaper."

"I understand that you have got a few hours dual in a Super Cub." "Yes, the deal is that I collect his avgas and set it up on a pallet, and then top his tanks up with his hand pump."

"Lucky you. That saves me some time, then. I know someone who owns a Fournier, hangared at Speke. There isn't much in the way of slope-soaring near there, and you hardly ever get unstable air, but he doesn't deed thermals, either. He motors over to Snowdon, and there is a slope to soar in any wind direction. And finally, haunted as you are by the Red Baron, you will be relieved that not merely the BGA Falke, but ours too, is built by Slingsbys under license. Now let's cut to the chase and get in the air!"

I heard another car arrive, and then a visiting tug pilot entered with Pete. He wanted to refuel before leaving. I wished them both good morning. "Young Ralph here has been jeering at our Falke. I propose to give him some field landing practise to widen his knowledge further." "It isn't time he could use for further solo, until the wind drops." "In that case, I would love an hour's dual in it, and then see what the afternoon will bring." "Right Bob, take it away! Fred has to refuel his Auster to tow the Nimbus to HusBos, but I'll jump the queue to do the daily weather check first." (He referred to Husband's Bosworth.)

We made our way to the hangar, opened the door, and wheeled out the Falke, in time to see Pete take off. Rob completed the pre-flight check, and we heard Pete's machine cough, and then pick up again. We both had our ears tuned to that engine, when it stopped finally. On the airstrip, the other Auster pilot was hooked up, and about to take off.

He should have got out, but Nimbus owners, almost to a man, have more money than time. He made it very clear that he saw no reason why Pete's engine problem was any of his business. His wife bent to speak to him, presumably to tell him that there was an Auster landing with a dead engine. Steve rolled to a stop, then leapt out, and waved his arms in an attempt to abort their take-off.

Despite her warning, he signalled to take up slack; the Nimbus left the ground after a very short run, followed by its tug, which immediately died. The Nimbus sailed gracefully over the fence, to settle on the other side, and the tug pilot hauled full flap on as the only possible way of avoiding the Nimbus. It passed just above, settling heavily, fully stalled, just ahead of him.

The Nimbus owner probably wasn't happy about elderly Austers playing leapfrog with his Nimbus, either, but he had brought it on himself! The tug pilot should have left his tug, and made a 'fait accompli' of his intention, rather than submit to bullying when safety is at issue.

Rob's comment was, "Kindly note, when Pete has just landed with a dead engine, and is waving his arms manically, one might be suffering from contaminated fuel, and should lie in a darkened room until recovered." He called Steve over. "Steve take your car, and collect engine tools, plastic tubing to siphon fuel with, a jerrican. Start with the visiting Auster, and it must have water in the carburettor, so clean that. The current avgas drum must have water in it, so tip it on one corner, and siphon all the water out from the bottom. That drum will then be usable. There is probably water in **both** tanks, so run it out of the drain cocks through transparent pipe until it runs clear. Then top it up till he's got a tank of clean fuel. Repeat with our Auster, carburettor and both tanks. We shall see to the Falke."

I had often helped Alec tend machinery. I tried hard not to get in the way, and hoped to learn something, like guess what he would do next. "I don't think we've got any water in the fuel, have we? If we've none in the carb, are we clear of it?"

"Not necessarily. If it has had the tank filled, and not been flown since, there could be water anywhere in the system. Hold on, Pete's come out with the

243

wrench for the hand pump. I'll go and have a look if he's found the problem."

He returned quite quickly. "All that was wrong, was that the flange wasn't tightened, and the rain and condensation have been collecting in the top. Every night the fuel cools, dropping the pressure inside. Because it isn't air-tight, it's gulped in nearly half a pint of water every night, until the water reached the pump inlet."

The Limbach motor was easy to work on. The top of the engine cowl was a length of piano hinge, much easier to access than when installed between two car wheel arches. As it is a flat-four engine, it needs two carbs, one on each side. Each had three non-return valves, not designed to fit only the right way round! They didn't take too long to clean and reassemble. There had been a little clean water in one carb, and in one tank.

Rob and Pete ganged up on me. Pete asked Rob, "Is the Falke serviceable?"

"Yes, we've been through the fuel system, cleaned both carbs, and made everything good!" "Are we allowed to do that?" "No sweat, Pete, Ralph is a certified aero-engine fitter." "In that case, let's have his moniker in the engine log." I had been taking myself too seriously again!

Even away from Tewitts' Field, determined gremlins can manage to lose a whole morning's flying! The only cool way to treat it is to accept the instruction and entertainment that comes in its place. The only reward the visiting pilot got for doing as he was bloody well told, was to find he had been 'volunteered' to de-rig the Cirrus, pass it over the fence, and then rig it again. Kind Rob then took pity on the owner, and used his car to tow him back to the end of the strip, while his wife held one wing-tip.

With one thing and anther, it was almost two thirty before we took off in the Falke. I **needed** a lengthy briefing on field landings, and briefing in the cockpit, which was dominated by a starting handle the size of the handbrake on a tank transporter!

"I'd like you to take everything loose out, or stow it, and sweep the floor. As you will already know, you must stop the motor to soar. Mainly because a windmilling prop creates as much drag as a solid disk of the same circumference.

"This handle is what you restart it with. It avoids not just the weight of a starter motor, but also of a heavier-duty battery. Do not mistake this for another Super Cub, that can sprint up as many flights of stairs as you like. This is a chair lift.

"Give her her due, she climbs at forty-five knots, under full power, gaining height at the rate of four hundred feet a minute.

"The Falke has to be flown a special way to give its best. It is very like orienteering, or navigating a sailing dinghy. Flying cross-country under power, one must divert into areas of lift to gain height, and dive off the height at increased speed between you and the next rising air. There is no need to beat up and down soarable slopes, or even to spiral upwards in thermals, when time presses. One may simply progress in one direction, diverting either sideways, or 'porpoising' slow uphill and fast downhill.

"I'll run through the checks, and we'll be off. I need not remind you after this morning, that whatever you fly, power loss might be a problem."

The engine started at the third pull, and Rob left it idling while he ran through the control checks. He gradually opened the throttle as he lined up, and then pushed it full open, rotating into the climb when the airspeed indictor read forty-five knots.

"While it can keep up with most two-seater gliders in a thermal, it sinks faster at higher speeds, thanks to much higher drag. This will present a problem as the older first-solo machines are replaced with newer models of higher performance.

"There are already pupils at Lasham who have done all their dual on Falkes, and they have problems dealing with the greater penetration offered by modern sailplanes. They don't see the problem until they leave Lasham, because it's such a vast landing area. When they go somewhere smaller, they are always in danger of running out of runway. This proves them to be unready for cross-country flying. That woke you up, didn't it? You dozed off while I was nattering, didn't you? Take over, and level out at two thousand feet.

"Yes, the purpose of field landings is to prepare for cross-country flight, so pin your ears back. This is the stuff every glider pilot should aspire to. Don't you think we might achieve two thousand feet an hour sooner beneath that cloud street?"

"Sorry, Rob. I don't know where we are heading." "You don't need to. Why do you think I've never shut up since we took off? I do it to reduce you to dull-witted torpor, before testing your observation, orientation, and speed of decision-making. We've climbed to seventeen hundred feet. Throttle back to idling speed, and find somewhere to land. Talk me through it." "We set off into wind, and at the time you directed me to the cloud street we were less than half a mile away from the airfield. We are in very weak lift, and I will continue turning right till I'm looking up the windsock. I can definitely reach the airfield from here, even considering that we must pass the airfield to turn twice onto finals."

"That's good. We'll assume the airstrip is obscured by smoke." "Right. I don't like anywhere near the base of the scarp. The only big fields without trees are near the top of the reverse slope, and while none are flat, they offer gentle uphill landing grounds."

"So pick one." "One has been cut for silage, so is smooth enough to mow, and is free of livestock. I'll make an S-turn to stay wide of it on my downwind leg." "How wide?" "Three fields clear. I'll turn crosswind two fields away." "What height do we have?" "One thousand feet on the clock, plus two hundred feet lower than our take-off point." "Aren't we a bit high?" "I'll do a tight circuit, six hundred feet above the threshold. I need speed in hand to prepare for an uphill landing, and intend to 'touch and go'. Having panicked when I did this for real, I feel I must commit, rather than make an unplanned landing." "That's a fair point." "I am ignoring the altimeter, and judge us to be at six hundred feet at the threshold, turning crosswind. Turning downwind. Turning on finals, mixture rich, side-slipping, wings level."

At this point Rob took control, and not before

time! The field was steeper than I had judged it to be, and he needed to make sure that it really was touch and go, because had I landed, we could not have taken off again! "How could you improve on that attempt?" "The field proved to be smaller and steeper than I had judged it to be." "You are dead right! You looked at the altimeter far too low (because it lags). It has been drummed into you to always judge your approach visually, and you are still not doing it! Had I not intervened, you would have overshot the far boundary to land in an even smaller field, or, even worse, gone through that barbed wire fence, causing a lot of damage to the aircraft!"

"I did much worse than I expected. It is difficult to snap-judge the size and slope of the field well enough in order to commit at a thousand feet." "But this is what you must learn, because you are demonstrably unsafe to fly solo until you have made progress at field landings!" I must have really looked upset by my dismal performance, and he did something about it. "There is a steep learning curve at this point in your tuition. Your grasp of technical matters will help you with this site assessment, but you must hack it now, or all your experience chalk-hill soaring will have been wasted. You **can** do it, so don't rush it. If your height gives you five minutes to choose, **take** five minutes. I saw two better fields before you picked that one."

We continued upwind at maximum climb speed, and he showed me his selection of fields, explaining why they were better. "You have seen little of the land downwind of the airstrip, so that's where we will look. You have control. Look around and pick a field. Give a commentary."

"I judge us to be eight hundred feet above our take-off point, maybe two minutes to pick a field." Rob started the stopwatch on his clipboard.

"I'll turn crosswind to extend my view downwind. You see that biggest field next to the road? While one **could** land on it, the overshoot is too dangerous, due to telegraph wires, so try again."

I thought he had picked something that I had missed. My dad used this tactic, so it was a fair bet that he was blocking my view. "The only pasture I can see is too rough." I was turning gently to my right, to see what he was concealing. "The access road beneath us ends at the big house, and the telephone wire ends there. Who's for cucumber sandwiches on the lawn?"

"Calm down, we don't want the neighbours upset." "I believe we've got five hundred feet beneath us, having taken off much higher." I whipped through the 'powered' landing checks, and turned onto finals rather high, so side-slipped down, letting the controls centralise at two hundred feet, and the ASI returning to 65kts. "Shall I overshoot now, rather than alarm the occupants?"

"Yes, and that effort was **much** better! You knew I was hiding this, didn't you?" "Yes, thanks to my deceitful dad. He ate so much off my plate that I should have been a 'seven-stone weakling' like Charles Atlas." "Well, he helped you out when you were at a low ebb, then." "That's why I'll never forget him." He chopped the throttle on me three more times, and I found a field each time, and achieved a well-planned approach. "Do you mind exceeding the hour, now you're progressing well?" "No. I've lost a lot of time because of poor weather, so there's plenty in the kitty." "Then how about soaring the nearest cloud street, just for fun, and then picking a couple more fields as we return?" "I'd love to. Shall I climb to a thousand feet and then chop the throttle?" "That'll do. Why waste fuel motoring up, when those clouds were put there just to do draw us gently into the heavens? There's the lift, switch off, and relax." "I seem to remember one of the Old Testament prophets being drawn up into a cloud. I'm pretty sure he wasn't paying instructional rates for dual instruction at the time, though."

"Having let it slip that someone else is paying for this, pulls the rug from under **that** gripe." "I was just testing your memory." With the motor off, the Falke quite changed in character. It was the first time today that turning off the motor had not put me under pressure. Soaring, it felt like a more solid, more comfortable T21b.

"In case you were wondering, 'cloud streets' occur at right-angles to the wind, on sunny days, in the presence of unstable air. In other words, you only get them when thermals are being created, but not always then!"

When they have formed their parallel streets, each street has become a huge roller of cloud, all rolling the same way. To cross the streets at right angles involves crossing sinking air (flowing down to a cloud shadow) followed by rising air (generated by warm air rising from a stripe of sunlit ground). "At Tewitts' Field, only private sailplanes and our Blanik have ever reached a cloud street from our winch, and we have nothing better." "How do you like the Falke now?"

"Much better. It is definitely not an under-powered light aircraft. When Tim used to tell me how much more fun the Super Cub is than the Trikes, I see that in one way, a Falke could be better again, in offering really economical flying, that you could operate it cheaply unaided, given a pasture for airstrip, and a barn to store it in. Not that that will ever happen!"

We turned at the end of the cloud, having gained six hundred feet from when I turned off the motor. My main complaints about my home site have always been the hopeless launch rate, and three-minute launches that result in mere winch-launched sledge rides. To accept a launch commits you to stay until last light, having stowed all the equipment away. Frankly, if you don't get to soar, it just ain't worth it. It **must** speed up instruction using a Falke, when every ball wins a coconut! And a cast of thousands is no longer required."

"Your tales from the Gulags bring a touch of colourful squalor to our decadent southern existence. We pride ourselves at Inkpen that even the vilest peasant (such as yourself) may redeem his serfdom to gain the freedom of the skies, given a big enough bag of gold!"

The first beat beneath the cloud took us to two thousand feet at the far end. "Isn't this a gentlemanly way to soar?" "It certainly beats marching up and down a working hill-slope, like prisoners exercising." "There I defer to your experience. Look, there's Sheepless Hill." "It is etched in my memory as 'Shitless Hill'." "Then let us exorcise that memory by landing there again."

"We'll be throwing a lot of height away." "You're

right. We'll do a loop, and maybe a spin recovery to follow, and then a mad moment following which you will land. Is that sufficiently action-packed for you?" "You got it, man!" He searched the sky, above and below.

"There are four things to remember about the loop. One, Vne, short for 'Velocity, never exceed'. You may dive the Falke at 90kts, which is enough to carry you over the top (you may dive the Blanik at 130kts). Two, always align your aircraft with a straight road or railway, so that you describe a ring, rather than a section of a spiral. You did it right when you hit the turbulence of your own slipstream. Three, never invert an aircraft that has not been cleared for aerobatics, because the battery will most probably fall out, to the detriment of your power (I have seen it happen). Four, check the cockpit, particularly the floor and under the seat for lost sandwiches, empty beer bottles, and cheques to bearer. All this stuff falling around you may remind you of snow falling at Christmas, but that beer bottle might fetch up behind a rudder pedal. You already did that. Down we go!" I lifted out of my seat against the harness as he nosed over. "We are diving towards that straight length of road. When I pull back into the loop, we will remain within Vne, which is what?" "90kts." "Correct." He eased the nose up, ramming us into our seats, and leaving my stomach behind until only the sky was visible, until it slid over our heads, leaving us held in our seats by centripetal force. The horizon reappeared from behind our headrests, inverted. Speed built up again, and then came the shudder as the Falke hit its own turbulence. As we shot upwards, Rob gently zoomed the excess speed off into height regained.

"We lost less than two hundred feet." "Check for other aircraft, then loop her. Ease her out of the dive, to avoid an excessive angle of attack, which would mush away height in a high-speed stall." I did a 360° turn, checking above and below, before diving. "All clear above and below, down we go." I don't think I managed too badly, but it was a somewhat egg-shaped loop.

As I eased out gently at the bottom, I rather overextended the top, which found us stalled and hanging from our harness, until the descent served as a stall recovery. This made it deathly quiet for the short period between falling nose-down and flying again. At least, it was less stomach-churning to be the clown at the controls oneself. "You ran off to the left, and stalled going over the top, when you should have been pulling G. It was more like a stall-turn" "Sorry. Could one initiate a flat spin while inverted?"

"No, that's limited to powered aircraft with a high polar moment of inertia, such as full tip tanks. A glider able to stabilise in a flat spin would never receive certification, in fact if that ever happened the test pilot would have to bail out, because you need power to get out of a flat spin. Every glider or aircraft I have flown has had enough inherent stability to adopt a right-way-up level flight when the controls were released. I would consider anything **less** stable to be unfit for training."

"The Tiger Moth can recover unaided from any attitude, given sufficient altitude, and resume straight and level flight at the speed to which it had been trimmed!" "I always suspected that most aircraft could manage better without my intervention."

"The two problems are, your aircraft might hit the ground, if left to its sort things itself. The other is, if a wing drops on finals, near stalling speed, it needs instant correction with the aileron, just a twitch but full movement. Otherwise a ground loop will happen while you are deciding what to do. This is the price we pay for the convenience of 'differential ailerons'. Do you know why?"

"This feature is intended to increase lift, and reduce drag. It uses leverage, by attaching the cables that pull the aileron down further from the fulcrum of the control column than the attachments that pull the aileron up. It is emphasised by the air beneath the wing sticking to the ground. The problem gliders have is a higher aspect ratio, and ailerons at the end of the wing have so much leverage for the drag they produce, that trying to pick either wing up can induce a yawing moment to that side."

"I'm sorry I asked! Should you ever suffer a ground loop, you've certainly got your excuse well-rehearsed! While turning, extra lift is required, so when we stabilise in a turn, we centralise the controls, while applying gentle back-pressure. We've got sufficient height for a spin now, so carry out all-round observation, and then spin her."

The Falke seemed readier to spin than the Barge, for which the weight of the engine must be responsible. It was still very quick and positive to recover, and then to stop rotation. "That was fine. Forget the field landing while your instructor has a mad moment."

We were upwind of Sheepless Hill at 1,300 feet, surely the worst situation from which to set-up an approach! Rob switched off the motor, pushed the nose down (while respecting Vne) to make a hedge-hopping low pass downwind. The ASI showed 90kts, and the wind speed of about 20kts meant we were going the wrong way over our landing run at 110kts! We wanted to be going the opposite way at 65kts.

This was exciting, what next? Rob eased the Falke into an ever-steepening climb, then a burst of throttle to ensure good response from the rudder respond to full movement of the left pedal that turned the wings like a windmill, so that the climb was converted into a dive within our own wingspan.

He selected rich mixture, applied full right rudder just long enough to stop rotation, waited for stall recovery to restore feel to the controls, and cross the controls in a slide-slip, which he had to change to fishtailing at about a hundred feet, because it is dangerous to side-slip too close to the ground because you might stall on finals. Then he applied full throttle to overshoot, and re-trimmed to climbing power.

"Your task now, is to show me a precautionary landing. This is the last resort of a cross-country pilot who has run out of lift while seeking a soarable slope, because if the slope isn't working, there is usually no other form of lift within reach. Powered pilots arrive at the same decision when they are contact flying, that is, navigating by map beneath cloud ceiling. Lucky them, they can always retrace their steps, and might even retreat to the last airfield they passed!"

We chugged slowly higher. "I'll level out here. The skill I want you to learn, is to quickly recognise a safe landing ground when you are flying into wind, and need to quickly assess a field ahead of you, even at a shallow angle ahead. You must be ready to land as you cross the threshold, which needs quick reactions and no turning back. Keep the power on. You are over Sheepless Hill, so it should be quite familiar!"

I knew the features we crossed during Rob's 110kts low pass downwind, and I passed parallel to that, a field away, turning crosswind at 700 feet and completing my powered pre-landing check. I then turned on finals at 400 feet, about quarter of a mile from the threshold, so we were just riding down the groove like a carrier landing, letting the Falke settle, with plenty of barley field ahead of us.

"That was good, I've got her." Rob pushed the throttle open for the overshoot, and motored round the top of the hill. "You would have touched down close to where you landed to claim it for the British Flag, if that was your intention. Once I saw where we de-rigged it, I found the neat little groove where you touched down. Return to the field and land."

That evening, back at the 'Plough', the forecast gave a succession of depressions, bringing high winds and rain for the rest of the week. I spent most of Thursday staring through the clubhouse window at the miserable conditions. I was glad to have the opportunity to think through the rest of my stay.

By the time the partners were ready to lock up for an early finish, I told them that I would return home on Friday. It was an opportunity, while they were not busy, to thank them for all their help. I told them that I had serious doubts whether I could afford the degree course that my mother was so keen on. I was now convinced that I could still get a living sheep farming, but not without a chunk of capital, and I couldn't afford to postpone farming to take a degree and incur debt doing so. "My mum is remarrying in Western Australia this summer, and it is her fiancé that stood me my stay here."

It was Rob who asked the obvious question. "What's that got to do with flying?" "I've already accumulated twenty-five hours of dual on his Super Cub, and Mum's giving me enough cash to take my PPL at Mount Isa. She and her partner have started an agency for Polish White Eagle light aircraft, what the Poles use for artillery spotting.

"I'm pretty sure they are hoping I will work for them, but it just isn't a real job to me. My dad and grandpa were hill sheep farmers, and our family will nearly all have been, and we've lived there four hundred years. My only other living relative lives and teaches ten miles away, and might well visit them every year, but there's no way I can, with livestock in my care."

"Does this mean that your decisions about a degree and what you intend to do will come as news to your mum?" "Yes, Rob." "Well, you had better break it gently. I bet she might expect you to stay there till September, when she'll be expecting you to start at university. You must at least hint at your intentions as soon as you get back, and it will make for a traumatic parting, if she thinks she may never see you again."

"I know, but she made the changes, and it is too much to expect of me to lead her life and postpone my own until she chooses to retire." As soon as I got back to the pub, I rang Helen to let her know that I would get back to Preston late Friday afternoon, and ring her to be collected.

"Whatever is wrong, to bring you back early?"

"Nothing worse than bad weather. I've got in a couple of hours solo, and about three hours of dual, but bad weather is forecast for the rest of the week." No problem then, other than Hazel is staying in your absence, so you'll be on the settee until the weekend." "That's great. I'll look forward to seeing you all and telling you my news." The return journey was a further opportunity to go over my plans for the next few years. Of course, Jane had her future planned before she sat for School Cert, and would still be committed to her law firm until she had worked there for a few years.

That would separate us by launching me into farming, not a degree, while she still had so many ties running on for years. It would be really important to keep in touch with both her and Aunt Hazel, and neither of them would be pleased that I will be more or less abandoning Mum in Australia. It was tempting to think of my weeks in Oz were just the prelude to launching myself into farming three years before it would otherwise happen. I settled back on the train with four hours stretching ahead of me, and let my thoughts roam.

My judgement had improved, resulting in better planned approaches. On as airstrip much smaller than Tewitts' Field, this was something to be proud of. My confidence had improved when I found that I enjoyed the simple aerobatics I had learnt as much as the spin recoveries that I was already familiar with. Three areas of my flying required improvement.

Firstly, I must avoid those switchbacks in confidence that could turn minor fumbles into near-misses, and make success the prelude to disaster. Other priorities were emerging in my life. There was the ever-present danger of losing touch with friends and relations through seldom seeking the company of others.

Let's face it. The small progress I have made in gliding has been at the expense of friends and family. I was over-borrowed on their goodwill, and it was becoming apparent that there was little point in pursuing the hobby further, because it couldn't coexist with stock-raising.

It dawned on me that Jane had long since worked all this out, and just as I was suddenly faced with the likelihood of what Helen would take to be a brutal disowning of her after her wedding, it was probably pretty obvious to Jane that there were any number of things that might separate us over the next four years. This would lead her to keep me at arm's length until each knew what the other wanted from life rather than take anything for granted years before it could ever come to anything.

The only thing I was willing to concede was that I would indeed sit HSC before I left. Great minds must think alike, because when I rang to announce my arrival at Preston, Tim answered the phone, and came to collect me. I was glad of the chance to thank him properly for paying for my time at Inkpen. I felt it had been most helpful in extending my skills. He listened to all I had to say about flying the Blanik and the Falke before making the points he was waiting to raise.

CHAPTER 15

Under Capricorn

———❧———

"I've managed to sort the problem of the two leased White Eagles in Ireland. It's been a lousy start to our dealership, and I was tempted to return to Oz or New Zealand and start afresh, where I reckon I could drum up enough new business to generate more turnover to get the agency off the ground than we could do here.

"Helen disagreed, and the long and short of it is, nothing will change till you leave school. She insists that we make our breakthrough in the UK, **before** moving to Oz. She insists that if success is possible, it is possible **here**, but should do better there. She told me very firmly that I am not going back to my folks with my tail between my legs, but having sold a going concern."

By now we were at the outskirts of Longridge, and Tim pulled into a lay-by to finish what he had to say.

"Before you start, Tim, I've changed **my** ideas. I realise that I've wasted hours slogging away at laying drains and digging ditches. Things aren't always good for you just because you don't like doing them. Your gift of two weeks' tuition at Inkpen has finally made all my efforts worthwhile. By soloing and some decent tuition, I feel I've got somewhere with my flying, which has led me to re-focus on my career."

He looked embarrassed. "I'm not sure I'm going to like what you have to say. You earned what I gave you. We reckon that we can consolidate the business, and prepare a set of accounts for selling the business around June. We won't get as much as we would get with three years' accounts to show, but we don't intend to put our lives on hold for that long.

"Hazel hopes to come with us, having asked me to give her an intro to the Kimberley Institute for a year's sabbatical doing botanical research, which will be great for Helen. If you get university entrance, Hazel will take you for vacations. When you graduate, we'd like you to spend some time with us to see whether you take a job there, or return here."

"I've had some thoughts about that, Tim." "Whoa there! I'm not your flamin' agony aunt, so save it for Helen, right?" "If you're **that** scared of her, I will." "D'you think she has the 'ute bugged, Ralph? Both our heads might roll if there was any hint of conspiracy!" He grinned slyly. "I almost forgot Jane! Helen invited her to dinner, and we are on the way to collect her, now."

"Then why am I sat here, pretending to listen to you? Convey me to my intended, and don't spare the horses!" Jane heard the Land Rover draw up, and ran to greet me as I got out. As she hugged me, I was reminded of my selfishness. I had only spoken to her once during my absence. It seemed unlikely that any interest of hers might shut me out of **her** life, but once at university this would certainly be more probable. "It's great to see you again, Jane." I sensed some reserve, and felt that a kiss might not be welcome. I gave her a peck on the cheek, and squeezed her hand.

We went in so I could say hello to Brian and Daphne. They eased my embarrassment by warmly congratulating on my achievements at Inkpen. They left me feeling that they, too, thought that I had seized a golden opportunity, which was funny, because **I didn't**. Jane said, "I suppose, in its way, it is as important as university is to me."

I could only reply, "Of course it isn't. **Sheep farming** is." "I needed to remind you that if I can get on the honours course, it will take an extra year." "So be it. That would be a much better launch to your career. It will focus my mind on keeping in touch with you, rather than living like a hermit."

Tim drove us back to the house, where we went inside to greet Helen and Hazel. Helen was in control, as usual. "Ralph, get everyone a drink. There's fizz in the fridge. I'll have our meal ready in quarter of an hour. Get your small-talk out of the way, because we have big issues that concern us all, that need airing."

The meal was like Christmas all over again, but without Chet. I don't think Hazel was the only one who missed him when she wanted to toast my success, and now the embarrassment about the leased aircraft had been dealt with, we all looked forward to meeting him again.

Hazel rose, and waited for silence. "Nothing I have to say is of much consequence compared with your impending marriage. I just wish to drink your health and wish you both well, and I am sure that Jane and Ralph share that wish."

I leapt to my feet to collect the two bottles and tray of glasses from the kitchen. I commenced serving the wine, as the toast must be drunk before anything else intervened. "Have your say, Aunt Hazel, while I pour."

"I heard that Tim had put Rachel Breslau in touch with the Kimberley Institute. I was already seeking permission from the school governors for a year's sabbatical in botanical research. I am corresponding with the institute to seek their assent. If I succeed, I can travel with you, and attend your wedding. We all want to hear what Ralph has to say, but it must wait while we drink your health before the fizz goes flat. Here's to Helen and Tim!"

We rose as one, and drained our glasses. Hazel spoke again. "I don't suppose Ralph considers his time at Inkpen to be much to boast about, but we think it merely puts the cherry on the cake of much-improved academic work since Alec's death. So I will top your glasses up to drink to him, while he has his say."

"I feel embarrassed to be toasted by you all, because it isn't such a big deal to me. When Dad died, I was certain that the most important thing he had done previously was to buy himself out of the army, at the peak of his career, where he had a great reputation, and was well respected. Short as his farming career was, that was what I intended to carry forward from what he had done, in Grandpa's footsteps.

"Several people have bent their efforts to get me through university entrance, but if I take that route, I will lose three years of farm experience, and be burdened by debt while needing an agricultural mortgage to buy or rent more pasture, and re-stock it. Never mind if that leaves me with no alternative job, this is the job I've been involved with for my whole life, so I'll willingly sink or swim!"

Helen was obviously upset by this. Hazel looked at her, and covered her confusion. "Chet had more to tell me. He has returned to Cuba to complete his national service, which he evaded by joining the US Merchant Service.

"I persuaded him to first send an open letter in the Guardian to the Cuban Ambassador in London stating that he felt that he owed this to his native country, but hoped that he wouldn't suffer as a result. The Guardian published a rather huffy letter from the Ambassador saying that they are a civilised country, and Mr Berrigan need not fear punishment, having served the twelve months conscription that was due from him."

"Good on yer, Chet! Never was a Cuban passport more dearly bought. That's as close as he'll ever get to sticking his head in a lion's mouth." Helen had now collected herself, and we all bustled about clearing the table while she made the coffee. She brought the tray in, and got discussion rolling. "Now, Jane, tell us what you will be doing a year from now." "I'm seeking sponsorship for an honours law degree. It would take three years, and having paid for that, my sponsors would of course expect a reasonable return for their money. As they are based in Blackburn, I will need to commute there when I finish at Aberystwyth."

Again, Helen had the wind taken out of her sails. Here was a girl of Ralph's age who knew what she could be doing in six years' time. Come to think of it, so did he! Had either of us bothered to ask her, we would already know, too. "Thank you, Jane. You seem to have been the one amongst us who had had most success with planning ahead. Tim has an announcement to make. The floor is yours, Tim."

"Helen and I are engaged!" We all clapped and cheered. "Of course, the sooner we marry the better, as far as I am concerned. St Bart's would be just the ticket, but Helen has been so generous as to point out that my family, who outnumber hers, might prefer us to tie the knot in Kununurra. Ralph and Hazel are her only close family, and it looks as though they are both able to be present at the end of the summer term.

"I s'pose I was a bit green when I started thinking about the agency, and it was Chet who was suggesting a bank that would help me, and how to go about setting up a business. I soon found out that Helen was better informed about business matters than either of us. It has not been a bed of roses. Still and all, I've chewed things over with our accountant, and we no longer seem to be harbouring any hot potatoes.

"I've bought back the two aircraft leased in the Republic. I've a dozen machines leased to flying clubs. No-one's sharing profits with us, and we're still chasing up new leases. So, everything is set to go, and there's champagne chilling if you would care to drink the health of a very happy pair of newly engaged youngsters."

Hazel rose, and waited for silence. "Nothing I have to say is of any consequence, compared to my wish to see your ring, and drink your health, and I'm sure that Jane and Ralph must feel the same." I rose to my feet. "Carry on, Aunt Hazel, while I bring the drinks and glasses in, and get pouring." "I heard that Rachel Breslau had asked Tim for a letter of introduction to the Kimberley Institute, and decided that a year's sabbatical on botanical research was just what I needed, too. I cleared it with the headmaster and the governors, and my job will be waiting for me when I return.

"While we want to hear anything Ralph might want to say, he has nearly finished pouring, and we don't want it to go flat while we listen to his blether. So here's to the happy couple, to Helen and Tim!"

We all rose to our feet and clinked glasses before drinking their health. I hovered around topping up glasses, as it looked mean to be left with any! Hazel tapped on her glass with a knife. "Quiet please! Let's hear what Ralph has to say!" "I took up gliding eighteen months ago. I soon realised that I was getting nowhere until Tim showed up, and asked me to collect his avgas for him, in exchange for a little dual instruction on his Super Cub.

"My fears that I might soon be splashed all over the front page of the 'News of the World' were soon allayed when it became clear that his interest lay elsewhere. I continued to learn from him, and when he was contracted to collect two Britannia College sailplanes from Sutton Bank, he demonstrated the whole navigational procedure from ordering a forecast from Air Traffic Control (Broughton) to calculating the Dead Reckoning to give us the elapsed time both to and from Sutton Bank to the average speed and the track made good and drift in both directions.

"As icing on the cake, he stood me two weeks' gliding instruction at a chalk hill soaring site at Inkpen. For a while, I was trying to see a possible livelihood in flying, but I was kidding myself. I will go ahead and take my PPL while in Australia, but with the least possible expense, and that will be the end of it. It is necessary to fly five hours a year to renew one's PPL, but why bother? It isn't worth the expense, and I'll have loans to repay. I still think it worth taking the PPL, because it keeps open the possibility of helping you if my own plans come to nothing, but that's it."

Helen had shown only her bossy side since my return, but now she redeemed herself. "Alec did leave a little money for you. I had hoped to have 3,000 for university, but I can't make you go if you don't want to. I was going to put aside two thousand for your PPL, if that's what it takes you." Helen rose to her feet.

"Ralph must be worrying about how everything will pan out for him. I can set his mind at rest, I think. Alec and I had discussed his future, and budgeted for the possibility of funding possible degree studies, with what we could scrape together towards working capital for the farm. In addition, I have included money from my savings to cover his training to PPL level. There is £3,000 set aside for your university course, and what remains is yours to reignite your stock rearing enterprise at Tewitts' Field. It will slightly reduce your borrowing."

She didn't want Alec belittled by Tim's generosity. She had received a life interest in Alec's estate, and clearly, a chunk of this has been sold. It was for me to trust that she would leave me what she was able to, which was all that Dad would have expected of her.

"Gosh, thanks, Mum! Then once I've sat HSC, we can light out for the territories. You two will find your new home and workplace, while I'll do my social butterfly bit at the Isa. I never wanted to disappoint you about taking a degree, but Alec didn't deserve **his** fate, either. We just have to play the cards we've been dealt."

It only dawned on me about this time, where I had misunderstood Mum's crack about the dairy herd delivering 'five per cent return from money borrowed at fifteen per cent', which was intended to deceive. If it was true of the cash-flow state, it certainly didn't describe the **capital** state. The dairy production depended on breeding from those cattle still capable, every year, to keep them in milk.

The milk cheque was the cash flow produced, and **in addition** we gained that annual increase in the herd, to either get more milk, or sell on. I thought it pretty low to insult Alec in that way. Helen went upstairs to get her engagement ring and pendant to show us. This moved Tim to address us.

"Mark this well, all of you. Alec deferred to Helen's financial decisions, as I too am ready to do. When we leave for Australia next summer, just remember that I told you today that this country is **going to Hell on a handcart!** I'm no genius, it must just take an outsider to see the way things are changing.

"I'm putting my money where my mouth is by stockpiling avgas. I'd sell up and leave, at any price, but that would leave Helen to see Ralph through A-Levels. Let each of you consider how your planned future might founder."

I rose to my feet to propose the toast. "We all know and love Tim and Helen. **His** message to Great Britain is, **'Prepare to meet thy doom!'** Our message to him is, **you're the one holding a tiger by the tail!** As we celebrate their engagement, let us applaud their reason for postponing their wedding. Tim wants me to sit A-Levels before spiriting Helen away to foreign shores.

"Helen wants Tim's family to enjoy those celebrations in **their** local church. I'm grateful for the extra time I've been given. In parting with Helen, I shall lose not merely a mother, but a scullion, washer-woman, and financial backer too! May their concern for others return to them like bread cast upon the waters and their union be long and happy. And not lacking in soggy bread, either."

Tim actually blushed, and avoided our eyes, as Helen returned with a red morocco jewellery case. We all expected something striking and colourful.

The ring itself he produced from his pocket and placed on her finger, giving her a lingering kiss. She opened the case to put on the enclosed pendant, and then walked around the room so each of us could have a good look.

The ring was a large fire opal, and the pendant a sun-burst with all the stones, of course, cabochon cut, a round one in the centre, with four elongated stones radiating from it. They looked opaque and milky in our cold northern light. Next day, I saw them in sunlight come to life in a blaze of green-edged scarlet and orange.

Because of high winds at the weekend, no-one showed at the clubhouse. A group-training scheme had commenced in my absence, and fate had struck again. One of my ewes (which would have been penned up had I been present) had charged the Blanik in a beam attack during its landing run.

It was away for repair until 1974, but with so much extra duralumin riveted on the rear fuselage that it was always lacking the nose-down trim available on the trimmer tab. With both two-seaters missing, the club was leaking cash, and I was OK, having converted to the Swallow.

We were soon to be reminded of Tim's words, firstly in October '73, when oil prices rocketed, and again in December, when the bank rate rose to thirteen per cent, and power economies were enforced. They even banned Sunday launches at gliding clubs. When we met again for another enjoyable Christmas holiday, Tim was big enough not to say, "I told you so."

In February '74, Ted Heath went to the country asking for a mandate to beat the Miners' Strike, and lost in March. Harold Wilson accepted the Miners' terms, and the price spiral commenced. By superhuman efforts (and helped by stockpiled avgas) Tim continued to operate profitably. Helen felt honour-bound to put her shoulder to the wheel. She had talked him out of selling up to make a fresh start in Oz, and so considered it to be her fault. To his credit, he had not overridden her wishes.

She charmed or bullied prompt payment from his clients, and hungrily canvassed his customers for sales prospects, or at least for leases. When an aero-club with three White Eagles was struggling to pay, she suggested that Tim buy one back, which he sold at a good profit.

They struck sparks off each other in their efforts to trade successfully in the most difficult circumstances that had yet occurred in the 20th century. Tim kept his airframe fitter busy, and pared expenses to the bone.

Among pilots of light aircraft the White Eagle was becoming familiar, and was considered far superior to those Austers that were still airworthy. As both were selected as artillery spotters, one important difference was that the White Eagle's body section at the cockpit was almost an inverted triangle, so that under each wing you could lean outwards to see things almost beneath you.

This became easier by banking slightly to each side. As Helen put it in her sales pitch, "It's all eyes and wings, like a dragonfly." Operators found it simple, rugged, and easy to repair. They also appreciated its low stalling speed, and the short landing run which this afforded. Simply due to the speed at which aircraft developed in WW2, it was stronger, lighter, had more reliable electrical components, and a lighter, more economical and more powerful engine. What was not to like?

"Next subject. You were bowled over by Rachel, by a combination of her quick brain, and her total confidence, based on being the spoilt child of wealthy parents. Had you chosen university, you would have met dozens like her. Jane would stand out from the crowd, even at Oxbridge. In fact you are probably her only weakness! Never mind, she will meet loads of guys anxious to take her off your hands."

"Thanks a bundle, Tim. I can't wait to make her mine, and feel inferior for the rest of my life! To be serious though, there's a fatal flaw in your kind offer to promote me cabin boy on the Clancy yacht." "Which one? I can think of thousands." "Having me around when you are married to my mother." "Let's face it mate, we're already living in the same house, and we've managed to dodge you so far. You'll find that in Australia, we don't all live on top of each other, like you Pommies. You'll also earn your keep, never fear. So you'll be financially independent, not forced to share the parental roof, like some less refined version of Harold Steptoe."

"Thanks, cobber. Helen's lucky to have bagged the last Australian gentleman!" "So I keep telling her!"

Silence reigned for a while. Eventually, I broke it. "Doesn't proper coffee give you a thirst? I'd better get a couple of beers from the fridge." "Those are the first unselfish words you have spoken today. Jump to it!" In all but my studying, that end-of-term feeling was dissolving my other commitments.

I couldn't be bothered with the gliding club, knowing that I would be in Australia shortly after leaving school, and light aircraft would get my total attention until I had my PPL. Then my attention would switch to how, under present circumstances, it would be possible to extract and income from the farm.

I had been considering accumulating a pedigree of Lleyn sheep, and was now weighing them against beef cattle. They would start paying in the first year, given decent pasture for them, a cattle trailer, and housing. I would also need to fully stock my herd on the fell, and 'fold them all on mangolds' while they were 'in lamb'. Then back to the fell till the next lambing season. The best way to seek beef pasture, would be to rent it from someone I know, who would care about the security of my cattle.

CHAPTER 16

Chet Lives!

—※—

Flying out to Darwin, we stopped over at Bombay, late in the monsoon season. For three months, it is washed by the same rainfall that Manchester gets in a year. We drove from Juhu Airport into town in a downpour, I couldn't wait to see what the city might offer. I first explored the old pedestrian part around Walkeshwar Temple, with its huge 'tank' for purification before entering. Hindu worshippers bathed in the pool after bathing to focus their minds.

It wasn't pedestrianised as a new feature, it was the legal area where judges and lawyers dwelt, and was still a no-go area to wheeled traffic because the steps and cobbles were the deterrent! There was so much worthy of colour photographs, the sky constantly washed clean, with vast pillowy cumulus clouds boiling up against a blue sky.

Yellow stone Victorian buildings housed the

chambers which bore the brass plates of judges and barristers. The rain pelted down, and then for a while it was all sunshine, blue sky, and piling clouds. Helen dragged Tim round the 'Khadi' stores, each one marketing the crafts of its region on a co-operative basis. This initiative had been favoured by Gandhi to compete with the factory-produced goods that Victoria's reign had brought.

You need people made wealthy by industry, of course, to have anyone who can afford hand-made goods, fabrics, and paintings from Kashmir, or brassware from Benares. I guess lots of the wealthier middle class who supported congress, bought khadi goods out of respect for Gandhi.

Helen lingered longest in the Kashmir emporium. She bought some Moghul lacquer ware, which mostly had the insubstantial feel of papier-mâché. It seems such a waste to expend costly hand work on a base that will eventually get wet, and return to being old newspaper!

Helen bought herself a salwar-khameez outfit, as favoured by the local students of all religions, although it was intended to protect the modesty of Muslim ladies. As the students all had them tailored as close fitting as possible, it doesn't work out that way.

They comprised a close-fitting shirt ending above the knee, with loose trousers ending in a cuff at each ankle. Comfortable to wear, and protection against dust and hot sun. Hers was made from sari-length dark blue silk, which had its end weighted with an ornate pattern woven in gold wire on the warp end, so that it formed the bottom front of the khameez.

We spent hours at the European swimming club at a rocky beach called Breach Candy. The European community had raised funds for the survivors of a 19th-century shipwreck. When the last survivor died, they bought this plot of land on Vir Narriman Road with the remaining capital, and built a sea pool cut into the rock, and above it a fresh water swimming pool with diving board surrounded by a garden with a cafe, and as much land again for a European hospital.

The really weird thing is, almost a hundred years later, and twenty years after independence, no Indians were admitted! The exclusive Willingdon Club near the race course, had long since admitted those Indians wealthy enough to afford it!

Our hotel, a functional-looking concrete block, served as a permanent base for British United aircrews sleeping over. It also served as a staging post for Cuban military advisers en route for China.

It was difficult to imagine anything other than rum and dancing that they knew more about than the Chinese did! They were difficult to tell apart, as they all wore olive fatigues with a cap more like a French képi than a baseball cap. Most of them had beards, which didn't help. They kept to themselves, possibly fearing that chatting to Americans or Europeans might arouse suspicion.

One evening at dinner, wondering how to occupy the evening, Tim suggested a taxi trip to Juhu Beach, next to the airport. It had been a popular venue for Gandhi's political meetings, because of the nearby shanty towns to serve as dormitories for labourers moving to Bombay to seek work. It had little else to recommend it, owing to the habit the jobless have in these parts, of finding someone to stand and stare at.

I took our driver to be a Sikh, as many of them proved to be. They were almost invariably well turned-out, and often sought work in the armed forces, or the police. His beard was evidently wrapped around a rubber band, which was hidden beneath his turban, and his eyes invisible behind large sunglasses.

He was silent during the long, slow journey. Tim paid him off, while Helen and I bought three coconuts from a vendor, who neatly pared away the husk with a machete, before opening it with the final blow. Helen and I had almost emptied the contents of our nuts before Tim caught us up.

"What kept you, sweetheart?" "The guy claimed he knew me from somewhere. Gawd knows how many countries he went through before I managed to extricate myself. I think it was a ploy to extract a bigger tip. Ready for a swim, anyone? Ready? I'll race you to into the sea. Keep to the right of that seine net, or that will be another entanglement!"

We'd had enough after a couple of hours. The fishermen had spread their net between boats that must have been their version of Arab dhows.

Rather than haul the catch aboard, they preferred to have their shore crew wade out and unhitch the net from the boats to haul it ashore. Why should it have filled me with such awe? It had to be because they still used nothing not available in biblical times. Almost immediately another ancient practice came to light. We heard bleating, and a shepherd approached along the beach with a mixed flock of sheep and goats, foraging for palm fronds and other greenery that had arrived with the tide.

I wasn't really interested in the nuclear power station at Trombay, although that was the image that the government preferred to advertise. There was a group of young engineers and architects with what seemed to me to be of more practical help to everyday folk. They looked at what was up for grabs in scrap yards, and set out to make bullock carts more effective by fitting them with car back axles from scrap yards. It reminded me that I come from a 'throw-away' culture, and this was in the spirit of the old naval 'make-do and mend' sessions that were part of their weekly routine in the days of sail. These carts ran with less friction, and the tyres rode over the mud rather than sinking into it.

When we returned to where we had left our clothes, people were actually waiting there for us, for want of better entertainment! Europeans who came here to swim, must often have had to get in the car wet, dripping sea water onto the upholstery. I think at that time there were around 70,000 Europeans resident in Bombay, including many Eastern Europeans. We were still a major attraction to beggars, though, who pursued us (I presume) in the belief that we were tourists, and fair game.

Talking about this, Helen said, "Tomorrow is our last day here! Let's try and have a short sail, with some sight-seeing and a picnic, so we don't feel that our time here has been wasted! Tim, is there anything we can do that will spare us the unwanted attention of other people?"

"We could take the boat trip to the caves on Elephanta Island. The boat has awnings to shade you from the sun, and there's an on-shore breeze, so it tempers the heat."

"That sounds ideal! I'll ask at the desk if we can have a picnic lunch for the three of us." She also got us straw hats, a posh one for Tim, and even we anticipated getting plenty of use out of ours at our destination. "Is that one of the outings featured in 'A Passage to India'?" "No. I've only seen it on the box, but that was to Malabar Caves. Mind you there's loads of Australian novels I haven't read yet." "What, proper **books**, not just comics and picture books?" I asked. "Nothing that would interest **you**, no. As I was saying, that is why I avoid all this crap about 'bearing the White Man's burden'. Who are they kidding? The whole idea hinges on **them** carrying **our** burden."

Helen chipped in. "Pardon me for breathing, but I only accepted you proposal of marriage on the understanding that you were a white man, too!"

Our boat trip was a great success. Surely, everyone must love to visit islands. Elephanta was unspoilt, after the Portuguese left. Their soldiers and sailors used the Hindu statuary for target practice. The Catholic priests with them had probably been affronted by the many and varied sexual activities enjoyed by the figures, and encouraged their destruction.

We managed to stay close to a good guide, and even Tim was impressed. The guide explained that Buddhism had spread until they were in by far the greatest majority. Then Hinduism began making inroads in their numbers, not by violence or dispute, but mainly by including tribal people by claiming that Hinduism shared some of their beliefs, such as fire or sun worship. They had sixty distinct languages, and

279

loads of different dialects, so although the Mughal invasion had unified much of the north of the subcontinent, it was little wonder that until the arrival of the East India Company, they had never been completely unified.

We emerged from the caves with still an hour to occupy before the boat returned. We found a good spot for our picnic. Tim bought some mangoes. Our guide reappeared, and asked if he might eat with us. Helen made room for him, and gave him a mango.

He asked if we were on holiday, and I said that Helen and Tim were on their way to Western Australia to get married in Tim's home town. We were soon deep in conversation. Our guide had studied at Leeds University, and was keen to inform us what India had given civilization in the past, and what it hoped to do in the future. Helen and I felt that we had to be very careful what we said, to avoid causing offence.

She said afterwards, "India makes me feel like a rampant colonialist! Thank goodness Australians have hides like crocodiles, if they're all like Tim! Darwin, here we come!"

Next day, in the bustle of loading the taxi for the airport, it dawned on me that it was a driver we had used previously, to visit Juhu Beach.

Having arrived at the airport, we checked luggage, tickets, and passports. We had finally broken free of the endless form-filling. Indian nationals, and European residents all required tax certificates to prove that they didn't leave the country owing tax. Each time one ragged porter put down one item of baggage, another would pick it up, and hold his hand out. Finally, we were in a queue on the tarmac, waiting to embark. The steps were placed against the entrance, and a stewardess opened it from inside. "Oh Gawd, what now?" said Tim. "Look over there, near the control tower."

A black limousine had stopped there. Strangely, it bore CD plates, and more strangely still, a police officer emerged. He was tall and slim, with a service cap bearing his police badge on a yellow band. He had a revolver in a webbing holster on a webbing belt, with khaki drill uniform. He had two pips on his shoulder, and a swagger-stick.

He saw the flight crew emerge from the terminal, and stood, legs apart, slapping his palm with his swagger stick. "Hey, Captain!" he shouted. "Come here, please. I wish to tell you one thing." The captain spoke to his crew, who carried on boarding, while he approached with leisurely dignity. The police officer showed him a photograph, and he shook his head, before moving more briskly to board.

"You will remain here, I tell you!" Another 707 commenced take-off, and the policeman was forced to run after the captain, unable to make himself heard. "Hi, Bruce, what's on?"

"Hi, Tim, long time no see. This joker is after someone, and hopes to delay the flight while he checks through all the male passengers. We've got more than a hundred." A shrill voice followed him. "I shall postpone your departure!" "Henry! Check the passenger manifest for a Peter Gomes, travelling on a Portuguese passport."

The irate officer caught up with him. "Don't dare turn your back on me when I am speaking to you if you hope to leave Juhu today." Tim intervened "Why? Who might you be?" "I am Inspector Parikh." "Yeah? Well it will take more clout than **you've** got to interfere with Air Traffic Control." Tim put an arm around the man's shoulder, and gave him his best false smile. "I'll be glad to help, if I can. What's the problem?"

Delighted that someone might take some action, the inspector took out his photo. I looked over Tim's shoulder. It was obviously Chet, with beard and moustache. Someone had concealed the Cuban uniform with a black felt-tip pen.

"He's wasting your time, Bruce. He's not on official business at all. He arrived in that limo with CD plates, parked next to the control tower, and is just running an errand for one of the Embassies. If it was official, the police headquarters would have contacted the airport authorities."

That did it. Abandoning dignity, he hid his face in his cap and ran for it. Once in the car, it reversed at high speed until it had put a hangar between our aircraft and the car. "Helen, meet Bruce. Helen and I are to be married in Kununurra!" Even as Bruce congratulated them, a jaunty, cleanly shaven figure joined our party. "Thanks, Tim. It was the luck of the Irish that you were there to stop his gallop. Hi, everyone! Me name's Sean Costello, and I hail from the Republic. I guess I'm just enough like that photo to have spent weeks here answering questions, had they lifted me!" Bruce shook his head as we fell about laughing in the queue to board the 707.

"Hi, Ralph. Enjoy the drive to Juhu Beach?" That really floored me. I couldn't believe that I could spend forty minutes in a taxi with him, without recognising him. It was a brilliant choice of disguise. Admittedly, he had never previously kept silent in my presence for that length of time!

In fact he was still gabbing away ten to the dozen, in what he took to be an Irish brogue when the stewardess gave him his seat number. "Hey, sweetheart! May I move to be with my friends?" I had no sooner stowed my flight bag, than he handed me his, and settled in the next seat. "You've blown it yet again, Sean!"

"You can't say that without knowing the circumstances, Ralph. The Cuban Embassy replied to my open letter in the Guardian, saying that all in required of me was to complete the period of National Service that my country required of me in Cuba, to wipe the slate clean. OK? What actually happened was, back in uniform one week, and the next en route for China as a 'Military Adviser', instructing Chinese troops in US Counter Intelligence tactics, thus blackening my character with Uncle Sam.

"I'd caused the Cuban Embassy to 'lose face', right? The best scenario was, they weren't going to turn me loose till the Military Attaché in London retired. The worst scenario was, I'd be buried there!

"I always have a hole-card up my sleeve, and when I arrived in Ireland I changed my name by deed poll, and applied for Irish nationality! That was before I met Tim, and now I am an honest-to-God, card-carrying, Son of Old Sod!

"I guess you thought I was failing to clear Customs, and entering the UK illegally, which I never have done and never will do. If you think I have let you down by not telling you my legal name, you have now seen for yourself how dangerous my government can be in pursuit of its citizens!

"I was logging all my flying hours, as required, but you didn't know my name because that snippet of information would mean that they could reach out and lift me whenever the wished. That minor deceit was less important than the fact that I have broken no law in either the Republic, or the UK, nor do I ever intend to!

"So thanks to my open letter in the Guardian, a handful of people know that I am back completing my service to my country, and all is back to normal, but now you know differently. When I got to Bombay I thought another passport would speed my flight, but chose the wrong guy to buy it from.

"He sold me out to the Cuban consulate in Bombay as well. Knowing what you know, few would blame me, an American ex-serviceman, for dodging a posting in which I would be teaching Chinese servicemen American Counter Insurgence tactics. They wouldn't like that. So it was just as well that as the net closed on Peter Gomes, Sean Costello was buying a flight to Darwin on his American Express card!" "Gosh, Sean, that was brilliant!"

"You are right, Ralph, in your understated British way! My next hurdle is to get a work permit, as they are very keen that one gets one **before** coming here. Once I've got one, I'll get crop-spraying to earn a crust."

Tim chipped in. "I know a guy in the legislature in Perth that served in Vietnam, as you did. I can give you a letter to introduce you to him, and I'm pretty sure he will help you."

"Well, if he can, I think I could earn enough on the strength of one work permit in Oz, to return to my land of mists and mellow fruitfulness, to restart my air taxi business in a better-equipped way.

"As for Castro's heavies, I have a snippet of Industrial Espionage that I happened on by chance, that could feed poor mountainous areas all over the globe, that could portray him as Father Christmas to the poor and starving. If they accept it, and let me off the hook, that's fine by me. The patent holder will lose out, but that's life! If not, I'll write a piece for the papers about how Cuba is working to spread communist subversion through South East Asia. The Russians have supplied fighter-bombers to Indonesia that are faster than anything Oz has to stop them with. By the way, how is Hazel these days?"

"She is coming for the wedding. Actually, she is fitting in a work permit at the Kimberley Institute, which conveniently expires before 'The Wet', when we will return together. Do you consider selling what I take to be American patents to Cuba to be a 'victimless crime'?"

"I won't be selling it, but giving it away. Do **you** consider that letting poor people starve is a 'victimless crime'?"

He was then distracted by a stewardess passing. "Champagne for four, please, and we've plenty to celebrate, so be generous!" As we sipped our wine,

Tim brought Sean up to date with all the news since we were last in touch with him. "How did you arrive at Sean Costello? It does have a certain gravity to it."

"Well, Helen, before it was Chet it was Ché. Close enough to answer to. Costello is one of the many Hispanic names from the survivors from the Armada, whom they describe as 'Black Irish'. Having arrived as flotsam on Ireland's shore, they lost their appetite for zapping English heretics, and just grew spuds, instead. I also prefer to settle quietly there, rather than cash in on my recent success as a Yankee Imperialist."

Helen replied. "I like that. You can reach me at Tim's mum's address, and I'll give you contact details, and a wedding invitation. Hazel will be delighted to find you here. She expected you to be digging latrines for the foreseeable future."

"The chow wasn't great. I seemed to be **filling** latrines that long. However, you can forget all that. I have. My tourist visa will tide me over well past the wedding, but never fear, I will keep in touch. In Ireland, I'd spend for ever working for the bank's benefit. We've all gone straight from famine to feast. It is really worthwhile slogging my guts out here, so I can be working with my own capital when I return."

Hazel caught my attention. "Could Sean swap seats with me for an hour or so? There's something I've been wanting to discuss with you for a while, and this long flight offers an ideal opportunity. "Do you mind, Sean?"

"Yes, sure, Aunt Hazel. I'm intrigued to hear what you have to say." "Well oddly, it is something that I have always held to be precious, but my own views about it are starting to change. This could be a long session." "I've nothing better to do, so take your time."

"I'm sure our last Christmas at Tewitts' Field is fresh in your memory, specially that afternoon's walk that nearly ruined Christmas for all of us. This is what you need to know, to understand the seeds of discontent between Helen and myself, although we share the same views on almost everything else.

"Both your parents were raised in families long established in our local community. As in all other such cultures, oral history was passed down, and until universal education arrived, there is good reason to believe that it was passed down verbatim, as it still is in parts of Ireland.

"Unfortunately, once we succeeded in learning to read and write, it is very doubtful whether we may still trust our oral memories. Some of this oral history was jealously guarded because whatever one learned about one's own craft, was regarded as 'money in the bank', but to other people, any 'secret' knowledge might be salacious.

"This gave rise to intense secrecy, possibly more than could ever be justified. So what we were told and sworn to secrecy about, came to be passed on, skipping a generation. It would mainly be trade secrets, or farming lore passed from grandfather to grandson.

"It was kitchen gardens, cookery, and herbal medicine from grandma to granddaughter. Because Grandpa was a widower, he wanted to pass on what he knew to Helen, who being in her teens at the time, was suspicious when asked to take on more learning of a very secret nature.

"Strong-willed as she was, she managed to offend Grandpa, who thought she was both treating him as a 'dirty old man', and lacking respect for what he rightly considered to be valuable local knowledge, and a tradition that should be respected. I was very fond of him, and when Helen told me (which she shouldn't have) I asked Grandpa to tell me, because he was so upset.

"Unusually, Alec also refused to involve himself, so the few people who knew of this lore, which started in pre-Christian times, realised that their marriage would break the succession of its inheritance forever in your family. Unless, of course, you are prepared to learn what I know."

"I think I can guess immediately how your feelings have changed. At that time of universal education, someone should have broken ranks and printed what they knew, because what they retained accurately as illiterate beings, will have been corrupted by every succeeding generation.

"Much as I would like to discuss this with Jane, I realise would not be permitted. That is a strong reason for me not to take on a secret which might cause future embarrassment between us. The main value of your knowledge in this field, is as an amateur naturalist and trained botanist, who will have done her best to spot which of these memories have suffered corruption.

"Sad to say, the best thing you can do with it is to publish it as an interesting bit of social history, and as a piece of intelligence, it should rank as originating from an extremely reliable source. I would be extremely surprised if you have not already earmarked several items that would repay proper scientific research. Now Grandpa is no longer with us, I'm sure he would understand that you have made an honest choice in 'breaking the chain' rather than pass on corrupted information.

"I am sorry if I have been presumptuous in speaking like this to someone of years greater experience, but I'm fairly sure that I am only reinforcing things that you have already considered doing.

"On an entirely different subject, it is dawning on me that I can't do what I intended to do, which is get a livelihood up and running before considering how to hold our scattered family together. It might be too late by then, so, do you feel like more champagne with me, or would you prefer a coffee?"

"You are growing up quickly! You guessed rightly about my misgivings, and I might even make a start while I'm at the Institute – once Helen is married I'll have time to kill on my own. As to maintaining our family life, I'm definitely up for it! I'll drink a glass of champagne with you for a start, and we must do some of the tourist stuff around Kununurra, whenever we are both around"

Tim had something to say to me, too. "I've been waiting for a word with you. I guess it would be easier for Kerry not to have us all at home at once. I can buy you a ticket from Darwin to Mount Isa, and give you a cheque to open your own bank account when you get there, and square up with Helen later.

"Give us a little time on our own, before we are

prospecting for a resort airstrip with a great home on it, awash with spendthrift prospective pilots! And you will get the bit between your teeth, with cash for up to thirty hours, plus enough cash to feed yourself for three weeks or so."

I told Helen later. "This is short notice." "You'll settle in faster, without me to bother about. Try and keep the pressure off Tim, Ma. You'll get along with Kerry like a house on fire. I'll be in touch, and we'll arrange some time together before the wedding."

On arrival at Darwin, things were hectic until I waved them off. Sean waited to see me off, before taking a taxi into town to do business. "I might look you up at the Isa, sport!"

CHAPTER 17

"To Wives and Sweethearts"

If you can still remember the first chapter, it ended with me in a police cell, writing a précis of my life so far. When I look at it now, it just begged more questions than it answered. Why had I banged on about Bud Maturin, when Tim was very obviously wooing my mother enthusiastically? It can have been of no concern to me. Any other explanation fails to fit. Mum wanted a flirtation.

I looked at everything through Dad's eyes, but I was still happy to ignore 'the elephant in the room'. From meeting Tim, I made steady progress with my flying, but to be honest, I was always clear that flying would never have any bearing on my livelihood. It was almost as if everybody else thought that my growing interest was worthwhile, and I was riding the bandwagon. My school work was definitely improving, and there was loads of stuff I was eager to learn.

I had never forgotten that Mr Bradshaw was certain he could get me a good GCE if I applied myself, which had always been the case. He was happy. I was happy. Up to Dad dying, I always knew what had to happen next, and that I would gradually spend more time occupied with the running of the farm, but suddenly nothing was certain any longer. I was not helping Mum around the place, but she was happy with what I was doing.

When Mum married and remained settled in Australia, she might expect that I would tag along eventually, even if I tried something else first. One problem was that I was far less 'street-wise' than my school mates, having no social contact outside school. So I went straight from being years behind my schoolmates socially, to finding myself in a foreign country with money in my pocket and sexual urges to satisfy.

There had never been any prospect that I would consider staying there, so if the consensus was that once I was recognised as one of the Clancy in-laws, I would have to behave like one – I knew different! I was all set when she married to hit the buffers with the throttle still open!

I never saw any problem with achieving my PPL, not least because it had never been important to me. The contracts came and went, and it was getting near enough to the wedding for Sean to leave a gap in our series of contracts, to get ourselves to Darwin for wedding suits, presents for bridesmaids, and the whole rigmarole.

Sean told me to volunteer to collect a wedding cake and take it with me, because he didn't reckon there would be much better than a cupcake to be had in Kununurra. Suitably equipped and attired, Sean flew from Darwin, while I drove, having been reminded to adjust my watch when crossing into Western Australia. Tim's mum found me a trailer caravan to stay in, beneath the shade of a eucalyptus tree in a paddock adjacent to the owner's bungalow.

Helen, Hazel and I did a furtive round of the local tourist attractions, which the Clancys slightly disapproved of, having known the place before it had been developed. She had lots to talk about, what with selling off the agency, and getting our property into good nick in case we wished to rent it.

"Tim promised me to find us a home to my liking, before immersing himself in the new business. So we are looking for a great place to live, bearing in mind that it has to work as a sales agency. He thinks we will most probably fill the bill in the Whit Sunday Islands, a popular destination, but none the worse for that. It clearly has to benefit from people coming and going, so what's wrong with a popular destination? They are always passing that way, to and from the Great Barrier Reef. It had what estate agents call 'a good footfall'.

"It certainly qualifies as a change from managing a Creamery in Chyppen." She sighed. "I never expected to be making a new start without Alec. I shall never forget the happiness we shared. Now I need to share this new happiness with you and Hazel, to make the most of your visit."

"I hadn't intended to rain on your parade. Just when you were looking like Sylvester, about to swallow Tweety Bird."

"Speaking of which, as soon as Tim and I leave, you will be after Rachel like a rat up a drain. Sean was telling me that you have been 'very physical' recently. Just because **he** thinks he has to sleep behind a locked door (the mad, impetuous boy!) doesn't mean that **she** is in any danger."

"Yeah? Well the fact that it worries **him** worries **me** to death!" "You don't doubt the reasons she gave, do you? That idiot Bruce, that she works for, expected her to feel flattered to be 'wooed by bronzed surfies' as he put it." "No, I accept that **that** happened. I definitely think she would be upset to get the same treatment from **you**."

Heeding my mother's words of warning, I kept things light-hearted when I called on her, one evening. This was difficult, as she only wore a white bikini beneath a sarong, as she put the poultry in their sheds at last light. "Would you mind taking me into town? I haven't visited for a while. I'll be changed in no time."

As we drove, she asked me how I had enjoyed the PPL course at Mount Isa. "Does that mean we could go sight-seeing from the airfield?" "Of course. I wasn't sure if you would be interested after the hours you must have flown with your dad."

"The thing is, here it is always going to be a pleasure, outside the Wet. It might impress these spotty adolescents at the Institute, to see me being squired around by a man! Oh no. Here are three of them now."

Easily parrying their suggestion that we should join them for a drink, she left them standing on the pavement while she flung her arms around my neck to kiss me, in an assumed show of affection for me. Was this to deceive them, or me?

Soon afterwards, she spotted Sean drinking coffee. It was that sort of town, I guess, where you might meet everyone you know. She suggested that we join him. As I planned my outing with her, she plied Sean with questions. To get back into the conversation, I tried to impress Rachel with the differences between driving and flying in Oz and the UK.

"You were right about one thing, Rachel. So often, when you'd leave the plane in the hangar, in the UK, it would be less effort to fly in Oz..." Of course, all this was new to me, but Sean had flown (and driven) in many countries. Before I had finished speaking, Sean had told her which aircraft hire firm had the best terms, the best viewpoints, how to string them together in the best order, so as to catch each in full sunlight.

He aroused my suspicion by draping an arm around my neck, so I looked around to find his reflection in a mirror. Sure enough, the hand on the end of the arm around my neck was making 'motor-mouth signs', which was bloody cheek when he had just spoken for ten minutes on end, without pausing to draw breath!

A swift squeeze on his windpipe shut him up, while I interjected. "I have the strange gift to play this man as if he was a stringéd instrument." He replied with sarcasm. "May I reply with a vote of thanks for your informative lecture?"

"As I recall, the lady chose to pick my rather more

adult brain on the subject of aerial sight-seeing. I had been vaguely aware of a faint bleating in the background, and courtesy would shortly have led to me yielding the floor to you. He went on to give her a concise and thorough briefing covering where to apply for club membership, and a 'blood chit', to a list of landmarks, arranged in a circuit."

Then Rachel had something to tell us. "Exploring, in my lunch hour, I've found a track clearly pre-dating the dam, that leaves the Duncan Highway in the direction of the dam, and disappears into it. There's easy access to the shore, and nobody using it. I thought if Sean could spare his pickup we could have a picnic there today?"

"You've no further demands, I trust? I've bought you coffee, been chewed out by Clyde, arranged hire of a Cessna 150 for Bonnie, and now she hijacks my truck! Am I in a hostage situation here?" Rachel fluttered her long, curling eyelashes at him. "You catch on real fast, Irish Gringo!" "I don't think my friend Hazel would approve of this, and I'm sure Helen wouldn't." "Do you think I stand the slightest risk from your apprentice? The keys!" With one last bluster, he surrendered them.

"I won't tolerate any complaints about your behaviour while it is in your charge, and I want it back as it is now, washed and gassed up!"

"You've got it, that's how you'll get it back." I could see he was upset, and sought some emollient words. What came out was, "Out you hop, Jiminy Cricket, I'll **always** let my conscience be my guide!" We left for the shops. "Let's grab a sandwich and go bush!" I shouted.

She cranked the eyelashes round to engage me. "A barbie is much more atmospheric. I won't eat again until the sun goes down. We can swim first, and then relax with a little wine. These spur-of-the-moment parties are always the best ones!"

With provisions and the barbecue on board, we parked on a bare red bluff overlooking the Great Water. "Let's see what the water's like. Grab the towels, and follow me!"

I grabbed the towels, and my trunks, and followed, already fifty yards behind, and losing ground. There were boulders near the water's edge, but they didn't slow her down at all.

She made for a sheltered inlet where a dry creek entered the lake. As I descended, she was skipping from boulder to boulder, screaming shrilly. Pausing to shed her clothes, in a flash she was diving in one hundred yards ahead. It didn't look as if she had a costume on, but if she hadn't, there was no way of telling, and no loss of dignity.

She was totally in control, as she was much faster, whether on land or swimming, so I was never going to get any closer than she intended me to. I thought discretion the better part of valour, and sought to put my trunks on, but they didn't look to have been worn for years, and the elastic was backed up with a drawstring, very tightly knotted.

They must have been last dried with chlorine in, perishing the cord, which snapped at the knot. I just got them on, but might have to cut them off with scissors after I got home. She zoomed around the lake like a wet bike, doing crawl, while I proceeded at a sedate breaststroke.

About an hour later she came within hailing distance. "I'm getting out now. Give me at least ten minutes before you follow, so I can dry myself, right?" "Yes. Take your time." I was generous with the time, and she was drying her hair still. One towel was kilted round her waist, while the other covered her breasts while she dried her hair.

She laughed at my pop-eyed ogling while she tossed me the towel she had been using on her hair. "Turn round, Ralph." She towelled my back vigorously. After a while she moved away. "You'd better light the barbie before you get dressed. That's your job. You coped with that better than you expected, didn't you? Because we're mates, you kept your schoolboy fantasies in check."

She had looked so fantastic with a towel around her waist that I had to remind myself that my future was with Jane, and there was no chance of spending my future with Rachel, and even less of having my wicked way with her.

During the hour or more we had swum together, I had spent only a few minutes within speaking distance, and naked or not, I had seen less of her than anyone could have seen had she been wearing a costume and walking freely about.

This was clearly not a new situation to her, and would be totally controlled by her whenever it happened. As I busied myself with the barramundi steaks, and foil parcels of peas and sweetcorn, she lectured me about my lecherous ways, and lack of respect for women. "No man shall share my company unless I can respect him. I've met a few womanisers, so wrapped up in themselves that they have little to offer any partner. I'd hate to see you wind up like that."

She didn't seem to have clocked that I hadn't yet got rid of my wet trunks. It was time I made a contribution. "When Neville flew us to Ronaldsway, you looked like a model in your scarlet catsuit and black suede accessories. Not only was it practical for a light aircraft, but it looked sensational! Cross my heart, I never thought, 'Cor, she looks like a good jump!'

"You set standards that left all those more obviously available beyond the pale." By now, I had got my trousers on, over my wet trunks. Despite my looking like an incontinent pensioner, she rewarded the insincere compliment with a chaste peck on the cheek. "As for being available, have you been making hay in the absence of Helen's beady eye?"

This deserved an honest reply, and I found it easier to reply having turned round to check the food. "Since you ask, no. The temptation is always there, but the opportunities are few. Clearly what I am failing to do, is to seek meeting places where there is no pressure, I suppose coffee-bar type places, which I have never felt drawn to.

"I occasionally get time off at roadside bars, but I suppose girls avoid such places like the plague! Just occasionally there are girls in such places, but not surprisingly, they are so obviously inferior to those I met at school that I have never felt attracted. My work demands total concentration, and often lasts from dawn till dusk, and takes place in very hot and dusty conditions. By the time I've cleaned up and eaten, if there were a church social, or village hop within driving distance, it wouldn't seem worth the effort.

"I usually wind up haunting the nearest bar, to Sean's oft-repeated disapproval. May I replenish your glass?" "No thanks. I'll make this last. Like Leah, I can get high sniffing a cork. By the way, how are things between you and Jane right now?"

"On the back burner, I guess. She made it very clear that her degree involves four years of study, broken by a year with her sponsors. She must then work for them for a while before considering other employment. I guess the fish and veg are ready now, if you would serve up for me, I'll just brown the naan bread and unwrap the corn cobs."

We were really hungry by now, and started the meal in silence, as the brief tropical sunset bathed the lake in orange and red.

"The more I get into bush flying the more glad I am to forget university, and cut to the chase. It seems that everything I want is within my grasp, here and now." I was being tested, and that very phrase must have been anticipated.

"You parried my question. You say you **might** assume commitments in five years' time." This was the tipping point. I thought long and hard before replying. "I'm afraid you hit the nail on the head. It has only gradually dawned on me that what came across as a lad's daydream of a seduction scene was the outcome of your high principles. I set out this afternoon with lecherous inclinations, which were never to reach fruition. When I heard myself selling

Jane short, it brought me to my senses."

She smiled, and applauded me. "No hard feelings, then?" "Well, definitely **lots** of hard feelings in the wrong place, but all doomed to be disappointed." "So tomorrow's joy ride is still on?" "And still eagerly awaited! As is a pair of scissors to free me from my cozzy!"

When I dropped Rachel off at her friend's bungalow, she returned with the scissors, true to her word. "I realised that borrowing scissors from Hazel might involve a lengthy explanation, and I don't want you sleeping in damp shorts!"

I arrived back at Hazel's bungalow a little earlier than expected, next day. "Sean, it occurred to me that you might like me to drop you at the airport before picking Rachel up."

"Thanks for that. I want to get all the spraying gear serviced, which will otherwise occupy our first working day." On to pick Rachel up. She was not only waiting, but carried a beach bag with what I hoped would include a packed lunch! As I went to collect the Cessna 150, Sean emerged from a hangar and collected his pickup.

"Where's Sean going with his pickup?" "He has to sort the spraying system, and he's doing it **now** so we can have it to go to the pool, after our pleasure flight." "Whoops! My apologies."

"Sorry. I shouldn't have snapped at you. I trust Sean absolutely, and hope he can trust me. Anything that involves courtesy, or helping others, he's already done before you ask him."

I went off to sign everything to do with hiring the

Cessna, including temporary membership, and a 'blood chit', to state that if it all ended in tears, it was your own stupid fault anyway. I proceeded to the control tower, where I logged a two-hour local flight sight-seeing.

The Kimberley Institute was our first port of call, and I throttled back to keep the noise down as I descended to six hundred feet for a good look. Hazel appeared, and waved to us. Rachel had never said much in favour of her colleagues, but I knew the girl who owned the bungalow got on well with her, and she started enthusing about working there now.

"May I have a closer look at the racing dinghies? There's Chris in his Hobie Cat. I crewed for him last week. She takes off like a rocket, every time a gust hits. Let's have a look at our secluded picnic rendezvous. Who knows what use we might find for it?" She giggled wickedly.

"Shall I move on, now?" In my head, I was composing a newsy letter to Jane. I really missed her, but looking at this place and enjoying this weather, no way would I wish away the time that would pass before Jane and I next met. I had a lot of flying to do, and I intended to enjoy every minute of it, because when it ended, it would be for ever.

I initiated a turn onto 84 magnetic on the gyro compass as I applied climbing power, and then rolled out on the new course. "Thirty minutes to our next turning point. This is magic! I've not seen **any** of this wilderness area before."

She put her arm round my neck, and gave me a peck on the cheek. I realised that this was the first time I had actually **enjoyed** her company, and that this had been my own fault, the result of unreal expectations.

When we landed back at the airfield and handed the Cessna back, Sean and Hazel were waiting to drive us to the pool. "Did you enjoy your spin? You sure look ready to cool off." We enjoyed going there together, and when we had had our fill of swimming, Rachel's packed lunch was enough for the four of us.

I noticed that Hazel's attitude to Rachel had grown friendlier now she had got to know her better. I could but hope that Helen's would change the same way once she realised that while Rachel was far better qualified than most to behave like a Scarlet Woman, she lacked the inclination!

Hazel asked us in to see her garden, before Sean drove Rachel and I home. They were like an old married couple. Hazel wanted to show us all the scented blooms, at their best in the evening, and Sean seemed most focussed on the compost heap, and a few rows of potatoes. "Would you believe me if I told you that I have a sport that bring might bring Oxfam beating a path to the Institute?"

Back to Rachel's bungalow. I had not noticed previously that a mature tree next to it was covered with pink blooms. I had not met Midge, but now she stood waiting for us on her veranda. She had a deep tan, and jet-black hair, and was dressed for tennis. "This is **him?**"

"**You** might not think highly of me, but my mummy does!" "You know what I mean, stirrer! Rachel's so notorious for rejecting the local talent, that we wondered if you were some kind of Superman!" "What you see is what you get!"

"Well, I'm out till late, so don't do anything I wouldn't." She got in her car, and left with a raucous screech of laughter. A cloud of pink parakeets left the tree, echoing her laughter!

Just as **I** had felt left behind when Jane accepted university entrance, so now **she** might have felt betrayed by my picnic with Rachel, but if I had set course with bad intentions, Rachel never intended that anything should come of it. As for me, having gained her friendship, I would never trade it for intimacy.

Raised from a deep sleep by my alarm, I rushed around like a scalded cock. I threw perishables into a bin bag, showered, washed, shaved, and put my toiletries in a ready-packed sports bag. I then bolted my breakfast and arrived at Hazel's bungalow half an hour early.

Sean opened the door in a surly mood. "So you **did** manage to make it then?" "I'm half an hour early, in case you hadn't noticed! And the top of the morning to you too, my sprightly Irish leprechaun! Once again we meet in comradeship to seek our pot of gold at the rainbow's end." He dragged me into the front room, and closed the door.

"Forget the comradeship! You will sweat blood earning pots of gold for **me,** your **master**, on this contract. You will work till you drop, and the nearest you will get to a bar will be to shake a tambourine outside one, while you peddle 'Warcry!' As a special treat, I might buy you a can of shandy from a vending machine. In short, your playboy days are over!"

Hazel opened the door. "What are you both lurking in here for? Come and be sociable in the kitchen. Have you eaten?" "No!" I lied. "I'd love whatever you are having!" Sean warmed visibly in her presence. I poured coffee, and stowed Sean's sports bag in the pickup, while Hazel cooked my eggs and bacon. "What's biting Sean? I've only ever known him to be easy-going?"

Sean returned, before she answered. "Sean wanted you to know that your responsibilities would be greater this time. For goodness sake, tell him why."

"I'm upping your commission to seven and a half per cent, and, by God you'll earn it!" I picked him up and gave him a big smacking kiss.

"Isn't he just a **living doll**, Hazel? Marry him quickly before I steal him from you." "**Lay off me**, you Pommy faggot. I was just demonstrating my masterful side to Hazel, before you started flinging me around like a rag doll. Go sit in the truck while we say our goodbyes."

I drove to the airfield, building speed on the road to get my eye in for the long drive ahead. Sean had more hours of contracts in hand than we had ever yet tackled, hence his efforts to increase my motivation. He was not yet ready to discuss them. "Any queries about the job, before you drop me off at the airfield?"

"I'm clear about contacting you, and where we'll meet. But with eight contracts to complete, might we run out of engine hours without completing them?" "Engine and airframe hours are **my responsibility**, and don't concern you." "May I draw your pickets then, my pocket Valentino, and stow them in your locker?" "No need. I'll be there before you are halfway. Hit the road, and leave me to complete my own tasks." "Then bon voyage! Perhaps someday, the Fates might arrange our paths to cross once more." "Should they fail to cross tomorrow morning, you'll be unemployed, and hitching back one hundred hot and dusty miles."

CHAPTER 18

Wedding Bells, at Last!

I mused that Sean certainly knew my failings. Assuming that my familiarity with the Pawnee might make me reckless. Sean had chosen this moment to boost my motivation, and the pressure on me at work. One result was that I now had locations recorded in my flight log which I could no longer recall!

I started to see a negative side to crop-dusting. I knew enough about biology to understand that populations of plant or animal, are limited by the food supply. Animal and insect 'pests' (and plant 'weeds') are therefore created by intensive farming.

It happens to be abhorrent to Aborigines, because they arrived (by land bridge) 40,000 years ago, accompanied by the dingoes that they had domesticated. It was their practice to make sure that the food plants they gathered should, when necessary, be replaced with seedlings or cuttings, to avoid removing plants (or animals) to the point of extinction.

Mostly, they would live a nomadic existence, but that did not cause them to exhaust food supplies wherever they happened to be, and then seek richer pickings elsewhere. This suggests that the tribe were ruled by what was best for the tribe, which is probably why they never developed further socially, or organised systems of ownership, and personal wealth.

So far, I had not even spoken to one, but the feeling came across that no-one considered what **their** opinion might be, because no-one cared. Obviously, they shared my grandfather's beliefs in a more extreme way, but very few of them were lucky enough to share his quality of life! That led me on to think that I could probably have achieved contentment shepherding as a lay-brother for the Prior of Furness for one loaf and a gallon of small beer a day!

Don't get me wrong, I loved my job, and just thought that eventually, farming would be organised to avoid explosions of pests, instead of repeatedly creating economic problems, and not bothering about them until they arrived. For the short time I was here, it was best to avoid touchy subjects, just as it would be if I lived in Ireland, or Scotland, for that matter. It's not as if it was really antisocial, like drug-dealing.

Here was a wedding about to arrive, which would launch Helen and I in opposite directions, and it must be obvious to both that it might be years before we saw each other again. I knew for certain that I would sink or swim raising livestock, as do many wealthy people. However wealthy, they would hesitate to leave their wealth in one hemisphere to visit the other, even briefly.

I enjoyed the job so much. My heart always quickened to hedge-hopping with the wind in my face and the roar of open exhausts in my ears. I would guess that if Helen ever mentioned fears of losing touch with me to Tim, I was sure that Tim would be ready to bet heavily on my eventually succumbing to Australia. I knew better.

Speaking of Tim, he sent letters to Sean and I to get ourselves to Darwin to acquire clothes for the wedding, and a proper wedding cake. Sean would also need gifts for the bridesmaids. He appended a shopping list of things that were not to be had in Kununurra. I decided to be guided by Sean regarding not only wedding wear, but leisure wear for afterwards. It was best to start with a haircut, as I didn't fancy trying on wedding suits while looking like someone who slept rough.

The last day of our contract arrived, and I took Sean to the farm airstrip to leave for Darwin, and book us into a hotel. I knew which hotel to drive to, but they wouldn't confirm the booking till I arrived with the luggage! Having spent lavishly on myself, I was in a mood to buy fire opal pendants for Helen, Hazel, and Jane. Sean liked them so much that, generous as usual, he bought matching earrings for each of them.

When we left Darwin for Kununurra, I felt like a different person with my hair cut, and wearing 'smart casual' clothes. When I rang Helen to say we were leaving, I told her that if lost in the desert for several weeks, I would start eating the wedding cake from the second layer down, with no writing or decorations on it. I don't think I would last more than that layer, washed down with water from the radiator (having emptied the water bags).

Sean told me to drive only in full daylight. "I'd rather you break your journey at Victoria Crossing, and charge it to expenses." He pointed out that it might put a damper on proceedings if everyone wore black armbands, and the wedding cake was heavily bloodstained. "What do you do west-bound at Victoria Crossing? **Put your watch back ninety minutes!**"

Back in Kununurra, I enjoyed the luxury of showering in my caravan, and changing into clean new underwear, shirt, and jeans. I called at Helen and Hazel's bungalow. Hazel opened the door to me, and Sean waved from the settee. "Aren't you the fashion plate? Auctioneer's boots, no less! Helen's dying to see you. Tell her I'm about to serve tea on the veranda. We have a spare bedroom, so move in for the wedding. It will be easier to keep in touch with everyone if we share the house."

Helen burst into tears when I walked in, which aroused an intense feeling of shame in me, thinking what she would feel when she found I would not leave England. "Don't mind me. Everything is going so well that I convinced myself that you would die in an accident, and never come back."

I had to sit hugging her. What was going to happen would be little better, if my livelihood was all that kept me from her. "I've never flown with greater care. Sean keeps me on a tight rein. Tomorrow is **your** day, and then you've got Tiny Tim to worry about, God help you! Let wiping **his** nose, and keeping **him** in line, be your first concern!"

"I heard that, young Swindlehurst! Welcome back." I showed him what I would be wearing, and asked him if there was anything I could do to help. "I'd better bring the cake in for a start, and see if it needs extensive repairs with Unibond." He passed me a long photocopied document. "I want you to memorise this, and then swallow it for fear it might fall into the wrong hands."

I stood, and saluted. "Wilco, out! I should add that Hazel is serving tea on the veranda." When I awoke in a strange bedroom it took me a moment to remember where I was. Then Hazel knocked, and came in with a mug of tea. "Nip in the bathroom while it's empty. This will still be hot enough when you come back. Your breakfast will be ready in twenty minutes." Time flew past until the wedding car arrived.

"Come in the living room, Ralph, while the bride makes her entrance." Helen's door opened, and the radiant bride glided out in primrose satin, covered with lace. Hazel held one corner of her train, who would the other bridesmaid be? Round the doorway, Jane appeared, looking even lovelier than I remembered.

I gazed, open-mouthed, then hurried to open the front door for them and help them into the car. I was full of pride to see Helen's many virtues rewarded at last. At the church, I squired her down the aisle, with head back and chest out, honoured to be giving her away.

Tim, with Sean beside him, looked around and

gasped. He smiled at all his friends, and his mother, Kerry, waved to me. I was instantly reminded of Alec's funeral and the comfort I found in the presence of so many friends who bore witness, and shared the grief. The date of that funeral was the last entry on the fly leaf of the family bible, in the roll-top desk back at Tewitts' Field. As soon as I returned I would record this event.

The torrent of emotions it aroused in me drove out some of the things I should have been thinking about and remembering today. Looking round the church, I found it had only been built in 1960. I had thought Kerry and Tim to have been long-established here, but **nobody** was. After all the ceremonies I had attended at St Bart's where both sides of the family had been burying their dead for four hundred years, I had always felt insignificant, a mere spectator.

I had had to travel halfway round the world to see myself finally as a **player** in the game, not an onlooker. As I left the church, the vicar expressed surprise at never seeing me before. I explained that I had qualified for my PPL, and never stopped working since. "I won't be here much longer, either, as I return in September."

I looked at Jane's face, watching me and smiling. I always felt as if she knew what I thought, as it happened! I kissed Helen, and put my arm round Jane to kiss her carefully on the cheek. Tewitts' Field filled my mind. It was the antithesis of this place. I heard Grandad's voice saying, "Dark, true, and tender is the north!" Not in Australia it ain't! Granddad's thoughts would have been of ancient paths, and holloways, and ancient long-distance tracks along bald ridges, used for thousands of years.

The only ancient artefacts for a hundred miles were aboriginal cave paintings. They were made by people who had accepted poverty and hunger in pursuit of a sustainable existence which had left their surroundings unchanged for forty thousand years.

In European eyes they seemed to have become mere paupers in their native land. Lack of money degraded them, in the way that Rachel's wealth added to her glamour. It brought to mind the beatitudes, 'Blessed are the meek, for they shall inherit the earth.' Surely a dire prophecy for the rest of us. Might **we** be the ones left devoid of livelihood, scavenging the garbage we have spent our lives producing? Then the ones who chose never to change **their** surroundings will enjoy the unspoilt parts of the same land that they found 40,000 years ago.

As soon as the photographer had finished marshalling the guests into every permutation that a genealogist could imagine, I found Jane, and took her to find Rachel. "What a lovely wedding, Helen looks great! Even our presence failed to make her look her age."

Rachel addressed Jane. "I don't know if you've spoken to Ralph yet. I've done my best to involve him in every possible social embarrassment, but nothing that he would be ashamed to tell you."

"Thanks Rachel, stay close. I'll need you to boost me up in a minute. Do you know any of the locals, or just us true Brits? Quick, both of you! Grab a leg each and boost me up!"

Jane had seen Helen stand in the wedding car and turn her back to the guests to fling her bouquet.

Rachel and I tossed her skywards, as in a rugby line-out, to pluck the bouquet from the air a good nine feet above the ground. Hefty Australian maidens went down like skittles in her wake, as she landed lightly as a kitten on her gold court shoes.

Rachel said, "The three locals approaching are colleagues I try to avoid! The three of them, Norm, Bruce, and Kevin stared pop-eyed as Jane and Rachel (as if by telepathy) each pressed one of my hands to their breast and winked at them as they passed. Helen and Tim stood at the entrance to the marquee. Once inside, the three of us split up.

I helped to serve wine, while the girls offered plates of canapés. Then we circulated, chatting to the guests. Then, while the girls cleared the tables, the men cleared all the chairs away to leave room for dancing. Helen and Tim started things off, to the music of a local quartet. Once things had warmed up, with most people on the floor, the couple left, to change for their departure. When they were ready, Sean called everyone outside to see them off for their honeymoon.

They were taking their new White Eagle to Queensland, to explore the islands of the Great Barrier Reef. Kerry reckoned they were most likely to choose Lindeman Island of the island chain as their base. Sean and Rachel showed the guests some spirited dancing, I took Jane on the floor, and Hazel excused Rachel, who was immediately seized by the despised Kevin.

Jane was ready for refreshment, so I collected two glasses of white wine, and sat with her on the veranda. "Why does Hazel address Chet as Sean?"

"As with 'Coronation Street', you have to keep in touch with the plot. A brief résumé follows. Vietnam veteran Chet Berrigan chose to honour his military service conscription in the Cuban Army, so as to maintain dual nationality.

"They aimed to compromise his US citizenship, by using him as a military adviser in the People's Republic of China, specifically to train their soldiers in US 'Counter Insurgency' techniques, what they call 'Co-In'. Hazel sent (under his name) an open letter to the Cuban Embassy in London, saying he was prepared to serve his period of conscription, in Cuba, like other conscripts.

"All those serving in China are regular soldiers who volunteered for that duty. The Ambassador replied by open letter in the Guardian to say that was all that was required of him. Chet agreed to this, but first (with devilish cunning) he changed his name by deed poll to Sean Costello, under which name he applied for citizenship of the Republic of Ireland as a third nationality.

"The sneaky Cubans promptly posted him to China, and they broke their journey at Bombay, using their block booking at the same hotel used by British United Airways, which we were using. He had his American Express card secreted about his person, and he promptly bought a ticket to Darwin, and did a runner using his Irish passport!"

"So, in short, it wasn't due to early-onset dementia on Hazel's part?" "Well, that's the way **she** tells it!" "I'm sorry I ever asked the question now." "Surely, what you call yourself often depends on a flight of fancy. I once called myself 'Chutzpah' Danziger in the

Isle of Man." "Obviously, when you went with the Breslaus!" "Top marks for geography, that girl!"

"You are probably unaware that the meticulous detail in which you described the events suggest that there is some other recent event about which you hope to keep shtum."

"Are you sure you **need** a law degree? You could be put in charge of interrogation at Special Branch right now! Well, through no fault of Rachel's, we went for a picnic along some hidden track she found, that ended in Lake Argyle. I last used my cozzy in the swimming bath, and dried it without washing out the chlorine. The cotton cord was perished, and when I tried to un-knot it, it broke at the knot.

"I had to wear my trousers over wet trunks, and was waddling along like an incontinent pensioner, back to the car. When we got back to her bungalow, she brought me a pair of scissors, to avoid being seriously chapped about the crotch for the rest of my life. She got a better afternoon's entertainment than she anticipated."

"There is **nothing** compromising in what you just described. I'll accept that you were safely trapped in your cozzy. I see Rachel as drying herself, and within reach."

"She was, but I can assure you I never saw a glimpse of her, because I turned around until she had finished drying herself. For the whole time we swam, she was only very briefly within quarter of a mile of me. I did a sedate breaststroke, and she zoomed round like a wet-bike, doing the crawl."

"You are thinking far faster than you used to. You

immediately confessed, because you **immediately** realised when you saw me this morning that if I was not interested, I would have returned the tickets she sent me."

"Yes, I was immensely flattered. Crop-spraying does wonders for one's reaction time." "You look different too. Like a Chyppen Young Farmer who has 'done time' on Devil's Island. Apart from the tan, you've lost weight, and your eyes are definitely sunken, like a hermit crab peering out of its shell.

"Get this absolutely clear, when I got Helen's letter, enclosing the tickets, I assumed that my role was to be the US Cavalry, there to chase marauding Breslaus back to their reservation. I reasoned that she wouldn't part with her money that easily otherwise."

"She wouldn't. Even though that money had been set aside for my education. If I suspected that my arrival has merely postponed your coupling with Rachel, I would drop you like a hot brick."

"Just ask Sean. He is constantly warning me off hanging around bars, courting trouble. Rachel quite honestly flaunted herself at me, and immediately lectured me that she had no interest in any man that failed to treat her with respect, and that she despised womanising men. I promise you, that once committed to each other, I will never weigh up another woman!

"That is not to say that we should behave as if we are engaged, because we are **not**. I had always thought that **you** would be the one exposed to temptation, over a hundred miles away in Aberystwyth, It never occurred to me that I might let **you** down. It is dawning on me that my family is about to explode, and that there could easily be whole years in which Mum and I never meet, so I shall be pressing you and Hazel and Rachel to all return (with me) together, hoping that we may bond. I will also make sure I see Hazel every month."

"Then I'll tell you if I feel committed, before we leave. You seem to have brought our future into focus remarkably quickly, for one who wasn't supposed to know I was coming." "That was completely genuine."

"Anyway, let's see where you live." "As I told you, I'm renting an old trailer caravan under a eucalyptus on a paddock behind someone's bungalow. When I want company, I drop in on Helen and Hazel, and if Sean is with me, Helen moves in with Kerry and Tim, and Sean moves in with Hazel. I enjoy my privacy, away from the phone."

I opened the caravan door, and ushered Jane in. I opened the windows, and a breeze stirred the curtains. It looked at its best. Living in a confined space had finally taught me to wash everything and put it away after use. This blessed the 'van with the un-cluttered look of a hermit's cell. The largest window with the table and upholstered benches inside, aligned with the best view. It looked over the rooftops of Kununurra towards the Ord Estuary.

"Shall we have a pot of tea?" "I'd love some. I make sure that I drink more than at home." Once she was comfortable, and her tea in front of her, I got out a red morocco case. "Did you like the fire opal earrings that Sean gave you? Here's a pendant to match them. When we return to Darwin to fly home, it is probably too early to announce an engagement, but I would like to give you a matching ring to wear when the time comes. If so, I will regard myself as a probationary fiancé!"

Jane flung her arms around my neck and kissed me warmly for the first time. "So you **had** thought of me before you knew I would attend the wedding." I was clearly so overcome that Jane changed the conversation. "Do you see Helen settling here?"

"Yes, I'm sure of it. Kerry thinks they will choose Lindeman Island. It is a beauty spot with loads of paths, rising to a mountain peak, from which seventy other islands are visible, and people have been building holiday homes there since the thirties.

"I know she can be a grabber at times, and has already misled me about Dad's dairy herd investment being money borrowed at fifteen per cent, that only earned five per cent, which is true, if you ignore the crop of calves that is produced each year to keep the herd 'in milk'. My other gripe was that I assume Alec intended me to inherit, not necessarily the whole estate valued at the time of his death, but at least a going concern. Which makes disposing of the land while I am a minor slightly dodgy, to say the least. "That left **me** in a grabbing frame of mind myself, and it is just dawning on me (but doubtless obvious to you for months) that my **main** problem at present will be to get a living while setting time and money aside each year to hold the family together."

"Has she given you the house?" I hadn't expected such a direct question. "Yes, that's right. If you will have me, I can offer you a home." "Well then, how can you think you are getting short measure? I'm sure your dad will have left her a life interest in the estate,

319

in which case she need not part with any of it in her lifetime. The other thing it indicates is that she hasn't felt it necessary to keep it as a bolt-hole. Will you go to Lancaster if you qualify?" "No, I forgot to tell you. It still seems possible to build a viable enterprise, but not if I accumulate debt getting a degree first. My overriding concern is to run a hill-sheep enterprise, and Tewitts' Field is no longer viable as such. I remember when I met Brian and Daphne, explaining 'Folding on mangolds'."

"Yes, I remember." "Well I'm thinking that the guy with the mangold field in Cumbria has a son who wants to farm. I've known him for years, of course, and you might be able to think of a partnership set-up whereby I could get an NFU agricultural mortgage to buy a field up there for our partnership.

"I've been racking my brain trying to find a way I could visit Australia for long enough to justify the cost. Stock rearing requires some involvement '24/7', as they say. I would take time out each year during the wet, when Tim and Helen will be less busy, and most of my flock will be in Cumbria, and the remainder on my open fell.

"Expecting some wage earner to take that responsibility for me is plain stupid. It has to be someone with a stake in the outcome, which limits you to a family member or business partner. Maybe he could work part-time for his dad, and augment his income with my partnership enterprise. If it leaves him working more hours in the partnership than I do, then I should pay that same proportion more to finance it.

"The other thing I had in mind, before I

considered a partnership, was to start either a beef cattle herd, or pedigree sheep. Either of those should yield more profit than our present hill-sheep enterprise. Anyway, that's all in the future. I reluctantly accepted her action, which was mainly prompted by my lack of progress at school, and it succeeded in that aim."

"I can't believe that you suspect your mother's motives. As I see it, you would never have had any chance of passing GCE if she hadn't disposed of the dairy enterprise. Apart from that, without the gliding club, and then Tim's help, you would never have found the motivation to catch up your school work. Both Mr Bradshaw and Miss Rossi commented on the improvement in confidence that resulted from your flying training.

"You tell me now, that you have abandoned the possibility of light aviation in Australia, in favour of hill-sheep farming, a choice you are very lucky to have had. Set that against the certainty that if still saddled with the dairy herd, you would be struggling now to repay the agricultural mortgage. Failure to meet the payments would have bankrupted you."

Next day, Helen called round to say she had been discussing my decision to make the farm viable with Tim. He had pointed out that my grazing tenancy of Tewitts' Field was conditional on all sheep being cleared from the landing area on every day flown.

My absence at university would have resulted in forfeiting that tenancy, which would then be lost to me for ever, making it no longer possible to manage the hill flock. Jane must have told them in confidence of my offer of a 'probationary engagement', which they both considered better than getting a degree! It seemed that this was very strong support for my efforts to maintain family contacts.

CHAPTER 19

The Dream Time

Four zombies struggled off the London to Manchester shuttle at Manchester International. Leah Breslau was there to collect Rachel. She winked at me, and gave me the 'thumbs-up' sign, when Daphne wasn't looking. I introduced Rachel and her parents to Brian and Daphne, and Hazel to Rachel's parents, before Brian and Daphne ran Hazel home. I carried her luggage in, and she only had time to say, "Don't push co-habitation too soon! Remember you are only a probationary fiancé!"

"Thanks Hazel. I'll do my best not to put their backs up!" We were to eat with Jane's parents. They took me home just to leave off my luggage and light the Aga. The Land Rover had been on the trickle charger in my absence, so I told them I would follow them home, to save them turning out again. I did explain that having firmly settled on planning a viable hill-sheep enterprise, that it depended on not starting with the debt that would result from taking a degree.

They did not ask how I planned to do so, and if they thought that to be my business, that was fine by me. "What about Jane's vacations?"

"While you are maintaining her university career, of course, she will spend most of her time with you. Of course, my farm routine has to continue whether she is on vacation or not. Because I have more space, I would be delighted if you all came to Tewitts' Field for the day. I will never visit her at Aberystwyth without inviting you to join me. We would like to spend our evenings together as a rule, but of course you may have some evenings planned for her."

"As far as visiting is concerned, we will include you, if you wish to come. I believe Jane's invitation to be a maid of honour came as a surprise to you?" "Yes. Mum loves planning surprises for others, but I find she isn't too keen on receiving them." "That makes us think that if Jane is to get a good degree, you must make sure nothing interferes with that." "I certainly intend to avoid that. I see no need to even announce an engagement until she wishes to." "As dinner is now ready, that seems the right note on which to conclude."

The next day I awoke in my own (warm) home. It was great just to be eating breakfast in my own kitchen. I washed up the breakfast things, and looked around to see if there were other chores needing my attention. I knew I was expected by Jane, but that she would fight her corner effectively, and her words would carry more weight with her parents than mine would. She heard the Land Rover draw up, and shouted through the window, "We're in the kitchen, Ralph. The back door is open. I'm glad you've come in time to hear this. Dad has been running through the arguments for me not to take my eye off the ball until my LLB is safely in the bag. This is being discussed as if I've returned from Lanzarote, besotted with some unsuitable yob, with whom I've experienced a holiday fling.

"I **really** know you. Through my school years, we have spent more time in each other's company than I have with my parents. I was most influenced by those who came across as being the best teachers, particularly Mr Bradshaw and Miss Rossi. Mr Bradshaw stressed that the hardships experienced by those whose ancestors were restricted by Forest Law bonded strongly together, and protected each other.

"It deserves the efforts of the present generation to make much smaller sacrifices to maintain this 'united we stand' posture. Both his parents had forebears living here 400 years ago, so St Bart's graveyard is full of them. That is why it is important to both of us to carry on with hill-sheep farming, whether or not there is more money to be made in some other place, in some other job. Ralph is clearly proud of my legal ambition, and all for it, but feels he has a vocation for livestock.

"His grandfather inherited **his** father's flock, and Alec bought himself out of the army to inherit it. You have always done your best for me, to make sure I did as well as I was able at school. Now cast your mind back to the circumstances that precipitated Helens remarriage. She was working at the creamery when she became engaged to Alec Swindlehurst, a regular soldier in the Paras. She was offered the manager's post there, by which time he was a sergeant.

"He served with distinction in the Suez invasion, although he always doubted the legality, and even more, the morality. That was his reason for buying himself out. To improve the cash flow of the farm, he took an agricultural mortgage to buy a milk herd, and equip a milking parlour.

"Right at the outset of this enterprise, he died in a road traffic accident. Helen held down her new job, while winding up the new enterprise, and sold the herd and as much equipment as she was able, plus part of the flock to pay off the mortgage. She also sold the land the house stood on.

"Having met Tim, and becoming engaged to him, she sat her PPL. This was to help her get a light aircraft sales agency off the ground, at the time of the Miners' Strike, followed by the Three-Day Week. She then helped him sell that as a going concern, to go to Australia and set up a similar agency there.

"The question is, what academic achievements did **her** parents have to swank about? You may be surprised to hear, just School Certificate! In legal matters, you don't get your nose through the door without the degree, but to succeed in business, everyone, even lawyers and doctors, won't get far without sheer force of character!"

"Thanks, Jane! That was telling them. If your mum and dad needed reminding, I did so even more, having recently questioned her motives!"

"Sorry I banged on at such length, Mum and Dad, but I really want to get back with Ralph and explore the house properly. As I have to return to Aberystwyth in a few days, I must avoid parting from you in a bad atmosphere."

Brian spoke up. "That is just **not** going to happen, love. Off with you now!" It still seemed strange to me to be entering an empty house. I picked Jane up to carry her over the threshold, and it was enough to arouse a storm of passion, but nothing must come of it. She sensed this, so I said, "Think of all the lovers who have felt this. In all the wars, this might have happened before they parted for the last time."

"I feel the same, but it's best not to think about it. I'll never be able to concentrate if I'm living some sort of fantasy life in my imagination."

Next day, it seemed weird to wake to an empty house, but it was warm, thanks to the Aga. I missed the presence of my mum, but then, she had such a commanding presence that it was more restful in her absence! Actually, Jane must return to Aberystwyth shortly, and her parents and I wanted to make the most of her time with us. From now on, I would get up when I chose, and eat what I felt like. I was at that stage of a farming career when I could lean on a gate and chew a straw, and tell anyone that chose to comment, "This is when the most important element of farming takes place."

I just had porridge and coffee for breakfast, and was wondering what Jane had in mind concerning the farm, as she had little time left, before her return. The phone rang, providing the answer. She was dropping her dad off at work, and would be with me inside half an hour.

She had one useful contribution to make, already. She had taken in what I had told her about self-launching gliders, and immediately taken the point that most long-established gliding clubs were better adapted to training their pilots in self-launching trainers, by virtue of owning sites on top of the slope that they soared, because all their solo pilots could use cheap winch-launching to get in the air, making money for the club!

It was therefore possible, once the time limitation imposed by the donors of the grant had expired, that they might seek to move. Her suggestion was that I should ask the club committee for 'first refusal' of the site, if the club ever sought to move. It would even be worth knowing when they were permitted to move, and what might attract their interest.

When she drove in and parked next to the house, her immediate interest was in our remaining outbuildings, and the sheep pound. She had made it very clear that she would never take sides in any disagreement between Helen and I. I guessed that she was planning a possible granny flat. The fact that she included the pin-fold among the possible sites suggested that she thought the club wouldn't care where the sheep were enclosed, so long as it didn't reduce the area available for landing and taking off.

There was a choice to be made about a possible partnership, and a choice between beef cattle and pedigree sheep as the additional enterprise. Obviously finding a partner should come first, so that he should be involved in the choice of enterprise. In short, there seemed no decision that could usefully be made right now, other than make a note in the back of my diary, headed 'To-do List', which should list these various delayed decisions, graded by their importance.

Suiting the word to the deed, I did so, as follows:

TO-DO LIST

1. Alec's headstone

2. Seek business partner (even for a short period)

3. Agree on new enterprise (preferably pedigree sheep or beef cattle)

While she was here at Tewitts' Field, I must get sorted about her preference about returning to college. "Jane, what are your wishes about my seeing you off to college?"

"Just to fix with Mum and Dad about spending the evening here, and for you to drive over in the morning to wave me off. The journey takes the best part of two hours, and if you are there too, I foresee many long embarrassed silences. With just the three of us, we usually find plenty to talk about."

"I was hoping that would be your choice. I haven't checked the flock yet, and Blue still thinks he's everyone's pet. He will be happier at work again, and it will do me good, also.

"Way back on our flight from Bombay to Darwin, Hazel chose to have a heart-to-heart discussion about family history, and I avoided commitment to get involved in an oral local history study of hers. Despite this bad start, I need to spend more time keeping in touch with her, so I want to ask her to show me the remains of my ancestors' deer pound he built for the Prior of Cartmel according to the priory records, six hundred years ago.

"I also want to tell her what I have in mind for Alec's headstone, and get moving on that." "I expected relief at not having spent a whole day getting rid of me, but not intimations of mortality! Have you suddenly realised the error of your ways?" "No, I've been aware of them for years, as it happens, but don't expect a neatly typed confession ready for our last evening until your next vacation." "I have no need to remind you what **you** needn't expect on your farewell evening!" "What! No country pleasures?" "Not from me, anyway!" "On a more serious note, I've been thinking about what your parents were saying, and come to agree with it." "That's good."

"There was more in what they said than I was able to accept at the time. They are not the only ones who might be put out by our getting married before you graduate. You employers might wonder if a good degree is your first priority. Your parents will be delighted that a home awaits you, but an income is also required, and I am clearly as far from that, as you are from graduation. Plan as I might, a mortgage will await the income to support it." "I agree. I thought you would meet them halfway." "The next thing worrying me is that I may not be able to afford visiting you before your next vacation." "No problem. I will invite them to visit me at half-term, and they will suggest including you." "So far, you have dealt with every problem I raise with an instant solution! The next thing on my 'to-do' list is Alec's headstone." "I believe the first step is to secure the vicar's permission, and he will explain what is, and what isn't permitted. Only then will you have enough data to seek quotations from memorial stone masons. They will tell you if the soil has settled sufficiently since the interment for the stone you choose to remain stable."

"I never thought of that. Plant it too early, and it might constitute a 'dead-fall trap' for emerging vampires." "Specially in St Bart's graveyard." "When I ask about the graveyard rulebook, I might suggest that they add one about having to drive a stake through the heart of new inmates." "I have nothing to add to that, so give me a kiss, and I will take my leave." I made sure it was a kiss which would last till half-term! The house fell silent as the grave. I took Blue to check the heafed flock, and then settled to an evening meal in front of the box, with a beer. Next morning, I received an early phone call from Hazel. "When does Jane leave for Aberystwyth?" "Brian and Daphne will take her on Saturday." "Will you be free for lunch on Sunday?" "Is twelve o'clock OK? I'll look forward to seeing you then." "I was hoping you might have a couple of hours to spare." "Certainly. Funnily enough, I was just telling Jane that I must spend more time with you in Mum's absence." "I shall certainly look forward to that, then." "Have you heard from Sean?" "Yes, I'll share his news with you when we meet."

Her garden had evidently received plenty of attention since her return, and her home was smelling of lavender furniture polish as usual. This time, it was somewhat overcome by the smell of roast lamb with all the trimmings. In fact, there was so much Sunday dinner requiring my complete attention that I ate it almost in silence until my coffee arrived.

"I imagine that Sean's work permit will have expired by now. Is he back home yet?" "He opted for a brief stay as a tourist. He'll be back at Shannon soon, with plans to trade his Cessna taxi in for something bigger."

"I was sorry to 'knock you back' concerning the oral local history, but I expect to be run off my feet trying to get a living from a seriously reduced hill-sheep enterprise. I did 'get the message' of what you told me, and realised that certain places I knew locally seem to have an atmosphere of their own, such as we all experience on entering an old church." "Then I guarantee that you will experience that if we visit what little remains of you ancestors' winter pasture for the deer of the forest."

We walked in silence between the trees, across rough pasture, towards open oak woodland. When a small stand of yews came in sight, she made for that. As we got closer, we could see that it had been fenced off with an ancient dry-stone wall to keep livestock away from the poisonous needles and berries. As soon as we reached it, Hazel pulled some branches aside to reveal a section of earthworks consisting of a ditch, the spoil from which has been used to steepen the uphill side of the ditch.

"John Swindlehurst dug this, with the aid of another unnamed lay brother, on the orders of the Prior of Cartmel Priory. It was intended to keep the deer from the forest 'in-bye' on winter pasture, until spring growth provided sufficient pasture for them back in the forest. At that time the verderers, would open a gategiving access to the Royal Forest, and drive them back where they came from.

"The Swindlehursts and Slingers walked these pastures, woods and fells, filling their minds with wonder at their surroundings. They came gradually to own their flocks, rather than work them on behalf of others. Eventually their fell sheep became heaf'd to the fell, and many of us did, too. Those who did lost the will to seek a living elsewhere. My grandfather showed me all that had been shown to him, passed verbally from 'time beyond ken'.

"You already know all that has transpired since then, so let's move on to the present. I believe you are thinking of your father now. I think it would be improper to involve Helen in the matter of his headstone when she is newly remarried, so what do **you** intend to do about it?"

Now that Robert Louis Stevenson is safely out of copyright, I thought to paraphrase his words:

Be it granted to me to behold you again in dying,
Hills of home, and to hear again the call,
Hear about the graves of the martyrs the Tewitts' crying
And hear no more at all.

The End

Printed in Great Britain
by Amazon